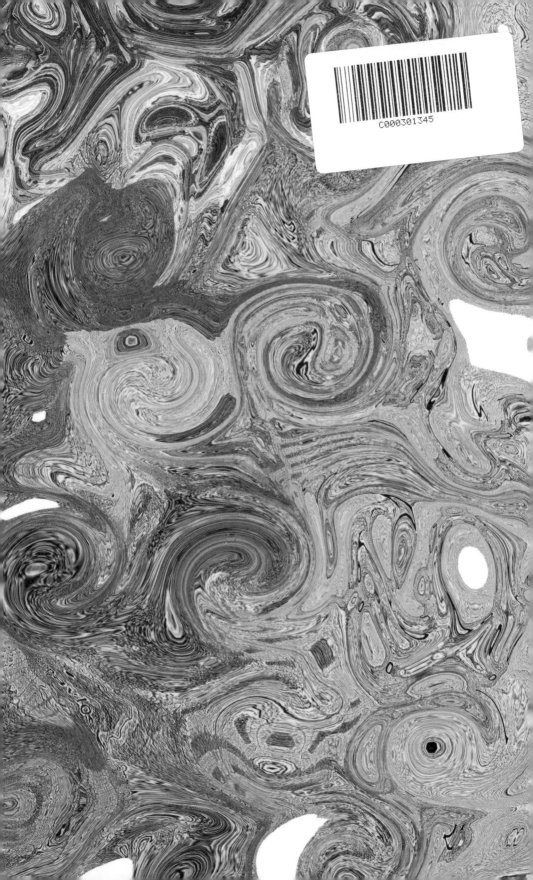

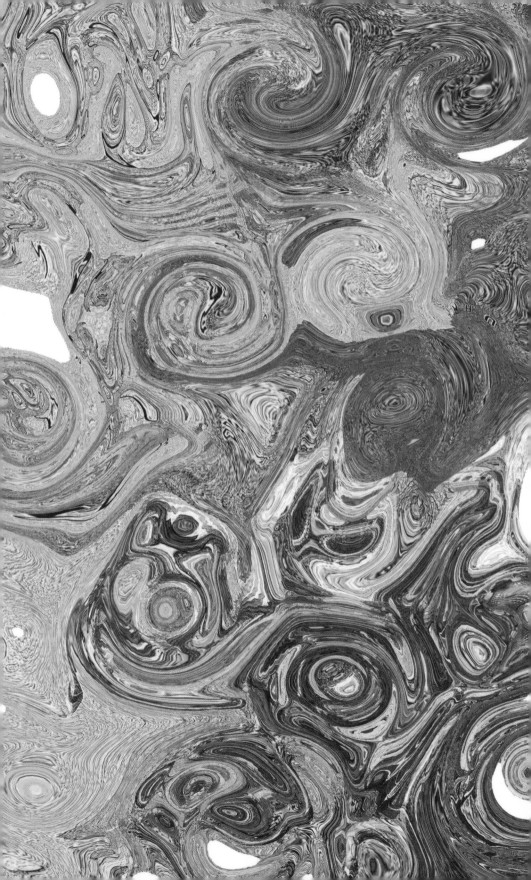

THE
EXTRAORDINARY
ADVENTURES
OF
FOUNDLING
MICK

JULES VERNE

The Extraordinary Adventures of Foundling Mick

The Extraordinary Adventures of Foundling Mick

Originally published as 'P'tit-Bonhomme' by Bibliothèque d'Éducation et de Récréation, Paris, 1893

First published in English by Sampson Low, Marston and Co., London, 1895 as *Foundling Mick (P'tit Bonhomme)*

This edition published 2008
by Royal Irish Academy
19 Dawson Street
Dublin 2

www.ria.ie

© Royal Irish Academy 2008

ISBN 978-1-904890-42-3

British Library Cataloguing in Publication Data. A CIP catalogue record for this book is available from the British Library.

This publication has received support from

Printed in the UK by Mackays

10 9 8 7 6 5 4 3 2 1

C O N T E N T S

INTRODUCTION

William Butcher[1]

VERNE IN IRELAND

Jules Verne (1828–1905) invariably sets his works in far-flung, exotic parts, while endeavouring in each new book to avoid revisiting territory. The novelist himself travelled intensively and extensively outside France, reaching Scandinavia, North Africa and North America. By far his favourite destination, however, was the British Isles, with a score of trips. This represented in some sense a homecoming, for part of his family tree came from Brittany—and another from Scotland.[2]

Verne's Celtic attraction takes on additional resonance in that he used the above locations, including Ireland, to set his novels. In the last case, it is true, his contacts were fleeting or debatable, with one contemporary account even reporting that Verne never went to Ireland.[3]

The first Hibernian visit was with his brother, Paul, en route for New York on the *Great Eastern*. From Liverpool, the huge ship skirted Holyhead before nearing Carnsore Point and following the coast down. On other crossings, the *Great Eastern* put in at Queenstown (Cobh), but perhaps not on this occasion:

> Wednesday, 27 March [1867]. Emerald Coast, follow [*sic*] the whole day—creamy sea, squally, dirty green—stiff breeze / many ships—steamers overtaken / frequent meals / Queenstown—fishing fleet— ships of all sizes ... the beacons [of Cape Clear and Fastnet Lighthouses] / sail up to WNW.[4]

These telegraphic notes are the only direct record we have of Verne 'in' the Emerald Isle. However, the lightly fictionalised narrative which grew out of them, *A Floating City* (1870), expands them into a poetic, if still low-key slideshow, demonstrating the novelist's appreciation of Irish coastal activity:

> ... this long stretch of shore, with an elegant profile, whose permanent greenness has earned it the name of 'the Emerald Coast'. A few lonely houses, the twists and turns of a customs route, a plume of white steam marking a train passing between two hills, an isolated signal-post making grimacing gestures to the ships at large ...
>
> Numerous vessels, brigs and schooners, endeavoured to claw off from the land; steamers passed, billowing their black smoke ...
>
> Soon we hoved in sight of Queenstown, a small port of call where a flotilla of fishing-boats manoeuvred ...
>
> At half past four the land lay still visible, three miles to starboard ... Soon a beacon appeared. It was Fastnet Lighthouse, built on an isolated rock; night fell, during which we were due to round Cape Clear, the last projecting point of the Irish coast (vi).

But in addition to this, there exist tantalising claims, in two other contemporary sources and in the two family biographies,[5] that the novelist subsequently revisited the Irish Sea and Ireland. The date might have been 1872, the route being simply the cryptic along 'the English coast and up the Ocean to Scotland'.[6]

INCEPTION AND PUBLICATION HISTORY

Little research has been done on Verne's sources, with the manuscripts not yet deciphered for the world-famous *Journey to the Centre of the Earth* or *Twenty Thousand Leagues under the Seas*. It seems hardly surprising, then, that the inception of *P'tit bonhomme* (*Foundling Mick*) has hardly been explored.

The surviving manuscript is kept at Nantes, with the first and last sheets freely viewable on the Web.[7] Verne's correspondence with his publisher, Jules Hetzel *fils*, shows that an earlier title, less sentimental, was '*Petit homme*' ('Little Man'), possibly derived from the expression 'Grand Little Man'. The constituent volumes of the novel were written separately, the first undoubtedly in the second half of 1891, the second by 30 July 1892. On 5 December Verne returned the proofs of the first two chapters, revised following discussions with Hetzel.[8]

In reply to queries from the printer, Verne writes that the peat bogs of Ireland do indeed occupy '96 million cubic metres'; that 'holy potatoes' is the correct phrase, being a quotation; that the first line of the traditional poem 'John Playne's Complaint' should read 'John Playne, take my word for it ...'; and that it is the printer who has lost the colour map of Ireland to be published in the novel.[9] Even after publication, in serial form in the *Magasin d'éducation et de récréation* (1 January–15 December 1893), Verne found new errors in the first volume, especially as regards the place names, resulting in further revisions for the book publication (small format, 2 October and 20 November 1893) and the illustrated edition (23 November 1893).

Sales of the French editions were reasonable: in addition to the *Magasin*, about 20,000 copies had probably been printed by 1904. Sampson Low and Marston brought out the book in London as *Foundling Mick* (1895), going through several editions.[10] This anonymous translation comprised 27 chapters and 75,500 words, compared with the original 31 chapters and 120,000 words. A new edition was published for school use by the Educational Company of Ireland (Dublin) as *A Lad of Grit* in about 1932, abridged by another 35,000 words.

In an interview of spring 1893, Verne talks about the inspiration of the book:

> In the novel *P'tit bonhomme*, I describe the adventures of a lad in Ireland. I take him from the age of two and give his life up to the age of fifteen, when he makes his fortune and that of all his friends, which is a novel denouement, is it not? He travels all round Ireland ... my descriptions of the scenery and localities have been taken from books ...

I have read the whole of Dickens at least ten times over
… I love him immensely, and in my forthcoming novel …
the proof of this is given and acknowledgement of my debt
is made.[11]

The orphan's ascent clearly shows the influence of *Oliver Twist* (1838)
and *David Copperfield* (1850), as do the overriding sentimentality and
melodrama and even many of the characters.

Three other novels depicting a boy's struggles and travels
undoubtedly influenced Verne: *Sans famille* (1878—*Nobody's Boy*) by
Hector Malot (1830–1907); *L'enfant* (1879—*The Child*) by Jules Vallès
(1832–85), a schoolmate of Verne's at the Collège Royal in Nantes; and
Le petit gosse (1889—*The Little Chap*) by William Busnach (1832–1907).
Within the novel itself, Verne cites one source three times, a certain de
Bovet. Marie-Anne de Bovet (b. 1855) was a well-known feminist writer,
who from 1889 wrote three books on Ireland, sympathetic to the
nationalist cause.

Foundling Mick has been disliked by many of the critics: 'one of Verne's
least good', 'a descent into pathos', the hero 'of only middling interest, the
action long and drawn out', its plotting 'contrived and facile', the novel, it
is claimed, 'presents little of interest', 'is not a very good book'.[12]

However, others have argued that 'many passages … are superb' and
that, as 'one of the best written of Verne's novels, through certain moods
it creates, it is comparable to the best of Dickens'.[13]

PLOT [14]

In 1875 poverty reigns across Ireland. The book opens with
three-year-old Mick working the hidden mechanisms of a puppet show
depicting Queen Victoria and her entourage, forced by a cynical
showman who hits and starves him. The boy is intelligent, industrious
and persistent, honest, generous and brave: 'It was as if he were born aged
20' (II x).

Mick had been found by the showman on a street-corner in Donegal.
His earliest memories are of a bad-tempered drunkard who starves the

orphans she is meant to be looking after; however, an older girl, Cissy, protects him.

He is saved from the showman's clutches by the good people of Westport, Co. Mayo, and eventually placed in the poor school in Galway.[15] This institution is full of bullies who make his life a misery. However, Grip, sixteen, naturally good-humoured and thin as a rake, befriends him. When the school is destroyed in a fire, Mick is back on the street. In Limerick, Anna Watson, a flighty, ageing actress, takes him in and pampers him, but soon tires of the boy.

Finally, at the age of four, a family of Kerry farmers take pity on Mick: he spends four happy years with the hard-working, warm MacCarthys. But in 1880 famine strikes and they are evicted for rent arrears, while the farm is demolished about their heads.

Mick is on the road once more, alone except for Ranger, the farmer's dog.[16] He prospers by hawking matches. He finds a wallet containing £100 and returns it to the arrogant Marquis of Trelingar. With the Marquis, he visits Cahersiveen, Co. Kerry, birthplace of O'Connell, and Valentia Island, the starting point of the transatlantic cable (1857–66). After working briefly as a groom for the Marquis's loutish son in Limerick, Mick leaves in order to save his dog's life.

Ranger rescues from suicide another young orphan, Dick, who has not eaten for 48 hours. The two boys walk together to Cork, set up another hawking business and soon make £30, invested in turn in wool.

Moving to Bedford Street, Dublin, Mick and Dick open a children's toy shop. Mick also makes money by acquiring exclusive rights on an ingenious new toy. Dick captures birds, puts them in cages and sells their freedom to rich children.

In one dramatic episode, Mick single-handedly saves his cargo from sinking on the Irish Sea. In another, he visits Belfast, witnessing Land Leaguers fighting pitched battles; however, the boy's only interest is in business. While there, he rescues Cissy, trampled unconscious in the struggle, and takes her back to Dublin.

In 1887, at the end of the novel, Mick has made his fortune, given the MacCarthys their farm back, taken his earliest friend Grip on as associate and married him off to Cissy.

THEME

The novel is unusual among Verne's series of *Extraordinary Journeys* in having little journey and no extraordinary aspect. It possesses instead a strong social and political dimension, being indeed the only book to represent the proletariat and the class struggle. Verne concentrates on the poorest people, the starving children, the cruelty of the overseers, the violence, the excessive taxes, the exploitation of the tenant farmers by the great absentee landowners, the evictions by the stewards. The national cause is hammered home: the most energetic and intelligent farmers, with a traditional poetic culture, are set against the aristocrats, without any positive qualities, being liberal in England and Scotland, but tyrannical in Ireland. The Marquis of Trelingar, who looks down on anyone of lower rank, is a ridiculous anachronism.

But the account may be exaggerated, and the ideology is certainly laid on too thick. In any case, having worked in his research on the tyrannical English, Verne lets the matter drop: no political solution is seriously proposed. Instead of the travails of the Irish people, the novel comes to emphasise instead the success story of the hero.

Notes

[1] wbutcher@netvigator.com, http://home.netvigator.com/~wbutcher/

[2] William Butcher, *Jules Verne: the definitive biography*, with a Foreword by Arthur C. Clarke (New York, 2006), 5, 7–9.

[3] Daniel Compère and Jean-Michel Margot (eds.), *Entretiens avec Jules Verne* (Geneva, 1998), 95.

[4] Verne's unpublished 'Notebook of the voyage to America' (kept in Amiens Municipal Library), cited without reference by Philippe Scheinhardt, 'Jules Verne: génétique et poïétique (1867–1877)', PhD thesis, University of Paris III, 2005, 293.

[5] Jean-Michel Margot (ed.), *Jules Verne en son temps: vu par ses contemporains francophones 1863–1905* (Amiens, 2004), 44; Compère and Margot, *Entretiens avec Jules Verne*, 216; Raymond Ducrest de Villeneuve, unpublished, untitled illustrated biography of Verne in typescript form (1930—kept in Nantes Municipal Library), 109; M[arguerite] Allotte de la Fuÿe, *Jules Verne* (Paris, 1928), 162 (trans. Erik de Mauny, London, 1954).

[6] Margot, *Jules Verne en son temps*, 43.

[7] Municipal Library, www.arkhenum.fr/bm_nantes/jules_verne (last accessed 31 January 2008).

[8] The manuscript version confirms that the opening chapters did undergo a considerable number of changes, for example, the identity of the town where Mick is first seen, Westport being finally chosen (I i—see letter of 4 January 1893). (References to Verne's works are to the French edition and consist of the chapter number—in lower case roman—and volume number if any.)

[9] I xii; I xiii; II xiii; letter of 20 April 1893.

[10] A facsimile of the 1895 translation was published on www.lulu.com in 2007.

[11] Compère and Margot, *Entretiens avec Jules Verne*, 93.

[12] Ghislain de Diesbach, *Le tour de Jules Verne en quatre-vingts livres* (Paris, 1969), 72; Herbert R. Lottman, *Jules Verne: an exploratory biography* (New York, 1996), 285; Marie-Hélène Huet, *L'histoire des voyages extraordinaires: essai sur l'œuvre de Jules Verne* (Paris, 1973), 103; Jean Jules-Verne, *Jules Verne: a biography*, trans. and adapted by Roger Greaves (New York, 1976), 179; Daniel Compère, *Jules Verne: parcours d'une œuvre* (Amiens, 1996), 106; Brian E. Rainey, 'Jules Verne and Ireland', *Proceedings of the Annual Meeting of the Western Society for French History* (Canada) 10 (1984), 154.

[13] Francis Lacassin, 'Jules Verne et le roman des larmes', in Jules Verne, *P'tit Bonhomme* (Paris, 1978), 11; Laurence Sudret, 'P'tit bonhomme', l'hommage de Verne à Dickens', *Bulletin de la Société Jules Verne* 161 (2007), 30. Other articles on *Foundling Mick* in English are: Roger Faligot, 'Jules Verne and Ireland', *Irish Times* 11 August (1978), 15; Maryann Gialanella Valiuilis, 'Comments on Session: literary images of the Jew and of Ireland', *Proceedings of the Annual Meeting of the Western Society for French History* 10 (1984), 160–3.

[14] This plot summary follows the original version—some of the episodes mentioned are absent from the English translation.

[15] In Verne's French text, it is a 'Ragged School', an institution linked with Dickens, following his visit to one in 1843.

[16] In the original French, the dog is called Birk, perhaps after Fenian Colonel Ricard O'Sullivan Burke (1838–1922), featured in Verne's *The Kip Brothers* (1903—II x).

PART ONE

CHAPTER 1

In Far Connaught

Ireland, which has an area of 31,759 square miles, or 20,326,209 acres, formerly formed a part of the insular tract of land now called the United Kingdom. This we learn from the geologists; but it is history and fact that the islands are now two, and more widely divided by moral discord than by physical barriers. The Irish, who are friends of France, are, as they always have been, enemies of England.

A fair country for tourists is Ireland, but a sad one for the dwellers in it. They cannot fertilise it, and it cannot feed them, especially in some of the northern districts. But although the motherland has no flowing breast to give to her children, she is passionately loved by them. They call her by the sweetest of names; she is 'Green Erin',—and indeed her verdure is unequalled—she is 'The Land of Song'; she is 'The Island of Saints'; she is 'The Emerald Gem of the Western World'; she is 'First flower of the earth, and first gem of the sea'. Poor Ireland! She ought to be called 'The Isle of Poverty', for that name has befitted her for many centuries. In 1845 the population of 'the most distressful country that ever yet was seen' reached its highest point, 8,295,061; in 1891 when the last Census was taken, it had fallen to 4,706,162, and the terrible preponderance of indigence is maintained at the old figures, 3 to 8.

The island is hollowed out like a basin, in which there is no lack of water, for the chief feature of the country is the beautiful series of lakes (Hibernice loughs). Lough Neagh alone—the lakes of the drowned towns and round towers—covers a surface of 98,255 acres. The harbours of Ireland are some of the finest in the world, and the Shannon is renowned among rivers.

The town of Westport, in the province of Connaught, is situated on Clew Bay, which resembles Morbihan on the coast of Brittany in the number of islets (365) which dot the surface of its waters. This bay is one of the most beautiful along the entire seaboard of Ireland; its capes, promontories, and points are ranged like so many sharks' teeth which bite the incoming rollers. Connaught—the birthplace of the MacMahons—produces those special Celtic types which are preserved in the families of the persecuted people of past generations, the original owners of the soil. The country is very poor and wretched; to behold it is to have the interpretation of the old saying: 'To Hell or Connaught!'

It is at Westport that we are to find little Mick in the dawn of his life's story; we shall see where, when, and how that story comes to its end.

The great majority of the population of Westport are Catholics. On Sunday, the 17th of June, 1875, most of the inhabitants were at Mass, and a large number of the congregation had come barefoot, carrying their shoes in their hands almost to the church door, partly to economise those articles of attire, although few of them were in good case, and partly because they walked more freely without the restraint of shoe-leather.

For the moment there was only one person in the main street of Westport, a man who was pushing from the back a queerly shaped vehicle drawn by a small and manifestly ill-used pony, and shouting, with wasted energy in the vacant space: 'Puppets! Puppets!'

This travelling showman had come from Castlebar in County Mayo. He had not journeyed by the railroad which places Westport in communication with Dublin; he had not conveyed his luggage by any of the carts or cars which traverse the country; he had 'footed it' like a stroller, 'crying' his puppets everywhere, and urging on his wretched pony with blows, and loud cracking of his whip, which was occasionally accompanied by a sort of prolonged moan from the interior of the vehicle. And then, after the man had sworn at the miserable beast, he would seem to address some other lower animal, saying, with a hideous prefix, 'You — will you hold your tongue?'

The moaning would cease, and the—shall we say covered cart? —would rumble on.

The man's name was Hornpipe. It matters little what was his birthplace; enough that he was one of those Anglo–Saxons, too frequently to be met with among the lowest classes in the British Isles, who have no more feeling than a wild beast, no more heart than a granite rock. The showman had passed through the outskirts of the town, and was now going along the principal street, which was lined with fairly good houses, and shops displaying pompous signs, but where customers would not find much to buy. Out of this street ran several dirty lanes, and the cobblestones with which it was paved bumped and rattled Hornpipe's cart, doubtless to the detriment of the puppets destined to afford a mild diversion to the people of the province of Connaught.

As the public still declined to put in an appearance, Hornpipe trudged along dejectedly, until he reached the entrance to the Mall which is crossed by the street, between a double row of elms. Beyond the Mall stretches a park, with well-kept sanded paths, which lead to the port on Clew Bay. This park is open to the public by permission of the Marquis of Sligo, and gives access to the port at the distance of a mile from the town.

Town, port, park, streets, river, bridges, churches, houses, hovels, in a word, the whole place, belongs to the Marquis of Sligo, one of those wealthy landlords, owners of the soil over almost the whole of Ireland. The Marquis is of old nobility, and is not a bad landlord.

Every few yards Hornpipe stopped his cart, looked about him, and shouted, in a voice which resembled the creaking of an ill-greased machine,—

'Puppets! Royal puppets!'

Nobody opened the closed doors of the shops, not a head was put out of window. Here and there a bundle of rags would appear at the top of a lane, and out of the bundle would peer a hungry, hollow, red-eyed face. After a while a group of half-naked children appeared from somewhere, and five or six of the urchins ventured up to the cart when it was halted on the 'broad walk' of the Mall, and began to whine,—'Giv' us a ha'penny,' in chorus. The poor brats addressed their pitiful prayer to a man much more disposed to ask than to give alms, and they scurried away from his threatening hands and feet, and put a safe distance between their ragged bodies and his whip. No responsible spectator responded to the blandishments of the showman, and the cart, wearily dragged by the half-starved pony, resumed its rumbling way, and soon reached the park, which was as empty of people as the Mall. That Hornpipe should have come there at the hour of divine service to seek spectators among Catholics, was sufficient to prove that he did not belong to that part of the country. Perhaps he might have a better chance in the afternoon. At any rate there was no harm in trying the port, and thither he proceeded, grumbling and swearing.

The harbour of Westport is but little frequented, although it is the largest and most sheltered on this coast, and no foreign ships put into it. Some trading craft and fishing boats were lying there at low tide. The ships, which had come from the west of Scotland, freighted with grain—the great scarcity in Connaught—would sail away to the east, having landed their cargoes. To see large ships in Irish ports, one must go to Dublin, Belfast, Londonderry and Cork, where the transatlantic steamers of the Liverpool and London lines call.

Evidently it was not from the pockets of the fishermen and sailors who were lounging and smoking on the quay that Hornpipe could extract the few shillings he was seeking, so he stopped his cart, and allowed the pony to slumber, with hanging head, between the shafts, while he took a parcel from under the dirty carpet-covering of the vehicle, and complacently surveyed its contents—a lump of bread, some cold potatoes, and a salt herring. Of these choice viands he disposed with the appetite of a man who is breaking a rather long fast. A slight movement in the interior of the cart attracted his attention, and he raised the covering which hid the box of puppets (having looked cautiously around to make sure that he was not observed) and slipped into it a piece of bread, saying in a fierce tone,—

'If you don't hold your tongue—'

He was answered by a sound of ravenous mastication, as though a famished animal, dying of hunger, were crouching inside the box. He returned to his breakfast; the fluid portion of the meal consisted of buttermilk, carried in a tin can.

Presently the bell of the Catholic Church announced that Mass was over. Hornpipe roused the pony by an application of his whip, and set off briskly towards the Mall, in order to catch the congregation on coming out of the church. There would be a good half hour to spare before dinner-time, and he might pick up, not shillings, but a few pence in that interval, and give a second entertainment under better auspices in the afternoon. He recommenced his cry,—

'Puppets! Royal puppets!'

In a few minutes Hornpipe was surrounded by a crowd of perhaps twenty persons; not the most important among the inhabitants of Westport indeed, but still typical of the place. The children were in the majority; the men and women for the most part carried their shoes in their hands, as we have already stated, chiefly because it was so much easier to walk barefooted, according to their usual custom.

There were certain exceptions to this rule, in the persons of a few of the trades people of Westport; for instance, the baker, who paused to look on at the spectacle with his wife and their two children. It is true that his coat was already of a respectable age, and that in rainy Ireland years count double in the case of garments; nevertheless, the worthy man was quite presentable. Was it not due to the pompous signboard of his shop, 'Central Public Bakery', that he should be so? And indeed so central was his bakery that there was not another in Westport. The druggist also was in the little crowd; he insisted on the title of 'apothecary', although his shelves were destitute of very ordinary drugs, but then his shopfront bore the inscription 'Medical Hall' in such resplendent letters that the mere sight of them might have cured his customers.

A priest also had joined the group in front of Hornpipe's cart. He wore the ordinary ecclesiastical dress, a plain black coat, single-breasted, with a high-buttoned waistcoat and Roman collar. He was the parish priest, and many and various are the functions of such an individual in Ireland, outside of the services of the Catholic Church and the administration of its sacraments. He is the adviser of his parishioners in their business and family affairs, their friend and helper in trouble and sickness, and as he is neither appointed nor paid by the state, he acts with complete independence. His 'dues', voluntarily subscribed by his flock, certain tributes in kind, and the fees which are paid on all occasions of religious ceremonial—what is called 'casualty' in other countries, secure to him a modest but easy livelihood. He is the natural administrator of the schools and charitable institutions belonging to his creed, and an active party to the public amusements of the place when the regatta or the steeplechase is 'to the fore'. He holds a foremost place in the family life of his 'people'; he is respected because he deserves respect, although there is not a trace of the puritan about him. Against the purity of his life no whisper of doubt has ever been uttered. Why, indeed, should not the influence of the priest be powerful in a country so deeply imbued with Catholicism that an Irish peasant dreads nothing that can possibly happen to him so much as he fears being refused the sacraments?

Hornpipe then had a public, and one possibly more productive than he had hoped. His show might even be a success, for Westport had not previously been favoured with one of a similar kind. So the showman again uttered his cry: 'Great attraction! Royal puppets! Puppets!'

CHAPTER 2

Little Mick

Hornpipe's Thespian cart was very simply constructed; it consisted merely of a pair of shafts, a quadrangular box, or body, placed upon two wheels, and a couple of projections at the back which admitted of its being pushed uphill; the body, was sheltered from the chary sunshine, and also, but imperfectly, from the liberal rain of the west of Ireland, by a canvas awning stretched on four upright iron rods. The whole thing resembled the barrel organs which travel through towns and villages uttering their strident sounds, but Hornpipe's machine was not a barrel organ, although, as we shall presently see, music of a sort had a share in the matter.

The body had a lid which fitted over one-fourth of its depth from the top. This cover being lifted off and turned down along the side, forming a kind of tablet, the public were admitted to the following spectacle, after a preliminary announcement from Hornpipe in the following words:—

'Ladies and gentlemen! You are about to see the Great Hall in the Queen's palace of Osborne, in the Isle of Wight.' And, in fact, the reversed cover presented a saloon in miniature, contained between the four sides of the square lid, on which draped doors and windows were painted; here and there articles of furniture of the highest style in cardboard were pinned down upon a strip of crimson baize, the tables, chairs, and sofas being so arranged as not to interfere with the free circulation of the princes, princesses, dukes, marquises, earls and baronets, who, with their noble spouses, formed the guests at this great Court function.

'At the end,' continued Hornpipe, 'you will remark the throne of Queen Victoria, with the canopy of crimson velvet spangled with gold, the exact model of that on which her Majesty takes her place during the Court ceremonies.'

The throne in question is three or four inches high, the velvet is flock paper, the spangles are spots of yellow paint, but the whole is quite satisfactory to the simple people who have never beheld the real and essentially monarchical article.

'On the throne,' resumes the showman, 'contemplate the Queen—a perfect likeness—in her robes of state, the royal mantle attached to her shoulders, the crown on her head, and the sceptre in her hand.'

His audience, entirely relying upon the statement of the speaker, were delighted with the royal image, especially with the sceptre, which was modelled upon the trident of Neptune!

'On the right of the Queen, I call the attention of the spectators to their Royal Highnesses the Prince and Princess of Wales, as they appeared on their last visit to Ireland.'

No deception in this! There was the Prince of Wales in the costume of a Field Marshal of the British Army, and the daughter of the King of Denmark, clad in a superb lace gown cut out of the silvered paper with which the contents of sweetmeat boxes are covered. On the other side are the Dukes of Edinburgh, Connaught and Albany, Princess Mary of Teck, and in short, the whole royal family, ranged in a semicircle round the throne. In a second group are the great officers of the Crown, and Hornpipe points out each of them with his wand, to the admiration of the little crowd, adding that each of these noble personages is placed according to his rank. These gentlemen are regarded with only a mild interest, but there is more than curiosity in the stir excited by the showman's indication of a figure to the right in the vicinity of the prime minister, for the figure is that of Mr Gladstone, even then an illustrious 'Grand old man'.

And then occurs an extraordinary anachronism, for Hornpipe, swelling out his gruff voice into a stentorian roar, shouts: 'I present to you, ladies and gentlemen, your celebrated patriot O'Connell, whose name will always find an echo in every Irish heart!'

Yes, there was O'Connell, at a Court ceremony in England, in 1874, although he had then been dead for six-and-twenty years. A number of other celebrities were included, starred and gartered, His Royal Highness the Duke of Cambridge in a *tête-à-tête* with the Iron Duke, the late Lord Palmerston smiling on the late Mr Pitt, members of the Upper and Lower Houses, and behind them a line of Horse Guards in full uniform on horseback in the middle of the Hall—a rare spectacle even at a royal *fête* at Osborne. Not only was the military, political and official life of Great Britain represented by this motley collection of painted dolls, but the English fleet was not forgotten. The *Victoria and Albert* was not there under steam indeed, but several vessels were painted on the glass of the windows, from whence the harbour of Cowes was supposed to be visible.

It must be acknowledged that Hornpipe had not deceived his public in declaring his exhibition to be unique. Great was the astonishment which it produced, not only among the assembled urchins, but among the older spectators, whose world did not extend beyond the province of Connaught, or, perhaps, even the confines of Westport.

'Well, ladies and gentlemen, that is nothing to what you are going to see,' resumed Hornpipe. 'You suppose, no doubt, that these royal and other personages can make neither movements nor gestures; but they are alive, I tell you, like you and me, and you shall see that it is so. First, I will take the liberty of walking round, trusting to the generosity of you all.'

This 'walking round' is the critical moment for the showman of all kinds of curiosities; when the wooden platter begins to circulate. As a general rule the spectators of strolling shows may be divided into two classes; those who go away to avoid putting their hands into their pockets, and those who stay on with the intention of amusing themselves gratis—the latter are much the more numerous. A third category does exist, but it is so limited as to be hardly worth mentioning, and therefore, on the present occasion, Hornpipe 'walked round', with a smile on his bulldog face, which he endeavoured to render amiable, but which was merely fierce, with evil eyes and a mouth that looked as though it were always ready to bite. Among the ragged crowd there was nothing to get. A few of the spectators, who had been attracted by the showman's harangue, merely turned away their heads. Hornpipe's receipts, extracted from a few of his decently clothed auditors, amounted to one shilling and threepence. He looked at the coins with a scornful grimace; but it could not be helped. Perhaps there might be more people about later in the day, now he must make the best of the position, and go on with his programme. Thereupon the admiration became demonstrative, and amid stamping of feet and clapping of hands Hornpipe struck a blow with his wand under the body of the cart, to which a moan, unheard by any but himself, responded, and a sudden animation pervaded the mimic scene.

The puppets, moved by an interior mechanism, seemed to be endowed with real life. Queen Victoria did not indeed descend from her throne, for that would have been contrary to etiquette, she did not even rise, but she moved her head, wagged her crowned cap, and waved her sceptre after the fashion of the conductor of an orchestra ruling the waves of sound with his bâton. The members of the royal family turned stiffly round, solemnly exchanging bows, while the dukes, marquises, earls and other personages passed before them with great demonstrations of respect. The prime minister bent towards Mr Gladstone, and Mr Gladstone bent towards the prime minister. The other figures moved about in their turn, and the horses pranced and flourished their tails.

The whole of this 'business' was accomplished to the accompaniment of the shrill and rasping sounds of a bird-organ minus several of its notes. Certainly, it was all very fine, and the audience, who were not familiar with European drama, were quite excusably delighted.

'I would like to know what it is that sets them going,' said the baker.

'Sure, it's the divil himself,' replied an old fisherman.

'Is it, then?' muttered a woman, turning her head towards the priest, who was looking on thoughtfully.

'Ah, then, how could the divil fit into that box?' demanded a young shop-boy, who was a well-known simpleton. 'The divil's a good size, ye know.'

'Well, as he isn't inside, he's outside!' retorted one of the old women. 'It's himself that's showin' it, anyhow.'

This remark passed unchallenged; the unfavourable impression produced by Hornpipe's personal appearance was general.

Whether witchcraft were in question or not, it had to be admitted that something inside the box was moving the puppets, and yet no one had seen Hornpipe turn a handle or touch a spring. And yet—a peculiarity which had not escaped the notice of the priest—no sooner did the motion of the little crowd slacken than it was quickened by a slash of the showman's whip against the bottom of the box. For whom was this slash, always followed by a moan, intended?

The priest meant to know, and said to Hornpipe, 'You have a dog in the bottom of that box?'

The man, who seemed to resent the question, looked frowningly at the speaker.

'No matter what I have there. That's my business; I'm not bound to tell it to you.'

'You are not bound,' answered the priest, 'but we have a right to suppose it is a dog that works your show.'

'Well, then, it is a dog,' growled Hornpipe, 'a dog in a turning cage. It took a lot of time and patience to train him. And what do I get for my trouble? Not half as much as you'd get for a Mass!'

At the moment when Hornpipe uttered these insolent words the mechanism came to a dead stop, to the vexation of the spectators, whose curiosity was not half satisfied. And, as the showman was about to replace the lid of his box, announcing that the performance was over, the druggist inquired whether he intended to give a second.

'No,' replied Hornpipe roughly. He perceived that he was regarded with suspicion.

'Not even if you are sure of getting at least two shillings?'

'Neither for two nor for three.'

His only object now was to get away, but the little crowd did not seem disposed to make way for him. He had begun to drag the wretched pony off the ground when a prolonged sobbing wail issued from the show-box.

Then Hornpipe, in a fury, shouted,—

'Hold your noise, you cursed whelp!'

'That is not a dog inside there,' said the priest, laying hold of the cart.

'Yes, it is,' growled Hornpipe.

'No, it is a child!'

'A child! A child!' echoed the crowd.

The feelings of the spectators had undergone a sudden revulsion. It was no longer curiosity, but pity that actuated them. A child, shut up in the interior of that box, where he could hardly breathe, and lashed with a whip when he ceased to turn the wheel, having no longer strength to move in his cage!

'The child! The child!' was the angry demand of the incensed people.

The popular sentiment was too strong for Hornpipe. Nevertheless he tried to resist, and pushed the cart from behind in vain. The baker seized it on one side, the druggist on the other, and it was well shaken between them. Never had the Court been placed in such a predicament. Hornpipe was quickly reduced to submission, although he fought fiercely. Everybody joined in. The cart was searched; the druggist slipped between the wheels and lifted a child out of the show-box.

Yes! a little creature of three years old, pale, sickly, wretched-looking, with legs covered with weals from the lash, and hardly able to breathe.

No one in Westport recognised the child.

Such was the entry upon the scene of Foundling Mick, the hero of this veracious history. How he had fallen into the hands of the brutal showman, who was not his father, is easily told. Hornpipe had picked him up nine months previously by a roadside in Donegal, and we know to what purpose he had put the unhappy foundling.

A good woman took him in her arms, and tried to revive him. All the people pressed around him. He had an intelligent and gentle little face, this poor human squirrel, condemned to keep his cage turning under the box of puppets, to earn his livelihood. To earn his livelihood—at that age! At length he opened his eyes, and shrank back at the approach of Hornpipe, who called out angrily, 'Give him back to me!'

'Are you his father?' asked the priest.

'Yes,' answered Hornpipe.

'No, he is not my daddy!' cried the child, clinging to the woman who held him in her arms.

'He is not yours!' exclaimed the druggist.

'He has been stolen!' added the baker.

'And we will not give him back to you!' said the priest.

Hornpipe made a rush forward, his face was scarlet and his eyes blazed with rage. But two strong fellows flung themselves upon him and overpowered him.

'Hunt him! Hunt him!' cried the women.

'Be off, you vagabond!' shouted the druggist.

'And don't let us see you hereabouts again,' said the priest with a threatening gesture.

Hornpipe gave a savage slash of the whip to the starved pony, and the cart rattled along the principal street of Westport.

'What a wretch!' said the druggist. 'He'll come to be hanged, sure enough!'

'What is your name, my child?' asked the priest of the trembling child.

'Mick,' was the answer. He had no other name.

CHAPTER 3

The Poor School

'And No. 13, what has he got?'
'The fever.'
'And No. 9?'
'The whooping cough.'
'And No. 17?'
'He's got the whooping cough too.'
'And No. 23?'
'I think it's goin' to be scarlatina.'

As each of these answers was made to his questions, Mr Mulvany inscribed them upon an admirably kept register under the heading of the respective numbers. There was a column devoted to the name of the malady, the hour of the doctor's visit, the nature of the remedies prescribed and the manner of their administration after the patients should have been taken to the hospital. The entries were made in a remarkably fine and legible hand, and the register was a model of accurate book-keeping.

'Some of these children are rather seriously ill,' added the doctor. 'Give directions for care to be taken that they don't get cold in the removal.'

'Yes, yes' answered Mr Mulvany carelessly. 'Once they're out of this, they're no more business of mine, and so long as my books are posted—'

'And then, if they are carried off by one thing or another,' interrupted the doctor, as he took up his hat, 'it will be no great loss, I suppose?'

'In that case,' said Mulvany, 'I shall enter them in the death column, and their account will be balanced. Now, when an account is balanced, it seems to me that nobody has anything to complain of.'

Then the worthy pair shook hands and the doctor went his way.

Mr Mulvany was the schoolmaster of the poor school of Galway, a small town on the coast of Galway Bay. He was a stout, fat man, one of those elderly bachelors who have never been young, and who will never be quite old, who have no life-troubles or family cares, are not moved by any sentiments of love, sympathy, or compassion, and possess just enough heart to enable them to live. He was one of those beings who pass through life doing neither good nor harm, and are never unhappy—not even in the unhappiness of others.

Such was Mulvany, and he was the right man in the right place as the master of a poor school. The establishment indeed merited the epithet ragged school, which was in use twenty or thirty years ago, but has now ceased to be employed. He kept its books with great accuracy, but his solicitude was confined to that branch of his business. His charges were indeed a 'ragged regiment'. He was assisted by an old woman called Chris, who was seldom seen without a black pipe in her mouth, and a former pupil, a boy of sixteen, named Grip. The latter was a cheerful, even merry fellow, with a good face, bright eyes, and a turned-up nose. The school was a sort of refuge for the destitute; the scholars were the poorest of the poor, many of them forsaken children of nameless parents; the funds were precarious, and the condition of the school was wretched.

Of the forlorn dwellers in Mr Mulvany's gaunt and comfortless abode Foundling Mick was the youngest. He was under five years of age, and so far he seemed to be set apart for misfortune. After he had been treated as we have seen by Hornpipe, then rescued from his tormentor through the compassion of some good souls in Westport, he was now an object of charity in the Galway poor school. When he must leave that dismal refuge, what was to become of him?

The parish priest who had rescued him from the showman had vainly endeavoured to discover the child's previous history. Foundling Mick was unable to furnish him with any clue to it. He remembered only that he had lived somewhere with an unkind woman, a little girl who kissed him sometimes, and another child who died. Where had this happened? He did not know. No one could tell whether he had been a lost child or one forsaken by his parents.

At Westport, he had been taken care of by first one person, then another. Women pitied him, and lamented over his wretched fate. The name of Foundling Mick remained with him. He lived for a week here, for a fortnight there; but the priest and his people were poor; there was no orphanage in which to place the little boy, and so he drifted into the poor school, where he had now been living for nine months among a pack of young ragamuffins, confided to the tender mercies of old Chris, Grip the good-natured, and Mr Mulvany, a human machine. He had not yet figured on Mr Mulvany's list among the cases of scarlatina or whooping cough, or his account would soon have been settled—at the bottom of a pauper's grave in the churchyard. But, although he had not suffered in bodily health, of what was the moral atmosphere composed in which the poor little boy lived? For the most part it was deplorable. There was in the school a boy named Carker, whose mother was 'doing' a long term of penal servitude, whose father had been hanged for murder, and whose own character and conduct indicated the probability of his following in the footsteps of his parents. He was only twelve years old, but his perversity was already remarkable; he was a ringleader in every kind of mischief and ill doing, and was, naturally, a person of consideration among the ragged crew of juvenile flatterers and followers.

This boy was Foundling Mick's special aversion, detested and feared by him, and yet regarded with constant wonder! A boy whose father had been hanged! Just think of it!

The school bore no resemblance to modern educational establishments, where cubic feet of air are mathematically distributed. The scholars had to breathe in the allotted space as best they could, and to be satisfied with straw to sleep on, and scanty food, rarely more choice than bread and potatoes, to eat. As for the instruction given in the place, Mr Mulvany was supposed to dispense that article to the poor scholars of Galway. His duty was to teach the three Rs, but as he did not compel any of his pupils to learn, it would have been difficult to find two of the number who could have read off a poster at sight after two or three years of education. Little Mick, although he was so young, offered a contrast to his schoolfellows by evincing a desire for instruction, and thereby laid himself open to much ridicule. The only part of the school-house which approached to being clean was Mr Mulvany's own room; this was not accessible to any other person. He was best pleased with his pupils when they were out of doors, ranging the countryside at their own sweet will, and when the pressing need of food and sleep brought the vagabond band back to their wretched headquarters, their return always took place too early for him.

The intelligence and the good instincts of Foundling Mick exposed him not only to the senseless ridicule of Carker and five or six others who followed his lead, but to rough treatment at their hands as well. He did not complain, but oh, how he longed to be strong enough to enforce respect, to be able to give blow for blow, kick for kick, and how fiercely the fire of anger burned in the heart of the little creature who was too weak to defend himself! Mick would remain in a corner of the sordid schoolroom when the others were away on their excursions of vagabondage and depredation, to enjoy the quietness, and to be with Grip.

'You don't go out?' said the latter to him.

'No, Grip.'

'Carker will give you a licking if you haven't brought home something this evening.'

'I would rather be licked.'

Grip reciprocated Micky's affection. He was not without intelligence, and he could read and write; so he tried to teach the child the little he himself had learned, and Foundling Mick began very quickly to do honour to his instructor, at least in the matter of reading. Grip was also a capital storyteller, and he would entertain his little pupil for hours together, while Foundling Mick's laughter cheered and brightened the dismal schoolroom. Presently, the others included Grip in their spite and malice, to the great distress of Micky, but Grip regarded this development with philosophical resignation.

'Grip,' said Micky.

'Yes; what is it?'

'Carker is very bad-natured?'

'Indeed he is—very.'

'Why don't you lick him?'

'What for?'

'Aye, and the others too.'

Grip shrugged his shoulders.

'Aren't you strong, Grip?'

'I don't know.'

'But you have big arms and legs.'

Grip was tall, and as thin as a ramrod.

'Well, then, Grip, why don't you beat them, the brutes?'

'Cos it isn't worth while.'

'Ah! if I only had had your arms and legs—'

'It would be far better, my little chap,' answered Grip, 'to use them for working with.'

'Are you sure?'

'Certain sure.'

'Well, then, we will work together; we will try. Shall we, Grip?'

Grip gave a ready assent.

Sometimes Grip would take the child out with him when he was sent on an errand. The two were on a par in point of clothing; their garments were mere rags. This did not so much matter in fine weather, but under the rain and the snow, their pinched blue faces, red eyes, and shivering forms were pitiable to behold, as hand in hand they walked or ran to warm themselves, along the streets of the little town. Foundling Mick would have dearly liked to see what was inside the houses. To him they represented untold splendours. And the hotels at which the travellers alighted, what a pleasure it would be to see the fine rooms, especially those of the Royal Hotel! But the servants would have driven them away like dogs, or rather like beggars, for dogs do get a friendly pat sometimes. And the shabby shops, with the poor displays in their windows, what wonders did they present to the hapless boys! A grand display of clothing, to them, who were in tatters; an array of boots and shoes, to them, who were barefooted! Was it ever to be the lot of either to have a new coat made for his own self, a new pair of shoes, for which he had been measured? No, doubtless, never, any more than so many other poor creatures condemned to live on the leavings of the more fortunate. What pangs of longing assailed the half-starved pair, as they looked upon the big joints of meat on the butcher's stall, and inhaled the odour of hot bread and delicious cakes which pervaded the neighbourhood of the baker's and confectioner's shops!

'How good cakes must be,' said Foundling Mick.

'They just are!' responded Grip.

'Did you ever eat any?'

'I did once.'

'Ah!' sighed little Mick.

One day a lady, taking pity on his pale face, gave him a cake.

'I would rather have a loaf, ma'am,' said he.

'Why, my child?'

'Because it would be bigger.'

Once, however, Grip, having earned a few pence by an errand, bought a week-old cake and gave it to Mick.

'It is good?' he asked.

'Oh!—it is, just as if it had sugar in it.'

'So it has,' said Grip, 'and good sugar too.'

On occasions, Grip and Foundling Mick went as far as Salthill, from whence the whole spectacle of the bay of Galway is visible, with the Aran Islands, the Burren, and the Cliffs of Moher. Then they would return towards the port, along the quays, and the docks which were begun at a period when it was contemplated to make Galway the point of departure of a line of transatlantic steamers. They always lingered to gaze at the few vessels in the bay or moored at the entrance of the port. These objects had an irresistible attraction for the two boys, who, no doubt, had a vague notion that the sea is less cruel than the land to poor people, that it promises them a more secure existence, that life is better in the fresh, free air of the ocean, far from the ill-smelling dens of towns, in which the toilers are packed, that the sea is of all sources of health and sustenance the best for the youth and the man.

'It must be fine, Grip, to go on those boats, with their great sails,' said Mick.

'If you only knew how I've been tempted,' answered Grip, nodding his head.

'Then why aren't you a sailor on the sea?'

'You're right. Why amn't I a sailor?'

'You would go far—far away.'

'Perhaps it may come to that,' said Grip.

On their way back to the school, they had to pass through narrow streets and a squalid quarter of the town. Their way lay in the midst of ruins, but not such ruins as possess interest, being the work of time. These produced only a mournful and wearisome impression, for they were but the ruins of half- or quarter-built houses, left unfinished for want of money, roofless and rotting.

There was, however, something worse than the poor part of Galway, more repulsive than the last straggling hovels of its outlying quarter; the wretched place that represented all those two disinherited ones knew of home; and Grip and Micky were in no hurry to re-enter the poor school.

CHAPTER 4

Concerning a Seagull

Did Foundling Mick, in the midst of his sordid existence, ponder at times upon his past and strive to call it up before his dim vision? A happy child, living amid plenty, care, and affection, may naturally be altogether given up to the mere happiness of living, without a thought of what may come, but it is not so with one whose past has been all suffering. To such a child the future is a pressing care, an ever-present terror; he has to look forward, having to look back.

In Mick's retrospect there was always Hornpipe's figure; the brutal, pitiless rascal whom he sometimes dreaded to meet at a street-corner, with his big, hard, cruel hands ready to clutch him. Then he would be visited by a vague, terrifying recollection of the woman who had ill-treated him, but also by a gleam of remembrance of the girl who had been so tender to him in his pain.

'I can remember now,' he said one day to his companion, 'she was called Cissy.'

'A pretty name,' replied Grip, who rather thought, however, that the said Cissy was a figment of Foundling Mick's fancy, for nothing had ever been ascertained concerning her. But, when he had seemed to cast a doubt upon her existence, Mick had grown angry. Yes, he could see her in his thoughts. Should he not find her again one day? What had become of her? Was she still with that hateful hag? He loved her and she loved him. This was the first affection he had ever felt before he met Grip, and he talked of Cissy as though she were a big girl. She was kind and gentle, she caressed him, she dried his tears, she gave him kisses, she shared her potatoes with him.

'I would have liked to defend her when the old woman beat her,' said Foundling Mick.

'So should I,' answered Grip, to please the child, 'and I think I'd have hit hard.'

And indeed, if this fellow did not defend himself when he was attacked, he could defend others at need, and he had given proof of his prowess in the case of Mick and his persecutors.

One Sunday, soon after he had been sent to the poor school, Foundling Mick, being attracted by the sound of the church bells, found his way into the Catholic cathedral of Galway. The child was timid, and ashamed of his rags, when he saw how large and grand the building was; but he forgot his shyness in the delight of the organ music, the singing voices, the golden vestments of the priest at the altar, and the lights that burned in the sanctuary. He had not forgotten that the good parish priest of Westport had told him about God—God who is the Father of all; but neither had he forgotten that when Hornpipe uttered the name of God it was to garnish his vile oaths, and this recollection disturbed his thoughts in the midst of the religious ceremonies. Hidden behind a pillar, he looked at the priests with the same sort of curiosity as soldiers inspired. Then, when the whole congregation knelt, at the tinkling of the bell for the Elevation, he stole away unperceived, as noiselessly as a mouse goes back into its hole.

When Foundling Mick rejoined Grip in the school-house he said nothing about the church, and indeed Grip had but vague notions of the meaning of Mass and vespers; but, some time afterwards, having made a second visit to the cathedral, and finding himself alone with Chris, he asked her *what* was God?

'God?' replied the old woman, suspending the activity of her pipe for a moment.

'Yes, God?'

'God is the devil's brother,' said she, 'and he sends him all the bad children to be burned in his fire in hell.'

Foundling Micky turned pale on hearing this, and although he wanted very much to know the whereabouts of this hell filled with flames and children, he did not venture to cross-question Chris on the subject. However, he thought a great deal about God, whose sole occupation seemed to be the punishing of babies in so horrible a fashion, if Chris were to be believed, and one day, being very anxious, he began to talk to his friend Grip.

'Grip,' said he, earnestly, 'have you ever heard tell of hell?'

'Sometimes, Micky.'

'Where is it?'

'I don't know.'

'But listen—if children who are wicked are burned there, they will burn Carker?'

'Yes, and in a big fire too!'

'Grip—there's me—I'm not bad, am I?'

'You bad? No. I should think not, indeed!'

'Then I shall not be burned?'

'Not a hair of you.'

'Nor you, Grip?'

'Nor I—you may be sure of that, Micky.'

This was all that Foundling Mick knew about God, the whole of his catechism; and yet he knew, in a confused way, the difference between right and wrong, good and evil.

Mr Mulvany was not pleased with him, and if he were safe from the penalties described by Chris, he was by no means secure from those entailed by the schoolmaster's private code. Foundling Mick figured in the books of Mr Mulvany on the wrong side, in the columns of expenses, not in those of receipts. Here was a brat costing—not much,

Mr Mulvany—and producing nothing! One day the schoolmaster called him up and severely rebuked him.

'You won't do anything, then?' he concluded, impatiently.

'Yes, I will, sir,' answered the child, while he bravely repressed his tears. 'Tell me what you wish me to do.'

'Something that will pay what you cost.'

'I wish I could, but I don't know how.'

'You can follow people in the street, and ask for errands.'

'I am too little, they won't have me.'

'Indeed! Have you hands?'

'Yes.'

'Have you legs?'

'Yes.'

'Well, then, run after the cars, and pick up ha'pence, since you can't do anything else!'

'Beg for ha'pence. Oh, Mr Mulvany, I could not do that!'

'Ah! You couldn't?'

'No, sir.'

'And can you live without eating? No. I thought not. Well, I give you notice that one day or another I will make you try, if you don't find out some way of earning your living. Be off with you!'

Earning his living! And he was not five years old! He shrank away into a corner and hung his head. When these little creatures are not utterly stupefied by misery in their infancy, no one can imagine what they suffer, and they can never be sufficiently pitied.

After the admonition of Mulvany came the incitements of the scamps of the school, who were enraged by the better feelings and conduct of the little boy. They delighted in urging him to evil, and did so, not by wicked counsel alone, but by blows. Carker was his most active persecutor, and brought to the task an amount of zeal only to be explained by his own depravity.

'You won't ask charity, then?' he said one day.

'No,' replied Foundling Mick, firmly.

'Well, then, you stupid fool, you need not ask—take!'

'Take?'

'Yes. This is the way of it. When you see a well-dressed gentleman with the end of his handkerchief sticking out of his pocket, you pull the handkerchief and out it comes.'

'Let me alone, Carker!'

'And sometimes a purse comes out with the pocket handkerchief.'

'That's stealing!'

'And it is not ha'pence that's in rich people's purses; it's shillings, and half-crowns, and pound notes, and sovereigns, and then you share them with your comrades, you little sneak!'

'Yes,' said another, 'and you run away and laugh at the policeman.'

'And besides,' added Carker, 'suppose you do go to prison—what harm's that? It's just as good as here, and better. You get soup and bread, and potatoes, and eat as much as you like.'

'I won't! I won't!' cried the child, as he struggled to get away from the young ruffians, who were knocking him from one to the other like a ball.

Grip, who had just entered the schoolroom, tore him from them.

'You let that child alone, d'ye hear?' cried he, doubling his fists. This time Grip was angry in good earnest.

'You know, I'm not fond of hitting,' he said to Carker, 'and I don't hit often, but when I begin—'

The young rascals drew off from their victim, but threw him parting glances, which promised that they would begin again when Grip should not be available for his protection, and settle their little account with him 'between themselves'.

'Sure, you'll be burned, Carker,' said the child, with a comical air of commiseration.

'Burned?'

'Yes—in hell; if you go on being so wicked.'

At this the whole band of miscreants set up a shout of ridicule; but this did not affect the fixed idea of the roasting of Carker which had taken possession of Foundling Mick.

The intervention of Grip in his favour was not likely to produce good results to little Mick. Carker and the others were bent upon vengeance on Grip and his favourite. Of this Grip was well aware, and he vigilantly mounted guard over Micky, keeping him under his own eye as much as possible all day, and at night sharing with him the garret which he occupied under the roof. This was a cold and miserable retreat, but it protected Foundling Mick from evil counsels and ill treatment.

One day Grip and he had walked out to the beach at Salthill, where they occasionally bathed. Grip, who was a good swimmer, gave Mick lessons in natation, and the little fellow loved to plunge into the limpid water on which floated the beautiful ships which he saw afar off.

They were in the midst of the long waves that broke upon the beach, and Grip, holding Mick by the shoulders, was showing him the first movements, when a band of the schoolboys appeared at the side of the rocks, howling like jackals. There were a dozen of them, the worst of the whole lot, and Carker was the ringleader.

The cause of their vociferations was their having caught sight of a seagull with a disabled wing, which was trying to fly away, and might have succeeded had not Carker struck it with a stone.

Foundling Mick uttered such a cry that it might have been thought he had received the blow.

'Poor gull! Poor gull!' he moaned.

Sudden anger seized upon Grip, and he would probably have inflicted upon Carker a chastisement that he would have remembered, but that he saw the little boy rush up the beach into the midst of the group, imploring pity for the seagull.

'Carker! Carker!' he cried, 'I beg of you—beat me, beat me, but don't hurt the bird!'

A roar of ridicule greeted him as he came along the sand, naked, with his delicate limbs, and his thin ribs showing under the skin. And still he cried, 'Carker! Carker! Don't hurt the bird!'

No one listened to him; they all mocked at his entreaties, and pursued the wretched bird, as it strove to rise from the earth, hopping lamely from one foot to the other, and seeking a shelter amid the rocks. Vain were its efforts.

'Cowards! Cowards!' cried Foundling Mick, with streaming tears.

Carker had seized the seagull by one wing, and now whirled it about in the air; it fell on the sand; another of the band picked it up and dashed it on the pebbles.

'Grip! Grip!' shrieked Mick, 'save it! save it!'

Grip rushed upon the boys, but he was too late. Carker had crushed the seagull's head under his heel, and his companions greeted the exploit with shouts of laughter. Foundling Mick was incensed. Blind rage took possession of him; he picked up a large pebble and flung it with all his strength at Carker, whom it hit full in the chest.

'Ah! You shall pay for this,' shouted Carker, and, before Grip could prevent it, he seized hold of Mick, dragged him to the edge of the water, and struck him repeatedly. Then, while the others held Grip by the arms, he pushed the little boy's head under the incoming wave and kept it there at the imminent risk of suffocating him.

Grip set himself free from the detaining grasp of the young ruffians who held him, by dint of kicks and cuffs, and ran towards Carker, who fled with his rabble rout. The wave would have carried Foundling Mick with it in its ebb, had not Grip laid hold of him and dragged him back, half-fainting. Then Grip rubbed him vigorously, and having brought him to, re-dressed him in his tattered clothes, and taking him by the hand, said, 'Come away.'

Foundling Mick found the dead bird among the stones, and making a hole in the sand, he buried it therein.

CHAPTER 5

More of the Poor School

On his return to the school, Grip thought it right to inform Mr Mulvany of the conduct of Carker and the other boys. It was not that he cared to tell of the tricks they were in the habit of playing on him, for these he hardly noticed. Foundling Mick was in question now, and the ill treatment to which he was exposed was quite otherwise serious. This time persecution had been carried so far that but for Grip's interference the corpse of a child would have been carried in by the waves upon the beach of Salthill.

Mr Mulvany's sole answer to the complaint of Grip was a surly nod of the head. Grip ought to have known that such things did not concern him. He had to keep his books, and he could not have one column for cuffs and another for kicks. So Mr Mulvany merely sent the superintendent about his business. Upon this, Grip resolved from that day forth never to leave his poor little friend alone in the schoolroom, and when he went out he locked him into the garret, where the child was at least in safety.

The summer was ended, September had come, and September is almost winter in Galway. With the last days of that month winter came in earnest that year.

The dwellers on the coast of the bay had a hard time of it. The days were short and the nights were long in the hovels where both coal and turf were sadly scarce. In the poor school the temperature was low in every room except Mr Mulvany's own. Now or never was the time to roam through the streets and along the roads, picking up everything that could be used as fuel, the fallen branches of trees, the bits of coal spilled at back doors or around cellar-gratings, the fragments for which the poor clamoured at the unlading of the lighters at the quay. The school children were employed in this humble harvest field, where the gleaners were so many.

Foundling Mick took his share in the hard task, and every day he brought home a little combustible matter. This was not begging, and, at any rate, there was some warmth on the hearth, and therewithal he had to be content. The whole school, shivering in their rags, crowded about the fireplace—the big ones got the best places, needless to say—while their supper was being prepared. What a supper! When it did not consist simply of 'stirabout' (oatmeal porridge), it was composed of crusts, potatoes, and scraps of coarse meat made into an unappetising Irish stew, with plenty of grease in the gravy, and a very slender allowance of the mess was given to each of the hungry crowd. The bigger boys, of course, fared the best; for Foundling Mick there was neither a place by the fire nor a bowl of stew as a matter of right or custom, but Grip would take the child into his own den and share his own portion of the meagre daily meal with him. There was no fire up there, but by cowering under the straw and huddling close together they managed to defeat the cold, and to go asleep. Perhaps they were warm in their sleep; we may hope so.

One day Grip had a real turn of luck. He was strolling along the principal street, when a traveller who was going into the Royal Hotel asked him to take a letter to the post office. Grip gladly executed the commission, and received a shilling for his trouble. A whole, bright, new shilling! The employment of his capital was indicated easily—much should be placed in the stomach of Foundling Mick, a little in Grip's own. He bought a goodly supply of cold boiled beef, which lasted for three days, and was safely consumed without the knowledge of Carker and the others. Naturally, Grip had no notion of sharing with those who never shared with him.

Moreover, the worthy gentleman so fortunately encountered close to the Royal Hotel observed the wretched clothing of his messenger, and presented Grip with a knitted jersey of his own in good condition. Grip did not dream of keeping this adventitious garment for his personal use. Oh, no! It would be 'splendid' for Mick to wear under his rags. 'He'll be like a sheep in its wool in the likes of that,' said the good fellow to himself, exultingly.

But the sheep did not wish Grip to give up his wool to him, and a dispute arose between them, which was ultimately arranged to their common satisfaction. The gentleman was tall, and the jersey would have covered little Micky from head to foot. It was not impossible to divide the ample garment between the two friends. They might as well have asked the drunken old woman, Chris, to give up her pipe as to unmake and remake the jersey, so Grip, shutting himself up in his garret, applied himself to the task, bringing all his intelligence to bear upon it, and so skilfully did he execute it that Micky had a warm body-covering out of the stranger's charitable gift, and Grip himself had a short sleeveless vest, which, after all, was something.

Of course, the child was carefully instructed to conceal the addition to his wardrobe from the others, who would have torn it to shreds rather than leave him in possession of it. He contrived to hide his treasure successfully, and we may guess how highly he appreciated it during the long and bitter winter which brought privation of many kinds upon the district, and in particular to the poor school.

The parish did what it could for the poor, but the demands of several charitable institutions had to be considered and met to some extent before those of the destitute children in that chill shelter could be entertained. There was nothing for it but that the children should beg from door to door, and beg they did.

Foundling Mick had to follow the example of his companions, but he departed from their methods, for it had seemed to him the first time he lifted a door-knocker to ask for alms, that the blow had fallen upon his own breast. Instead of holding out his childish hand he falteringly asked —could they give him something to do? Such a question from an urchin of five years old was easily answered; he was given a hunch of bread, and ate it with tears. What would you have? He was hungry.

At last the hard winter of 1876 came to a close. The spring of 1877 was mild, and summer came early. It was very warm from the beginning of June. On the 17th of August Foundling Mick, who was then five years and a half old, had an adventure which brought about most unexpected consequences. He was returning to the school at seven o'clock in the evening in a melancholy mood, for he knew he should be ill received as he was coming back empty-handed. Unless Grip chanced to have some odd crust or other in reserve, there would be no supper for the little fellow that evening. He was within a few yards of the door when he stumbled and fell at full length, but without hurting himself. He got up and looked around him for the object which had caused his tumble; it proved to be an earthenware gallon jar, lying unbroken on its side in a soft mud puddle. The cork had been drawn, but replaced, and the jar had probably rolled off the sloping back of one of the low cars of the locality, unnoticed by its proprietor, who had made himself too familiarly acquainted with its contents. Micky set the jar up on end, and twitched out the cork. He did not know many of the good things of this world by sight, but he did know whiskey when he smelt it, and this was whiskey. Nearly a gallon too! What a welcome he should have now! All the ragamuffins might have their fill of Foundling Mick's find. Nobody was in the street, nobody had seen him, and he was close to the school.

But then certain ideas occurred to Micky—ideas which would not have come to Carker or the others. This jar did not belong to him, it was somebody's property and had evidently been lost. It might be difficult to discover the rightful owner; but no matter, his conscience told Micky that he must not dispose of other people's goods. He knew this by instinct only, for neither Hornpipe nor Mulvany had ever taught him the difference between right and wrong. Happily, there are children in whose hearts that lesson is inscribed by a Divine hand.

Micky, much disconcerted by his find, resolved to consult Grip, who would surely be able to return the jar to its owner. The great thing was to get the awkward receptacle up to the garret without its being seen by the young scamps, who would not trouble themselves about its proprietor. If it got into their hands, there would not be a drop in the jar by nightfall; but Micky could answer for Grip as he could for himself. He would not touch the jar, he would hide it under the straw, and tomorrow he would find out who had lost it, or if he could not do that, the two of them would go from house to house and inquire—they would not be begging this time. So Foundling Mick approached the school, laboriously endeavouring to hide the big jar with his tattered clothes.

Unfortunately, just as he reached the door, Carker came rudely out and bumped against him. The bully had seen the child coming, and thought it a fine opportunity for paying him off for the interference of Grip upon the beach at Salthill. He seized hold of Micky, felt the jar, and snatched it from him.

'Ha! What's this?' he cried.

'That! It's none of yours.'

'Then it's yours?'

'No, it's not mine!'

Micky tried to push past Carker, but he, with a savage kick, sent him reeling against the doorpost, and rushed back into the schoolroom, whither Micky limped after him, crying with anger.

He tried again to protest, but as Grip was not there to protect him, he was pushed, struck, and kicked. Chris joined in the fun so soon as she saw the jar.

'Whiskey!' she exclaimed, 'and enough for every one of uz!'

What could the little fellow do? To go to Mr Mulvany and tell him what was taking place would have been to ensure a warm reception for himself. And as for the jar, what would have happened to it? Mr Mulvany would have sent for the jar, and nothing drinkable that went into the schoolmaster's room ever came out of it.

Micky could do nothing else but hasten up to Grip's garret and tell him what had occurred.

'So it's Carker that took it from you, is it?' said Grip, threateningly, when his little friend had told the tale. 'We will go down, and I'll soon see who'll keep it!'

But when Grip got to the door he found it bolted on the outside. He shook the door vigorously, but it resisted all his efforts, to the great joy of the rabble rout below, who shouted,—

'Ha, ha, Grip!'

'Ho, ho! Foundling Mick.'

'We're drinking yer good health.'

Grip, finding that he could not burst open the door, resigned himself to facts, according to his custom, and endeavoured to quiet his angry companion.

'Let them alone,' he said, 'never mind the fools.'

'Oh, if we were only the strongest!'

'Yes! but we're not, you see. And what good would it do? Look here, Mick, I've kept some potatoes for you. Come and eat them.'

'I'm not hungry, Grip!'

'Never mind, eat all the same, and then we'll get into the straw and go to sleep.'

The very best thing to be done after such a supper.

Carker had bolted the door of the garret, because he did not mean to be disturbed that evening. With Grip securely shut in, the boys could drain the stone jar at their ease. Chris would not interfere, provided she had her share of the whiskey. So the liquor, which the young wretches sipped raw out of mugs, went round merrily, and as none except perhaps Carker were accustomed to the taste of spirits, they rapidly became intoxicated; in fact the jar was still more than half full when the whole company was drunk, some noisily, some stupidly. The noise did not arouse Mulvany from his usual indifference. He cared nothing for what might be going on downstairs, provided he were left undisturbed.

Nevertheless, he was about to be routed out of his den in a very summary manner, not without damage to his cherished account books.

The greater number of the young scamps had succumbed to their potations, and were lying about the schoolroom; there they would have fallen asleep had it not occurred to Carker that it would be great fun to set fire to some whiskey and drink it burning. This device, he thought, would 'finish' Chris, and two or three others who were not yet quite drunk; accordingly, he poured a good deal of the spirit into a saucepan—the only one at Chris's disposal—lighted a match, and set fire to it. The room was illuminated by the ghastly blue flame, the ragamuffins—such of them as were able to stand—took hands and danced round the blazing saucepan. Had there been any passers-by they would have thought a legion of devils had invaded the school; but the place was lonely at night.

Suddenly a great light appeared in the interior of the house. One of the dancers had tripped, and kicked over the saucepan; the blazing spirit, spilt upon the straw, instantly ignited, and the flames spread to the farthest corners of the room. The fire was everywhere in a moment. Those who were not quite drunk, and those who were startled out of their stupor by the glare and the crackling of the flames, had barely time to open the door and rush into the street, dragging old Chris with them.

At that moment Grip and Foundling Mick, who had just awoke, were endeavouring to get out of the garret, which was filled with suffocating smoke.

The flames had already been perceived, and some inhabitants of the quarter ran to the spot, bringing buckets and ladders. Fortunately, the poor school was a detached building, and as the wind was blowing from the opposite quarter the houses in front of it were not in danger. There was little hope of saving the school; it was on those who were shut up in it, and whose egress was barred by the flames, that attention was turned. Then a window on the first floor was opened; it was that of Mr Mulvany's own room, and the fire was approaching it. The schoolmaster appeared, staggering with terror and gesticulating wildly.

'My books! My books!' he cried, and tried to get down the stairs, but was driven back by the dense smoke. Shouts from the street warned him that he had not a moment to lose; he hastily collected his cherished registers and account books, and threw them out of the window. Those treasures fell into the street, were promptly trampled on by the men who were placing a ladder, by which Mr Mulvany was to be rescued, against the wall, pounced upon by the urchins outside, and torn to atoms, most of which the wind carried away and dispersed far and wide, to the high glee of the perpetrators of this act of mischief.

Mr Mulvany had been able to get out, not so Grip and Foundling Mick. The garret was lighted by a small window in the roof, and the staircase leading to it was already a prey to the flames. Presently the school-house would be merely a big bonfire. Then Grip's cries rose above the noise of the conflagration.

'There is some one in that attic!' exclaimed a person who had just arrived at the scene of the catastrophe. The newcomer was a lady, dressed in travelling costume; she had left her carriage at the end of the street, and was looking on at the fire. Her maid stood, pale and frightened, at her side. By this time the fire had spread so widely that it could not be subdued, and, the schoolmaster having been rescued, no farther effort was made to save the house, which was supposed to be empty.

'Help! Help, for those who are there!' cried the lady, throwing her arms up with a grand dramatic gesture. 'Ladders, ladders, my good people, and to the rescue!'

'Who is in the attic?' asked some one of Mr Mulvany, who was stooping over the poor remains of his books.

'Who? I don't know,' he answered in a bewildered voice; he was conscious only of his own disaster.

Then, with sudden recollection, he added,—

'Ah, yes! Two boys—Grip and Foundling Mick.'

'Poor creatures!' exclaimed the lady. 'My money, my jewels, all I have shall be theirs who save those lives!'

It was, however, no longer possible to get into the school-house, the walls were wrapped in flames, and the interior was burning fiercely.

Suddenly the thatched roof gave way at the side of the little window. Grip had contrived to tear away a rafter at the moment when the fire had reached the floor of the garret. He squeezed himself through the hole thus made, dragging the half-suffocated child after him, and crept along the sloping thatch to the edge of the side wall of the house. There he steadied himself against the abutment and looked down, holding Mick in his arms. At this moment a jet of flame burst upwards from the roof, carrying fragments of the thatch with it, which were dispersed around in glittering sparks.

'Save him!' cried Grip, 'save him!' and he threw the child from him on the street-side, where, happily, he was caught in a man's arms before he reached the ground. Then Grip flung himself down, and rolled, almost stifled, to the foot of a wall which immediately afterwards came down in a heap.

The stranger-lady advanced to the man who held Foundling Mick, and asked him in a voice which trembled with emotion,—

'To whom does that innocent creature belong?'

'To nobody. He is only a foundling,' was the man's reply.

'Then he is mine! Mine!' and she took the child and pressed him to her bosom.

'Madam! Madam!' said the maid, in a tone of remonstrance.

'Silence, Eliza! Silence, I say. Heaven has sent me an angel.'

As the angel had neither parents, relatives, nor friends, it was just as well to leave him in the hands of this lovely lady, who had so generous a heart, and she was heartily cheered by the crowd as she carried off her prize at the very moment when the last remnants of the poor school crumbled to the earth in a swirl of flame.

CHAPTER 6

Limerick

The charitable lady who had come upon the stage of our story in rather melodramatic fashion, but had played her part with so much scenic earnestness that nobody was surprised by her performance, could hardly have treated Foundling Mick with greater tenderness had he really been her own child. She carried him to her carriage in her arms, although the maid requested permission to relieve her of the precious charge.

'No, no, Eliza,' said she, in a tone vibrating with emotion. 'He is mine. Heaven has permitted me to snatch him from the ruins of that burning house. Thank God! Thank God! Ah! the darling! the darling!'

The darling was half-stifled, his eyes were closed, his mouth was open, his breath was coming in gasps. Plenty of space and fresh air would have been better for him than the tumultuous tenderness of his benefactress.

'Quick! to the station,' she cried to the driver when she was seated in the vehicle—a sufficiently shabby cab—'double fare if you don't miss the nine forty-seven train.'

And now, who was this providential traveller? Had Foundling Mick fallen into hands which would not let him go?

Miss Anna Watson, the leading lady of an important London theatre, was on tour just then, and engaged to appear at Limerick, after a short trip for recreation to Co. Galway, which she had just made, accompanied by her maid, a staid person named Elizabeth Corbett. The actress, a good-hearted, impulsive woman, who was always acting off as well as on the stage, open-handed, generous, but very vain and sensitive on every point where her self-appreciation was concerned, was on her way to take the train for Limerick, where she was to appear on the following day, when cries of distress and a volume of smoke and flame attracted her attention. The poor school was on fire.

What a chance! To see a real conflagration, so different from the stage mimicry! Notwithstanding the observations of Eliza, Miss Watson persisted in forcing her way to the front row of the spectators, with the result which has already been narrated.

The spectacle had not lacked interest, and the 'situation' had been admirably worked up. Two human beings shut up in a garret, a staircase in flames, and no outlet! Two boys—one big, one little (a little girl would have been more scenic, perhaps)—but it all did very well. And the cries which Miss Watson had uttered—how heart-rending, how ear-piercing! She would have rushed to the rescue in person only that her dust cloak might have fed the flame anew. And besides, the roof had already been rent asunder. The two poor boys had appeared in the midst of the smoke, the big one carrying the little one! Ah, what a hero was that big boy! How artistic was his attitude! What skill of gesture, what truth of expression! Poor Grip little thought he had produced so much effect. As for the other, the nice little boy, how pretty he looked! 'Like an angel coming through the flames of a hell,' said the complacently retrospective Miss Watson to herself. And this was the very first occasion in his life on which any cherubic or celestial idea had been associated with Foundling Mick. Miss Watson's quick eye had caught the stage effect in every particular. She had cried, as she would have cried on the boards: 'My money, my jewels, all that I have to him who saves them!' but nobody could have scaled the tottering walls to reach the crumbling roof. The cherub had been received into arms that were opportunely there to receive him, and had passed from those to Miss Watson's. And, now, Foundling Mick possessed a mother; nay, it was even rumoured among the crowd that Miss Watson was a great lady who had recognised her son in the midst of the fire at the poor school.

It is characteristic of actresses to imagine themselves always on the stage; for them the most ordinary circumstances of life are 'situations.'

When Miss Watson found herself comfortably installed in a first-class compartment in the train which the driver had caught without any trouble, with her maid and her newly acquired treasure, she indulged in all the transports of a real mother on a similar (stage) occasion.

'He is my child … my blood … my life!' she exclaimed. 'None shall tear him from me!'

'We shall see how long this will last,' said Eliza to herself.

For some time after the train started, Foundling Mick remained in a state of stupor, notwithstanding the efforts of Miss Watson to arouse him, and her outpouring of the traditional phrases of endearment. With the calm and deliberate assistance of the unemotional Eliza, the child was undressed to his woollen vest, the only article on his body that was not ragged, and provisionally attired in a warm dressing-jacket taken from Miss Watson's travelling bag, and a thick shawl. But he did not seem conscious of the process of getting rid of his smoke-tainted clothing, or that he was wrapped in warm garments and cradled in soft arms.

At length a junction was reached, and there was a short delay.

'Eliza,' said Miss Watson, 'you must see whether there is a doctor in the train.'

Eliza made inquiry; there was not a doctor.

'Just like the wretches,' said Miss Watson; 'they are never at hand when they're wanted.'

'I assure you, ma'am,' said Eliza, 'there is nothing the matter with the child. He will come round at once if you will only not smother him.'

'Do you really think so, Eliza? Ah, the darling! I am so inexperienced about children. Do as you think best, Eliza, for the sweet, sweet baby.'

Eliza released the child from Miss Watson's arms, and deposited him comfortably on the well-cushioned seat; then, after looking at him attentively, she replied to her mistress's anxious observations upon his long-enduring quiescence.

'May I tell you my opinion, ma'am?'

'Yes, yes.'

'Well, then, I believe he is asleep.'

Not only was this the case, but Foundling Mick and Miss Watson also slept soundly all through the remainder of the journey. At five o'clock in the morning the train ran into the station at Limerick, and Foundling Mick, awakened from his restorative slumber, sat up and gazed with great eyes filled with wonder upon the lady who was gazing at him. Then she kissed him repeatedly, exclaiming, 'He lives! He lives! God, who gave him to me, has not been so cruel as to take him away again.'

Eliza assented to this remark, and so it was that our poor little boy passed, without any intermediate experience, from the garret in the Galway poor school to the fine rooms occupied by Miss Watson at the Royal George Hotel, Limerick.

The fair and fashionable actress, who was not averse to being talked about, certainly had no reason for desiring to conceal the leading incident of her tour in Galway. Discretion was not enjoined upon or practised by any of the people of the hotel or the theatre, and the day after her first appearance all Limerick had heard of the romantic adventure of the poor school and the rescued foundling. The story ran that the heroine of so many dramas had rushed into the flames to save the little fellow, and Miss Watson did not contradict this improved version.

It was, at least, indisputable that she had brought with her to the Royal George Hotel a child whom she meant to adopt, an orphan to whom she would give her name, since he did not possess one, for 'Foundling Mick', that by which he called himself, could hardly rank as serious. In the meantime, she called him by all sorts of caressing baby-names, not at all appropriate to the poor child who had already served so rude an apprenticeship to life; but it must be remembered that Miss Watson knew nothing about this, and also that Foundling Mick was a very little fellow.

He was profoundly puzzled by his novel existence; he understood not at all the objects that surrounded him, or the ways of his new friends. He submitted to everything; he was not used to caresses, and he was caressed; or to kisses, and he was kissed; he was not used to fine clothes, and he was well dressed and well shod, moreover, his hair was curled. Besides all this startling novelty, he was fed like a prince, and given dainties in profusion.

The actress's friends of both sexes flocked to her rooms at the Royal George Hotel. What compliments she received, and how graciously she accepted them! The story of the fire at the poor school assumed such dimensions that it was only a wonder the whole of Galway had not been burned down before the subject was exhausted.

Of course, the child was not forgotten during these visits, and Miss Watson 'trotted him out' with rare dexterity. Nevertheless, his memory was at work; he remembered that if he had never before been petted he had at least been loved. And one day he asked suddenly,—

'Where is Grip?'

'Who is Grip, my baby?' said Miss Watson.

He made her understand not only *whom* but *what* Grip was. But for him, Foundling Mick must certainly have perished in the flames; but for Grip, only the corpse of a child would have been found amid the ashes of the school-house. This was very well indeed on the part of Grip, but his heroism—the word was accepted—could not at all diminish Miss Watson's share in the rescue. Supposing that admirable woman had not providentially appeared on the scene of the conflagration, where would Foundling Mick have been now? Who would have taken him? In what wretched hovel would he have found shelter with the other houseless outcasts, his former companions?

The truth was that nobody had inquired about Grip. Nobody either knew or wanted to know what had become of him. Foundling Mick would forget him, at last he would leave off talking of him. This was a mistake; the image of him who had fed and protected the helpless foundling would never be effaced from his heart.

And yet the life of the adopted child might well have diverted his mind. He accompanied Miss Watson when she went out in her carriage at the fashionable hour, and showed herself in the fair city of Limerick. Never was a more beribboned, a more dressed-up, a more decorative child offered to the public gaze. He had as many costumes as an actor; and as he had replaced Miss Watson's late spiteful little lapdog, no doubt she would have put him into her muff, with his curly head protruding, if he had been of a convenient size. Everybody looked at the little figure seated by the side of the actress, now attired in a Scotch costume, again as a Court page, and sometimes as a sailor-boy after stage fashion, and everybody spoke of him as 'the angel saved from the flames'.

Now and again he was taken to the theatre, where he was a sight to behold, in a velvet tunic and white gloves!— sitting up primly in a box under the stern eye of Eliza, hardly daring to move, and striving to keep awake until the end of the play. He did not understand a great deal that he saw, but he thought it was all real. When Miss Watson appeared in the costume of a queen with a crown and a royal mantle, and afterwards as a 'woman of the people' in cap and apron, or as a poor person in ragged garments, he could not believe that it was she whom he should presently find at the hotel. Hence the profound disturbance of his childish imagination; he knew not what to think. He dreamed of the plays at night, as though the sombre drama were continued; with it were mingled the puppets and the showman, Carker and the other wicked schoolboys, and he would wake in terror, but not daring to call anyone to him.

A few days after her arrival at Limerick Miss Watson had a grand opportunity of exhibiting Foundling Mick at the races, a favourite institution of the place. He was more gorgeously dressed than ever, her affection was more lavishly displayed; the 'angel' and his 'saviour' enjoyed a complete triumph.

Well, we must accept Miss Watson for what she was; a little extravagant, a little 'cracked', but kind and compassionate when she could be so with the accompaniment of display. The attention she paid to the child was visibly theatrical, the kisses she showered on him were the conventional kisses of the stage, but Foundling Mick was not capable of discerning the difference. And yet he did not feel himself loved as he would fain have been, and perhaps he said to himself unconsciously what Eliza oftentimes repeated to herself,—

'We shall see how long all this will last—supposing it to last at all.'

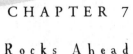

CHAPTER 7

Rocks Ahead

Six weeks elapsed, and it was not surprising
that Foundling Mick became accustomed
to his pleasant life. Poverty grows easy, or at
least endurable, why not wealth? As yet
things were taking their usual course, but
was it not probable that Miss Watson
would tire of her own exaggeration of
sentiment and prodigality of petting? To
use a phrase of her own, she had had a
'craze' for the child, who served her as a
pastime, a plaything, and an advertisement,
and although she continued to take
excellent care of him, her caresses fell off in
number and effusiveness. At first she had
the 'cherub' brought to her room before she
rose; she played with him, acting the part
of the young mother, and acting it very
well. Then, as this pretty performance
curtailed the hours of sleep, an indulgence
very dear to Miss Anna Watson, she
discontinued it, sending for her live
plaything at the luncheon-hour only. She

was quite pleased and amused to see him seated on a tall chair which had been bought expressly for him, and eating with a fine appetite.

'Ha! That's good, isn't it?' she would say. The first time she put the question to him he replied,—

'Oh, yes, ma'am, it is good, like what we get to eat at the hospital when we are sick.'

Foundling Mick had not been taught manners, as may be supposed—it was not from Hornpipe or Mr Mulvany that he would have learned them—but he was by nature reserved, discreet, and of a gentle and affectionate disposition, very different from the scamps of the poor school. He was, in fact, superior to his condition, just as he was beyond his years in his feelings and his ways. Flighty and futile as she was, Miss Watson had not failed to remark this. She knew nothing of his history beyond what he had been able to tell her of his little life with the puppet-show man. He was really and truly a foundling. Miss Watson longed to prove him what she persisted in declaring his 'natural distinction' gave her reason to believe he was, namely, the son of some great lady whose social position had obliged her to desert him after the fashion of the current drama. Thereupon she constructed a whole romance, not remarkable for its novelty, imagining 'situations' which might be 'adapted' for the stage, and composing in her imagination a fine 'piece' with 'tearful effects' in it. She would bring out the piece, play the chief part, and make it the most brilliant success of her dramatic career. In it she would be overwhelming, and why not sublime?

Then, having reached these heights of fancy, she would seize the child and strain him to her heart as though she were embracing him on the stage, amid the applause of a crowded audience.

One day, Foundling Mick, who was disturbed by these demonstrative proceedings, said to her,—

'Miss Anna!'

'Yes, darling, what do you want?'

'I want to ask you something.'

'Ask it, my pet, ask it.'

'You won't scold me?'

'Scold you? No!'

'Everybody has had a mamma, haven't they?'

'Yes, dear; everybody has had a mamma.'

'Then why don't I know mine?'

'Why? Because—' Miss Watson was somewhat embarrassed— 'because—there are reasons. But a day will come—yes! I believe you will see her.'

'I have heard you say—isn't it true?—that she must be a lady?'

'Yes, to be sure, a beautiful lady.'

'And why must she be a beautiful lady?'

'Because your face, your air—ah, what queer questions the darling asks!—Then the situation, the situation in the piece requires her to be a beautiful lady, a great lady. You cannot understand.'

'No, I do not understand,' answered Foundling Mick, very sadly, 'and sometimes I think my mamma must be dead.'

'Dead? Oh, no. You must not think such a thing. If she were dead, there would be no piece.'

'What piece?'

Miss Watson gave him no answer beyond a kiss.

'But if she's not dead,' persisted Mick, with the logical tenacity of his age, 'if she is a beautiful lady, why has she gone away from me?'

'She must have been forced to do it, my pet, against her will. But, at the end—'

'Miss Anna!'

'Well, what do you want now?'

'My mamma—is—not you?'

'I? Your mamma?'

'Since you—call me your child?'

'That is what everyone says to little people of your age. Poor little fellow! So he actually thought—No! I am not your mother! If I had been, I would not have deserted you. I would not have doomed you to poverty! Oh, no, no!'

And Miss Watson, who was much moved, ended the conversation by another stage embrace of Mick, who went away downcast.

Poor child! Whether he belonged to a rich or to a poor family, he was no more likely to learn anything about his origin than many another waif picked up at a street-corner.

One day, Miss Watson, who perceived that Foundling Mick's intelligence was developing itself rather rapidly, conceived the notion that it would soon become necessary to have him taught something. She began dimly to see that she had undertaken a future charge by her impulsive adoption of the child, who would grow up in time and have to be provided for. What was to become of him? He could not be taken in her train from town to town, from theatre to theatre, especially on the foreign tours which she intended to make. She would be obliged to place him at a boarding school. Of course it should be a very good boarding school, first-rate in fact. The only thing certain was that she never would desert him.

One day she said to Eliza,—

'He grows more and more charming; his nature is so affectionate. He will well repay me for what I shall have done for him. And then, he is so precocious, he likes to know things; indeed, I think he is even too thoughtful for his age. And to fancy that he was my child! Poor little fellow! I do not imagine I am like the mother he once had. She must have been a grave, serious sort of person. We must think well, Eliza.'

'About what, ma'am?'

'About what we shall make of him.'

'Now?'

'No, not now. Now, we have only to let him grow like a plant. But later on—when he is seven or eight years old. Don't children usually go to school at that age?'

Eliza was about to suggest that as the little boy was already used to school life—(we know, although Eliza did not, what sort of life he had found it)—the best plan would be to send him back to it, under far different conditions, of course; but Miss Watson did not give her time to reply.

'Tell me, Eliza,' she resumed, 'don't you think he ought to have a turn for the stage?'

'He?'

'Yes. Just look at him! He will be very handsome, he has magnificent eyes and a fine carriage. I am sure he would make a first-rate stage lover.'

'Dear bless us, ma'am; there you are, off again!'

'Not at all! I am quite in earnest. I will teach him to act. The pupil of Miss Anna Watson. You perceive the effect?'

'In fifteen years.'

'In fifteen years, Eliza, if you like; but I tell you again he will be the most charming young man that can be imagined. All the women will be—'

'Jealous! Ah, yes! I know that old tune. May I tell you what I really think, ma'am?'

'Yes. Tell me.'

'Well, then, I think that child will never let you make an actor of him.'

'And why?'

'Because he is too serious.'

'Perhaps that is true,' said Miss Watson; 'however, we shall see.'

'We have plenty of time, ma'am.'

Eliza was right; they had plenty of time, and if Foundling Mick would but manifest an inclination for the stage, all would be well.

In the meantime a splendid idea occurred to Miss Watson, one of those brilliant ideas which were hers alone; it was to bring Foundling Mick out at once at the Limerick theatre.

She must have been mad! will be the natural exclamation of the reader; but she was not mad in the ordinary sense of the word, and under the circumstances. Miss Watson was just then rehearsing a machine-made play of a kind which is not rare on the English stage. It was a drama, or rather a melodrama, entitled *A Mother's Remorse*, and it had already drawn copious tears from the eyes of a whole generation of playgoers.

In this work there was, of course, a part for a child,— the child whom the mother could not keep, whom she was forced to desert a year after its birth, whom she finds in a wretched state, and who is the object of a secret enmity, and in danger of being again torn from her, etc., etc., etc.

The part was a 'dumb' one, of course. The little person who was to play it would merely have to allow himself to be embraced, pressed to the maternal bosom, wept over and pulled from one side to the other, without uttering a word.

Evidently Foundling Mick was cut out for the part. He was of the right age and size, he still had a pale face and eyes that were used to weeping. What an effect he would produce when he should 'come on', with his mother by adoption! With what force and fire would Miss Watson carry off Act 3 Scene 5, the great scene, in which she defends her son at the moment when he is about to be torn from her arms. Would not the imaginary situation be doubled in intensity by the real situation? Would not the cries of the persecuted mother be genuinely inspired cries, and her tears real tears? Here was a sure success for Miss Watson, perhaps the most brilliant of her dramatic career.

She set to work at once, and Foundling Mick was taken to the last rehearsals.

During the first he was much astonished by everything that he saw and heard. Miss Watson called him 'my child', in speaking her lines, but it seemed to him that she did not press him very closely to her breast, and that she did not cry over him at all. In truth, it is quite unnecessary to weep at rehearsals. Tears ought to be strictly reserved for the public.

The little boy was a good deal disturbed. The 'behind the scenes' aspect of the place, the gloom and vagueness overhead, the crowd of objects which he could not make out, the spacious, empty house, the grey light filtered through the distant windows of the far-off corridors, made him uneasy. Nevertheless, Harry—he was Harry in the piece—did what was required of him, and Miss Watson confidently foretold a great success for him, and for herself.

Miss Watson's confidence was not shared by the company generally. Among her fellow actors and actresses some were envious of her, and she also gave a good deal of offence by her somewhat aggressive personality, and her incessant parade of her 'leading' position. And now she made herself more than usually obnoxious, by asserting, with her customary exaggeration, that under *her* training this child would one day excel Kean, Macready, and every leading actor on the modern stage.

This was, really, going a good deal too far.

At last the great day arrived. It was Thursday, the 19th of October. Needless to say that Miss Watson was in a state of excusable nervous excitement. Now she would lay hold of 'Harry' and kiss him repeatedly, with a good deal of shaking thrown in, again he would irritate her by his mere presence, she would send him away, and the child understood nothing at all about the matter.

A good 'house' might fairly have been expected, but as a matter of fact the doors of the theatre were besieged, so widely was the story of the rescued foundling known, and so attractive was the announcement of—

'A MOTHER'S REMORSE.'
A thrilling drama by the celebrated John Smith.
The Duchess of Kendal—Miss Anna Watson. Harry—
'Foundling Mick', aged five years and a half.

Our little lad would have been proud had he stopped before the big poster. He knew how to read, and there was his own name—such as it was—in great red letters on a white ground.

Unfortunately, his pride was very soon hurt; real trouble was awaiting him in Miss Anna Watson's dressing room.

Until that evening he had not rehearsed in costume, and indeed it would hardly have been worthwhile. He had come to the theatre in his ordinary handsome attire. But now, in the dressing room where the rich toilet of the Duchess of Kendal was performed, lo! here was Eliza proceeding to dress him in a whole suit of shabby clothes. Mere rags were these, clean underneath it is true, but on the outside soiled, torn, and patched. In the thrilling drama, Harry is a deserted child whom his mother finds in his wretched livery of poverty; his mother, a duchess, a beautiful lady in silk, velvet and lace.

At sight of these garments, the idea occurred to Foundling Mick that he was about to be sent back to the Galway school.

'Miss Anna! Miss Anna!' he cried.

'What's the matter?' she answered.

'Don't send me back! Oh, don't send me back!'

'Send you back? What for?'

'These ugly clothes—'

'Why—he actually imagines—'

'No, no, you little fool! Keep still,' said Eliza, giving him a by no means gentle shake.

'Ah, the darling!' exclaimed Miss Watson, in a fit of tenderness, as she daintily arched her eyebrows by the aid of a camel's-hair brush.

'The dear angel—if they only knew that in front!'

And then she put some rouge on her cheeks.

'But it shall be known, Eliza. It shall be in the papers tomorrow. He actually thought—'

She paused, and passed the 'white' puff over her shapely shoulder.

'No, no, you extraordinary little darling! Those ugly things are only for fun.'

'For fun, Miss Anna?'

'Yes, and you must not cry.'

She would have cried herself, had she not been afraid of damaging her artificial complexion.

Eliza shook her head, and obstinately repeated,—

'You see, ma'am, that we shall never make an actor of him.'

Meanwhile, Foundling Mick, in growing trouble, with a beating heart and tearful eyes, had his fine clothes taken off, and was arrayed in 'Harry's' tatters. Then it came into Miss Watson's head to console him with the gift of a new sovereign. The coin should be his 'handsel' she said, and in fact it did console Mick, who took the piece of gold with evident satisfaction and pushed it well down into his pocket after he had minutely inspected it.

This done, Miss Watson gave him a last kiss and went down to the green-room, having charged Eliza to keep Mick in the dressing room, as he had not to 'go on' until the third act

The first act went off well. Miss Watson was warmly applauded, and she deserved it. She played with great fire and spirit, and created a strong impression upon the audience.

After the first act the Duchess of Kendal returned to her dressing room, and, to the great surprise of 'Harry', she took off her grand dress of silk and velvet, and assumed the plain attire of a servant. It is unnecessary to explain the dramatic complications which made this transformation imperative. Foundling Mick contemplated the velvet woman who turned into a woman of serge, with great uneasiness, and a sense of confusion, as though some fairy had wrought the fantastic transformation before his eyes.

When the call-boy's stentorian voice summoned Miss Watson, it made Mick start. The 'servant' made him a sign with her hand, saying,—

'Wait, my little fellow, it will be your turn soon.' Then she disappeared for the second time.

In the second act the servant had a success equal to that of the duchess in the first, and the act-drop descended amid loud applause.

Clearly, no opportunity of being disagreeable was open to the good friends of Miss Watson and their allies in the 'house'.

On reaching her dressing room she threw herself on a sofa, a little tired, although she had reserved her great dramatic effort for the third act.

Once more she changes her costume. This time she is not a servant, but a lady, a lady in mourning, not so young as formerly, for five years have elapsed between the second act and the third.

Foundling Mick sat still in a corner of the room, with wide open, wondering eyes, not venturing to move or speak. Miss Watson paid no attention to him until she was completely dressed. Then she said,—

'Now, child, it's going to be all for you.'

'For me, Miss Anna?'

'And remember that your name is Harry.'

'Harry? Yes!'

'Eliza, you must keep reminding him that his name is Harry, until you leave him with the stage-manager close to the door.'

'Yes, ma'am.'

'And take care he does not miss his entrance.' No, he should not miss it, even if she had to help him with a good slap.

'You know,' added Miss Watson, shaking her finger at the child, 'your sovereign might be taken from you if you are not good. So beware the fine!'

'And prison too!' added Eliza, making a face at him which he knew well.

'Harry' felt for his sovereign at the bottom of his pocket, and resolved that it should not be taken from him.

The moment had come. Eliza took Harry by the hand and led him downstairs to the back of the stage. He was dazzled by the flaring gas-jets, and the great circles of light overhead, and confused and frightened by the coming and going of actors, supers, and scene-shifters, all of whom looked at him and laughed.

No wonder! He was a shameful object in those ragged clothes of a beggar boy!

The bell rang, and 'Harry' started at the sound.

The curtain rose, and the Duchess of Kendal was 'discovered', alone, in a cottage interior, soliloquising. Presently the door at the back would open, a child would come in, advance towards her, and hold out his hand to beg, and that child would be hers.

It must be noted here, that at the rehearsals Foundling Mick had been much annoyed by finding himself reduced to the necessity of asking alms. We remember his repugnance on a former and real occasion. Miss Watson had told him that it was 'not in earnest', but still he did not like it at all. In his innocent ignorance, he took things seriously, and ended by believing he was really the unfortunate little Harry.

While waiting for his entrance—the stage-manager holding his little hand—the child had been peeping through the doorway. He regarded with bewilderment the vast space filled with people, the clusters of lights over the boxes, the enormous lustre like a fire-balloon suspended in the air. It was all so different from what he had seen when he had sat in the front of a box, looking on at a play.

'Attention, Harry!' said the stage-manager.

'Yes, sir.'

'You know what you have to do. Go straight before you to your mamma, and take care you don't fall.'

'Yes, sir.'

'And hold your hand out well.'

'Yes, sir, like that.'

And he showed a shut hand.

'No, you dunce! That's a fist! Stretch out an open hand; you are begging.'

'Yes, sir,'

'And, above all, do not say one single word—remember, not one.'

'Yes, sir.'

The cottage door opened, and the stage-manager pushed 'Harry' in at the cue.

Foundling Mick had made his *debut* in the dramatic profession! Ah, how loudly his heart beat!

A murmur ran all round the house, a touching murmur of sympathy, while Harry, with faltering steps, downcast eyes and outstretched trembling hand, advanced towards the lady in mourning. It was easy to see that he had been accustomed to wear rags, and was not ill at ease in his tattered garments.

Suddenly the duchess rises, she looks around, she throws herself back, then she opens her arms.

What a cry she utters! One of those traditional cries which tear the chest.

'It is he! It is he! I recognise him! It is Harry! It is my son!'

And she catches him to her heart, she covers him with kisses, he quietly submits. She weeps, real tears this time, and cries,—

'My child, it is my child—this wretched creature, who begs from me!'

Poor Harry is stirred up by this, and forgets that he has been ordered not to speak.

'Your child, ma'am?' he says.

'Hush! hold your tongue!' mutters Miss Watson, under her breath.

Then she continues:

'Heaven took him from me to punish me, and today brings him back to me.'

She devours Harry with kisses, she bathes him with tears, her words are interrupted by sobs.

Never, never had Foundling Mick been so fondly caressed, never had he felt himself so maternally loved!

The duchess rises, as though a sound from the outside had startled her.

'Harry!' she cries, 'you will not leave me!'

'No, Miss Anna!'

'Hold your tongue! Hold your tongue!' she whispers, at the risk of being heard by the audience.

The cottage door is pushed open, and two men appear upon the threshold.

One is the husband of the lady in mourning, the other is a police officer.

'Seize that child! He belongs to me!'

'No, he is not your son!' replies the duchess, drawing Harry away.

'You are not my father!' exclaims Foundling Mick.

Miss Watson's fingers nip his arm so sharply that he can hardly restrain a cry. After all, what he has said fits into the piece; there is no harm done.

Now it is a mother who holds him with fierce tenacity. None shall tear him from her. The lioness is defending her cub.

And in fact the cub, who takes the scene seriously, is very well able to resist. The duke lays hold of him, but he struggles manfully, escapes from his Grace, and, running to the duchess, he cries,—

'Ah, Miss Anna, why did you say you were not my mamma?'

'Will you hold your tongue, you little wretch? Will you be silent?' she whispers, while the duke and the police officer are manifestly disconcerted by these unexpected 'lines'.

'Yes, yes,' says Harry, 'you are mamma. I told you so, Miss Anna, my real mamma!'

The audience begin to see that all this is 'not in the piece'. Whispers and jests go round. Some of the spectators applaud ironically. In truth, they ought to weep, for there is pathos in that improvised 'situation', a drama within the play upon the stage.

Nonetheless the piece was ruined! If for any reason laughter be heard where tears ought to be seen, the play and the players are done for.

Miss Watson keenly felt all the absurdity of the position. Some cutting remarks reached her from the actors standing about at the sides.

Bewildered and overcome, she was filled with sudden fury. She would gladly have killed the little wretch who had done the mischief; but her strength failed her, she fell on the stage in a dead faint, and the green curtain was lowered amid the laughter of the entire audience.

That same night, Miss Watson left the town with Eliza Corbett. She refused to give the performances announced for the week, preferring to pay forfeit. Never again would she appear at the Theatre Royal, Limerick.

As for Foundling Mick, she did not trouble herself about him. She left him there as she might have left any object that had ceased to please and become odious in her sight. There is no affection that can stand before injured self-love.

Foundling Mick had been pushed aside in the confusion, and left alone, understanding not at all what had happened, but feeling that he had been somehow the cause of a misfortune. He got out of the theatre unperceived by anybody, and roamed about the streets of Limerick until at length he found himself in a churchyard, and close to a huge building which was very dark at the side on which the moonlight did not fall. That building was St Mary's Church, and the weary child crouched down upon a flat gravestone in the shadow, trembling at the slightest sound, and wondering whether that wicked man the Duke of Kendal was searching for him, to take him away to a place where 'wild beasts' were. And there was no Miss Anna to defend him! He should see his mamma no more.

Shortly after it was light in the morning Foundling Mick heard a voice calling to him.

A man and a woman were standing near him. In crossing the road they had perceived the child, and paused to ascertain what he was doing there. The kindly couple were on their way to the coach-office, intending to take places in the public conveyance which plied between Limerick and the southern part of the county.

'What are you doing there, my boy?' asked the farmer.

Foundling Mick answered by sobs only.

'Come, tell me! What are you doing there?' said the farmer's wife.

Foundling Mick did not speak.

'Where's your father?' she continued.

'I have no father,' stammered the child.

'And your mother?'

'I have not got one any more.' And he stretched his arms towards the farmer's wife.

'He is a deserted child,' said the man.

If Foundling Mick had been dressed in his fine clothes, the farmer would have inferred that he was a strayed child, and taken steps to restore him to his people; but in 'Harry's' costume, the poor little fellow could only be taken for one of those unfortunates whom 'nobody owns'.

'Come along, then,' said the farmer, taking the child by the hand, and then placing him in the woman's arms.

'A little mite like that won't make much difference at the farm, will he, Mary?'

'No, indeed, Murtagh,' replied the good woman with hearty assent, and she instantly dried Mick's tears with motherly kisses.

CHAPTER 8

Kirwan's Farm

The experiences of Foundling Mick in Ulster and Connaught had not been very pleasant, as we have seen. He was now destined to an entirely new scene of existence, for his new-found benefactors conveyed him to the County Kerry, at the south-west of Ireland. This time he had fallen into good hands; would he be allowed to remain in them?

Kirwan's Farm lies within twelve miles of the town of Tralee, and in a district of the country which is almost exclusively held by 'foreigners' that is to say, by landlords who are not Irish, but English and Scotch men. 'Ireland for the Irish' has little meaning in any part of the 'distressful country', in Kerry it is a vain saying indeed. Nor were these stranger landlords ever resident; they expended the large sums which their agents extracted from the tenant-farmers in the English capital, and in foreign places of resort, on their families and their pleasures, and furnished striking examples of the absenteeism which is the great grievance of Ireland, leaving the people whose labour produced their wealth to the tender mercies of the agent or 'middleman' who is her curse.

Kirwan's Farm, with several others, was the property of the Earl of C——, a Scottish peer, who had not even once taken the trouble to visit the estate since it had come into his possession, and his lordship's tenantry were metaphorically ground into fine dust by Mr John Eldon, his agent.

Kirwan's Farm was a small place, only 100 acres in extent, and the land was stiff and difficult of cultivation. It was by severe toil alone that the farmer forced the soil to yield sufficient produce to pay the heavy rent of one pound an acre.

There are good landlords in Ireland, no doubt, men with consciences, who make themselves acquainted with the fellow men who earn the gold of which the toiler's share is so small; but these good landlords form a meagre minority, and for the most part the people are in the hands of persons who, as a class—in their case also exceptions must be admitted—are hard and pitiless.

Murtagh MacCarthy, the tenant of Kirwan's Farm, was one of the best, and most hardworking of the farmers on Lord C——'s estate. He was a naturally intelligent man, he had received a good education for his station in life, he thoroughly understood the business of agriculture, and he had managed, being well seconded by his strictly brought-up sons, to lay by a little money, notwithstanding the heavy charges that fall upon the budget of an Irish peasant. His wife, whose name was Mary, was an excellent housewife, and as active at 50 as she had been at 20 years of age. She was a dexterous spinner, and the hum of her spinning wheel might be heard in the cottage sitting room all through the winter months.

The MacCarthy family consisted, first and foremost in every sense, of the farmer's mother, a venerable woman of 75, whose husband had formerly farmed the land. 'Granny' had no other occupation now than spinning, in her daughter-in-law's company, and no other desire than to be of as little cost as possible to her children.

The eldest son, Murdoch, was 27, and still better educated than his father. He was deeply interested in the questions which always have interested and will ever continue to interest Ireland, and his parents felt considerable anxiety at times lest he should get into some trouble by his devotion to the party of Home Rule. Murdoch, who was a strong, good-looking young man of a rather silent and reserved disposition, had recently married the daughter of a neighbouring farmer. His young wife was a beautiful woman, such as may frequently be seen among persons of her class in Ireland. Her features were regular, her face was singularly proud and calm, her complexion was like milk and roses, her eyes were of the deepest blue, with long, black lashes, and her 'raven's-wing' hair lay in shining masses upon her well-formed head. Her carriage was noble and distinguished, and she walked with the free, unembarrassed tread which has come down with the Spanish strain in them to the women of many families in the south of Ireland. Kitty MacCarthy loved her husband devoutly, after the fashion of her countrywomen, and Murdoch, albeit not given much to smiling, would smile when he turned his dark, serious eyes on her. Kitty had a salutary influence over her husband, and she employed it by restraining him from unwise action each time that the emissaries of political agitation came into the district, to proclaim that a good understanding between landlord and tenant was impossible.

Murdoch attended the meetings, and Kitty's heart sank when she saw him setting out for Tralee, or some small town in the nearer neighbourhood. On these occasions he would speak with the eloquence so often found among the better educated of his class, and on his return, Kitty could read the thoughts by which he was pervaded, in his troubled face. To her exhortation to patience and resignation, most gently urged, he would reply:

'Patience—when time is passing, and nothing is done! By dint of patience and resignation, Kitty, people come to putting up with everything, to losing all sense of their rights, and putting their necks under the yoke. That I will never do! Never!'

MacCarthy had two other sons, Patrick and Peter, aged respectively 25 and 19 years. Patrick, or Pat, as he was more generally called, was a sailor on board of a Liverpool trading vessel. Peter, like Murdoch, had never quitted the farm, and the two rendered their father most valuable assistance. A perfectly good understanding existed between the brothers, although they differed widely in disposition and temperament. Peter was a jovial, happy-minded fellow, full of fun and frolic, the life and soul of the house, and his quick, though sunny temper contrasted with the more sombre nature of his brother Murdoch.

Such was the family into whose bosom Foundling Mick was about to be taken. What a difference between Kirwan's Farm and the poor school in Galway! Would not the contrast strike the child's precocious imagination forcibly? No doubt it would. It is true that our hero had passed a few weeks in bodily comfort with the capricious Miss Watson, but he had not enjoyed real affection; her theatrical caresses had brought him no conviction that he was loved, they were as uncertain, fugitive, and ephemeral as the stage-scenes themselves.

The dwelling-house of the MacCarthys was small; it consisted of two 'floors' only. The ground floor consisted of a large room which was at once kitchen and family sitting-room, and three sleeping-rooms, appropriated respectively to 'Granny', to MacCarthy and his wife, and to their son and daughter-in-law. Above, was a spacious garret, and a bedroom, occupied by Peter, and shared by Pat in the intervals of his voyages.

On one side of the house were the farm buildings, heavily thatched, and much in need both of substantial and ornamental repair. Capacious pigsties, a duck-pond, a big manure-heap, a haggard with two large haystacks, well protected from weather, a poultry-yard, and a fruit and vegetable garden, divided by a hedge from the farm land proper, formed the chief points in the aspect of Kirwan's Farm, which was anything but picturesque. Of course the potato was cultivated on a large scale, also turnips and huge cabbages. The potato, as everybody knows, is the basis of food in Ireland, especially in those parts of the island where the land is poor and hard to cultivate. We may well ask on what the rural population lived before Parmentier had made known his precious edible tuber? It may be that he rendered the cultivator imprudent by accustoming him to count upon that product, but at least it saved him from famine, unless all the chances were against him.

Murtagh MacCarthy owned four cart and plough horses and a strong, well-fed ass, at no loss for thistles; in that respect at least Kirwan's farm was productive. Half-a-dozen milch cows, about a hundred sheep, a few goats, and a dozen pigs, kept chiefly for consumption by the family, as MacCarthy did not care to enter upon the bacon business, complete the list of the livestock, without reckoning the noisy tenants of the poultry-yard.

Fowls, geese, ducks and eggs found a ready sale at the Tralee market, but turkeys and pigeons were not reared on Kirwan's farm. These are but rarely found in the poultry-farms in Ireland. A Scotch collie, kept as a sheepdog, was a great pet at the farm. No sporting-dog was to be seen there. Sport is a pleasure for the landlords and their agents exclusively.

Kirwan's farm was not the worst on the estate of the Earl of C—, but it was of only middling quality. Indeed, the whole county of Kerry, with its superb scenery in places, its renowned lakes of Killarney, and its beautiful expanses of richly-timbered country, is a stern land to the farmer, and he who has to extract his livelihood from it after the terrible exactions of the lords of the soil have been satisfied must be prepared to work hard, and to live frugally.

CHAPTER 9

Foundling Mick's Installation

On the 20th of October, at about three o'clock in the afternoon, a joyful stir was manifest about the farmhouse.

'Here they come!' cried Kitty and Peter, who espied Murtagh and Mary MacCarthy from the turn of the road.

The farmer and his wife had left Limerick by that primitive vehicle known as 'the long car', and as they had 30 miles to travel and the weather was cold, they were glad to arrive at their journey's end, to see and smell the cheerful turf fire which had been maintained at the point of perfection to greet them. The 'long car' having set down its passengers at the corner, went on its way to Tralee.

While the four were exchanging greetings in the porch, Murdoch came in from the back of the house.

'You have done well, father?' asked Kitty, after she had embraced her mother-in-law, 'Did you get the cabbage-plants in Limerick market?' said Murdoch.

'Yes. They will be sent to us tomorrow.'

'And the turnip-seed?'

'Yes, of the best sort.'

'That's right, father.'

'And a new kind of grain, Murdoch; a good sort too, I think. Look at it.'

Murdoch and his brother stared at the child, half-hidden in Mary's skirts, to which he was clinging.

'Here's a fine boy,' Murtagh went on, jocosely 'while we're waiting for Kitty's.'

'The little fellow is frozen,' said Kitty.

'I had him well wrapped up in the shawl,' replied Mary, 'but the drive was cold.'

'Put him before the fire and warm him well,' said MacCarthy, 'and the mother and I'll go see Granny.'

Kitty took charge of Foundling Mick and in a short time the whole family was assembled in the common sitting room where Granny's old armchair with cushions occupied the warmest corner of the fireplace.

The child was presented to her. She took him in her arms and set him on her knees. He made no resistance, but turned his eyes solemnly first upon one then upon another of the little group. He did not understand what was going on. Today was not like yesterday. Was this a sort of dream? He saw kind faces, young and old, around him. Since his waking he had heard none but kind words. He had been amused by the drive in the car which carried him quickly through the country, and the sweet morning air, laden with the scent of shrubs and flowers, expanded his chest. He had been given a good meal before the car started, and Mary MacCarthy had supplemented it with biscuits on the way, while he told her all he knew how to tell of his life—his existence in the poor school, the kindness of Grip, whose name recurred frequently in the narrative, then Miss Anna, who had called him her son and who was not his mamma; a gentleman in a passion, who was called 'the duke', and wanted to take him away—he could not remember the duke's name—lastly, his being forsaken, and how he had wandered all alone into the churchyard at Limerick. Mr and Mrs MacCarthy did not make much out of his story beyond the facts that he had neither parents nor friends, and was a deserted child whom Providence had confided to their care.

Granny, who was much moved, kissed the poor little waif, and he was caressed by all in turn.

'And what is his name?' asked Granny.

'He can tell us of no other name than Foundling Mick,' answered Mary.

'He does not want any other,' said Murtagh; 'and we will continue to call him by the name he knows.'

Such was the welcome accorded to our hero on his arrival at the farm. The old clothes in which he had been dressed for the part of 'Harry' were taken off, and clean, warm garments were substituted for them. These were not new, indeed they were the last that Pat had worn at little Mick's age, and had been carefully preserved by his loving mother. Then he had his supper at the table of these good people, seated in a high chair too, and all the time he wondered whether everything were not going once more to vanish!

What a feast that homely supper was, where none but pleasant faces were seen around the table, except, perhaps, that of the elder brother, always serious, even sad. And yet, all of a sudden Foundling Mick's eyes were suffused, and tears ran down his cheeks.

'What ails you, Mick?' asked Kitty.

'You mustn't cry, my child,' said Granny. 'We will all be good to you here.'

'And I'll make playthings for you,' said Peter.

'Come, come,' said Murtagh, good-humouredly, 'that's all very well for once, my boy, but you must know that nobody's let to cry here.'

'I won't cry any more, sir,' said Foundling Mick, and he drew closer to Granny's side.

Murtagh and Mary were tired; besides, bedtime came early at the farm, where all the family rose with the sun.

'Where's the child to sleep?' asked the farmer.

'In my room, and I will give him the half of my bed,' said Peter.

'No, no,' said Granny; 'make a bed for him near mine; he will not disturb me, and I'll like to see him sleeping.'

No wish of Granny's was ever contested. A bed was arranged for the little waif alongside of hers, and he was soon fast asleep, peaceful and happy in the shelter which Providence had provided for him.

The cold season had come, harvest time was over. There was not much to be done on the land, but no one at the farm led an idle life, as Foundling Mick soon found out. From the first, the little fellow tried to make himself useful. Early in the morning he went to the farmyard, thinking he might find something to do. Why not? At the end of the year he would be six years old, and at six a little chap can keep geese, cows, even sheep, with the aid of a good dog.

Then, after having had a good look round, he went into the house at breakfast-time, and being seated in front of a plate of stirabout and a mug of milk, he gravely requested to be allowed 'to begin'.

'Very well, my boy,' replied Murtagh; 'you want to work, and you are right. Everybody ought to learn to earn a living.'

'And I will, sir.'

'He's very young,' said Granny.

'Never mind that, ma'am,' said Mick, firmly.

'Call me Granny, child, like the rest.'

'I will. Never mind about my youngness, Granny. I shall be so glad to work—'

'And you shall work,' said Murtagh, wondering at the sense and intelligence of the child, who had known only the most wretched kind of existence.

'Thank you, sir.'

'I will teach you to take care of the horses,' said Murdoch, 'and to ride them if you are not afraid.'

'I'd like that.'

'And I'll teach you to mind the cows,' said Mary, 'and to milk them, if you are not afraid of their horns.'

'I'd like that well, ma'am.'

'And I'll show you how to mind the sheep in the fields,' said Patrick.

'That'll be grand,' said Micky, with beaming eyes.

'Can you read?' asked the farmer.

'A little, and write large hand.'

'And reckon?'

'Oh, yes! up to a hundred, sir.'

'Good!' said Kitty, with a smile. 'I'll teach you to reckon up to a thousand, and write small hand.'

'I'll like that, ma'am.'

He was quite serious about it all. To be the little servant of the farm was the height of his ambition.

Murtagh laughed heartily.

'You're going to be a broth of a boy, entirely, Micky,' said he. 'Horses, cows, sheep, if you mind all those there will be nothing left for us to do. Tell me, now, how much wages will you ask?'

'Wages?'

'Yes, wages. You're not going to work for nothing, I suppose.'

'Oh, no, sir.'

'What!' exclaimed Mary; 'he is to be fed, lodged, and clothed, and he wants to be paid as well?'

'Yes, ma'am.'

They looked at the child, seemingly a little shocked.

Murdoch, observing him attentively, said,—

'Let him tell us what he means.'

'Yes,' said Granny; 'tell us what you wish to have. Is it money?'

Foundling Mick shook his head.

'Come! Is it five shillings a day?' asked Kitty.

'Oh! Ma'am!'

'A month?' said Mary.

'A year, perhaps,' suggested Peter, laughing. 'Five shillings a year.'

'Well, now, what is it you do want?' inquired Murdoch, gravely. 'I see, you have the idea of earning your living, as we all have. However little you get, it will teach you to count. What do you want? A penny a day?'

'No, Mr Murdoch.'

'Then tell us.'

'Well, Mr MacCarthy, I want you to give me a little stone every evening.'

'A little stone?' cried Peter. 'Is it with little stones you'll make your fortune?'

'No; but I would like the master would give them to me all the same, and afterwards, when I'll be big, if you have always been pleased with me—'

'I see, I see,' said MacCarthy; 'we'll change your little stones into shillings and pence.'

Everybody complimented Foundling Mick on his excellent idea, and that very evening MacCarthy gave him a little pebble from the river's bed, where they lay in millions. Micky deposited it carefully in an old delft jug which Granny gave him to serve the purpose of a money-box.

'A queer child!' observed Murdoch to his father.

Yes, he was a queer child, and his good disposition had not been spoiled by either the ill-treatment of Hornpipe, or the evil communications of the poor school. Day by day, as time went on, the family at the farm found out more and more good in the foundling, who was not wanting even in that lightness of heart which lies at the bottom of the national Irish temperament, and exists in the poorest sons and daughters of poor Ireland. He was of a thoughtful and inquiring turn of mind; he sought into 'the whys and wherefores' of things, questioned everybody intelligently concerning the particular business of each, and delighted in gaining knowledge. His eyes were ferrets—nothing could escape them. He never let anything be lost or mislaid, were it of ever so little value; he would pick up a pin or a shilling with equal care. He took great care of his clothes, and was exceedingly orderly in all his ways, keeping everything that belonged to him, and the simple articles of his toilet, neatly arranged. Order was innate in him. He replied politely when he was addressed, and did not hesitate to press for farther explanation when he had not fully understood the answers made to his questions. It was plain that his progress in writing would be rapid, and he learned figures with ease. More than by these evidences of capacity, Murdoch was surprised and interested by the reasoning power which seemed to direct all the little boy's actions. Before long he was thoroughly instructed in the Catholic religion, so deeply rooted in the hearts of the Irish nation. This he owed chiefly to the zealous care of Granny.

The winter came, very hard and cruel. The farmhouse and the outbuildings were woefully out of repair, but John Eldon, the agent, would do nothing in that matter; to make and keep them habitable was for the overtaxed farmer alone, and he and his sons worked at the task almost incessantly.

During this time the women were variously employed; Granny

spinning at the fireside, Mary and Kitty attending to the cows and the poultry, helped to the best of his ability by Foundling Mick. He kept accurate account of everything relating to the house and the farm. He was too young to be allowed to look after the horses, and so he formed a close friendship with the ass, an excellent, willing and indefatigable animal, who returned his affection in dumb but eloquent fashion.

He wished his donkey to be as clean as himself, and this pleased Mary greatly. He would have had the pigs equally natty, but in that direction he was forced to confine his efforts to very elementary principles. After he had reckoned the sheep over and over again he entered the total of their numbers in an old pocketbook which had been presented to him by Kitty, and his taste for figures and methodical account-keeping developed gradually, until he might have done credit to the lessons of Mr Mulvany, had he ever received any.

One day, Mrs MacCarthy brought a dozen eggs out of the place where they were stored for winter consumption, into the kitchen.

'Not those, not those, ma'am!' cried Foundling Mick.

'And why, Micky?'

'Because they're not in rotation.'

'What rotation? Aren't all the eggs alike?'

'Of course not, ma'am. You have taken the forty-eighth; it's the thirty-seventh you ought to have begun with. Look!'

Mary looked, and found on every shell a number written in ink by Micky. She ought to have taken the eggs according to their numbering—from 37 to 48 and not from 48 to 59. She immediately rectified her mistake, and praised the little fellow for his good sense.

When Mrs MacCarthy told the story at dinner, Murdoch said,—

'It is to be hoped, Micky, you have reckoned the hens and chickens in the hen-house?'

'Certainly.' He took out his pocketbook. 'There are 43 hens and 69 chickens.'

Thereupon Peter remarked,—

'You ought to reckon the grains of wheat in every sack—'

'Don't joke him, boys,' said MacCarthy. 'If he's orderly in little things, he'll be the same in big things, and in life.' Then addressing the little boy, he said,—

'And your pebbles, the little stones I give you every evening—'

'I put them away in my jug, sir. I have 57, already.'

He had been 57 days at Kirwan's Farm.

'Ha!' said Granny, 'that makes fifty-seven pence at a penny a pebble.'

'What a lot of cakes you can buy for all that,' said Peter.

'Cakes, Peter? No, no. Copybooks. That's what I want to buy.'

The year was drawing to a close, and the weather was very cold. This was no novelty to Foundling Mick, he had seen harder winters than this one in Galway. At that miserable period of his life he had run barefoot in the snow, and the cold wind had penetrated his wretched clothing. And when he returned to the poor school, there was no place for the little waif by the fireside. How well off was Foundling Mick now! How pleasant it was to live with people who loved him! It seemed to him that their affection warmed him more thoroughly than the clothes which kept him from the wind, the wholesome food he ate, and the cheerful fire that burned upon the hearth. And it was better still, now that he was beginning to make himself useful, to feel that kind hearts were all around him. He was truly one of the family. He had a grandmother, a mother, brothers, kinsmen, and it would be among them, never leaving them, that his life should be passed. There he should earn his livelihood, as Murdoch had said to him one day. To do this, was his constant thought and desire.

Christmas came, a great event for Foundling Mick, who was, indeed, not ignorant of the meaning of the season, but had never shared in the 'keeping' of the day as a family festival. Great was his pleasure when his particular friend, Peter, presented him with a many-bladed knife as his first 'Christmas-box', and he ate plum pudding for the first time in his life.

CHAPTER 10

What Happened in
Donegal

Murtagh MacCarthy had made some attempts to discover the birthplace and parentage of his adopted child. The only clue he possessed was Mick's vague recollection that he had lived with an old woman and two little girls in a village in Donegal, and on following this up he ascertained that a child, eighteen months old, had been found on a doorstep in a small town, taken to the workhouse, and afterwards placed with a woman of the class now known as baby-farmers, in the outskirts of the town, which we shall denote by the letter R— and which was chiefly supported by the manufacture of linen. We are in a position to supplement the scanty information obtained by the farmer, and can give our readers a brief sketch of the history of the poor deserted infant, between the period of his being found by a policeman at R—, and his falling into the cruel hands of Hornpipe.

The woman to whose tender mercies the child was committed, at a time when there was much less care bestowed on such arrangements, and when inspection was very rare and superficial, if indeed it was exercised at all, was a bad specimen of a bad class. Her name was Murphy, she passed for a widow, but she was not a native of the place, and her previous history was unknown. Her neighbours described her as 'a hard sort of a woman', and her features justified the definition. She was an ill-looking hag, between 40 and 50, tall, thin, and big-boned; her small eyes were half-hidden under bristling red eyebrows; her big hands had fingers like claws, her nose resembled the beak of a bird of prey, and she invariably exhaled an odour of whiskey.

With this female dragon the poor little workhouse waif was destined to remain until he should be five or six years old, when he would be taken back to the prison of the poor, until he might be put out in the world in some self-supporting way. We have seen that the official programme was not carried out in the case of Foundling Mick; a simple incident prevented its fulfilment.

Mrs Murphy was in no dread of the visits of inspectors; no such impertinent intruders had darkened her door since she had added the profession of 'caretaker' to the industry by which she had previously lived, that of flax spinning. Neither had she to fear the interference of her neighbours on behalf of her unhappy 'boarders'; the district was very poor, and its inhabitants were immersed in and hardened by their own struggle for a bare existence. The hag had two little girls in her charge when Foundling Mick was sent to her. One of these children was four, the other was six years old. We need not dwell on the former, she was soon to die; the latter, who was called Cissy, was a pretty, fair-haired child, with large blue eyes, soft and intelligent, but already dimmed by tears, while her features were pinched, her chest was hollow, and her limbs were emaciated. To such a condition had she been reduced by ill-treatment. Cissy was a gentle, patient, resigned little creature; she accepted the life to which she was condemned without a notion that it might have been otherwise. Where, indeed, could she have learned that children existed who were petted by their mothers, cherished with care and caresses, to whom good clothes, good food, and good kisses were never denied? Assuredly not at the workhouse, where children like herself were treated no better than the young of the beasts of the field.

Foundling Mick—this name had been given him in the workhouse nursery, and it had stuck to him—the youngest of the 'boarders', was a dark-complexioned child, with bright eyes which promised intelligence and energy some day, if death did not close them prematurely, a constitution which would become robust if the bad air of the hag's hovel and insufficient food did not stunt his growth. The boy possessed strong vitality, and no ordinary endurance. He was always hungry, and weighed half what he ought to have weighed at his age. He was half-naked and barefooted, but he stood stoutly on his chilblained feet, and his legs were straight and sturdy.

A word will suffice in the case of the younger of the two little girls. She was consumed by a slow fever; her life was ebbing away like water out of a cracked jar. She ought to have had medicines, but medicines cost money; she ought to have been visited by a doctor, but a doctor has to be paid. So, the 'hard sort of a woman' did not go out of her way to provide either for her little boarder. After all, when the child should be dead, the workhouse would send her another; she would be no loser by the event.

Whiskey and porter cost money even in the little town of R—, and the drinking propensities of Mrs Murphy laid a heavy tax on the pitiful sum which was paid to her for the maintenance of the children. At that moment only a few shillings of the pittance remained, and although she need not suffer from thirst, seeing that there were some hidden bottles still in reserve, it was certain that the boarders would have to suffer from hunger. Such was the situation upon which the hag was musing, in so far as her half-drunken condition permitted her to reflect upon anything. Should she ask for an advance from the workhouse? No, it would be refused. Should she restore the children to the care of the legal guardians of the poor? No, she would lose her little income. And yet the children had not been fed since yesterday.

As the result of these reflections, Mrs Murphy took to one of the hidden bottles, and then she beat the starving children, being disturbed by their moans.

It was October, and the hovel was very cold; the wind whistled through the chinks in the walls, and the rain dripped from holes in the roof. The meagre turf fire did not suffice to warm the chilled limbs of Cissy and Foundling Mick, who sat in a corner on the floor, huddled together and shivering. The sick child lay on a truss of straw, burning with fever; the hag was staggering to and fro, holding on by the wall now and then, and muttering to herself as she cast angry glances towards the hearth. There was no pot upon the turf sods, and for a good reason, there was nothing to put in it.

A grunt was heard outside, and the door was pushed open by the intruding snout of a pig. Mrs Murphy looked stupidly at the animal as it began to root in the corners, grunting, but made no attempt to turn it out. Cissy and Foundling Mick stood up to avoid the pig, and the animal made for the hearth, where it routed out a big potato from beneath the turf ashes, turned it over with its snout, and took it in its mouth. Foundling Mick sprang at the pig, tore the potato out of its jaws at the risk of being bitten and knocked down, and, calling Cissy, he and she devoured the choice morsel between them. The drunken woman then seemed to awaken to what was happening; she seized a ragged old broom, and chased the pig, not without hitting poor Micky a hard blow in the process.

As the angry animal bolted out of the door, a man who had just reached it, narrowly escaped being thrown down, and Mrs Murphy was partly sobered by her surprise and alarm on perceiving that a stranger proposed to enter her abode. Whom could this intruder be? She had no visitors, her habits were to the last degree, and for sound reasons, unsocial. What if this person should be the inspector from the workhouse, and the children should betray their famished state to him. She made a stealthy threatening motion with her hand to Cissy and Foundling Mick, and planting herself in the doorway addressed the stranger abruptly—

'What do you want? Who are you?'

He was one of those persons who travel through the towns and villages in England and Ireland, getting insurances upon the lives of children, in other words ensuring their death.[1] The monthly payments of a few pence secured to the parents, guardians, or kinsmen, or to horrible creatures like Mrs Murphy, a sum of three or four pounds on the death of the children insured by companies who employed these agents. A notable amelioration in this system has been produced by the law of 1889, and the creation of 'The National Society for the Prevention of Cruelty to Children', is a decided step in the right direction. But, how sad it is to think that a law should be required in a case where the natural instincts alone ought to suffice!

The agent who had called on Mrs Murphy was a man between 45 and 50, smooth-faced, smooth-tongued, of sly and hypocritical demeanour. His business was to inveigle this hag into becoming a customer, by affecting not to perceive the neglected and abject condition of the children, and pretending to believe that they were treated with affection and solicitu0de.

'My good lady,' he resumed, 'if it's not troubling you too much, will you step outside for a few minutes?'

'Do you want to speak to me?' said the hag, who was always suspicious of a stranger.

CHAPTER 11

Life Insurance

'I am an agent, my good lady,' replied the man, in an insinuating tone.

An agent! Whose? From whence? What did he mean. Had he come to report on the children sent to the country in the R— district? Impossible to tell, so Mrs Murphy proceeded to overwhelm her visitor with her volubility.

'Excuse me, sir, excuse me. I am just cleaning up, after the children's dinner. You can see how well they look; the boy and this little girl, I mean, for the other is sick. Yes, indeed, she has a fever that can't be stopped. I'm just going to the town for a doctor. The darlints! I just doat on them.' All this, while she looked like a tigress trying to pass for a tame cat.

'Mr Inspector,' she went on, 'if the guardians would allow me some money for medicine—we have only just enough for their keep—'

'I am not an inspector, my good lady!'

'Who are you, then?'

'An insurance agent.'

'I do, ma'am. I want to speak to you about these three children, and I can't very well speak before them.'

She went out, closing the door of the hovel, and the two walked a few paces in silence. Then the man began,—

'You have three children?'

'Yes.'

'Are they your own?'

'No.'

'Are you any relation to them?'

'No.'

'Then they have been sent to you from the workhouse in Donegal?'

'Yes.'

'I'm sure they could not be in better hands. And yet, in spite of the best of care, these little creatures sometimes fall sick. Children are delicate, and I notice that one of your little girls—'

'I do the best I can, sir. I mind them day and night. I often go hungry myself that they may have full and plenty. I'm badly paid for them—three pounds a year, sir, only three pounds a year.'

'It's not enough, ma'am; it's not near enough. You must be the kindest of women to mind these dear children at such a loss. You have now two girsheens and a little boy in your care, I think?'

'Yes.'

'Orphans, no doubt?'

'I believe so.'

'I'm so accustomed to seeing children that I guess the age of the little girls at four and six years; and the boy's at two and a half.'

'Why are you asking me these questions?'

'I'm going to tell you.'

Mrs Murphy looked askance at the insurance agent, who continued,—

'The air is good hereabouts; it's a healthy place, but the children are sickly, in spite of all your care, and it might happen you to lose one of them. You ought to insure their lives.'

'Insure their lives?'

'Yes; for your own advantage. It is easy to understand that.' He noted the gleam of greed that came into the woman's eyes. 'By paying a few pence monthly to my company, you would secure a sum of from two to three pounds if one of the children were to die.'

'Two to three pounds!'

The agent perceived that the job was nearly done.

'It is generally done, ma'am, I assure you. We have several hundred children insured in Donegal, and although nothing can be a consolation for the loss of an object of so much care and affection, still there is a compensation—of course only a slight one—in having a snug sum to take from our company.'

'And can it be got—without difficulty?' asked the hag, casting a stealthy look around her.

'Without any difficulty, ma'am. As soon as the death is certified, there's nothing to do but to apply to our representative.'

Here he produced a folded paper, saying,—

'I have some policies all ready, and if you consent to put your signature to them you will be more easy in your mind for the future. And in case one of these children was to die—a thing that may happen any time, the money would help you to keep the others.'

'What would it cost?'

'Threepence a month for each child. Ninepence in all.'

'You would even insure the youngest girl?'

'Certainly; although she seems to me to be very ill. If your good care does not save her after all, it will be two pounds. Listen to that now! Two pounds! And mark this, ma'am, what our company does is for the good of the children. It is our interest that they should live, for they bring us in money? We are very sorry when a child dies.'

No, the insurance company was not sorry on such occasions, provided that the mortality did not go beyond a certain point. In offering to take the dying child, the agent was actually doing good business. Had not a director who knew what he was talking about, stated that 'the day after the interment of an insured child they took more "lives" than ever'?

This was true, and it was also true that wretches existed who did not hesitate to resort to crime in order to obtain the insurance money; these, it must be freely admitted, were very few.

'Come,' said the agent, in an insinuating tone, 'don't you see where your interest lies?'

Nevertheless the woman hesitated to give the ninepence, even with the prospect of her gain by the little girl's death to encourage her. She tried to bargain, to get a reduction.

'It cannot be done,' said the agent. 'Just think, ma'am, that in spite of all your care, this child may die tomorrow, or indeed, today, and our company have to pay your two pounds. Come, now, sign your name. Be advised by me.'

He produced pen and ink, the woman signed the paper, and reluctantly placed in the agent's hand ninepence out of the little hoard in her pocket. While the man walked away from the cabin, Mrs Murphy stood near its door, motionless, for some minutes. The children had not ventured to come out. Until now she had thought only of the few pounds which their existence was worth to her each year, but their death would bring her in more than that. Did it not depend upon herself whether she should have to pay any more ninepences?

The hag flung the look of a poising hawk at the bird in the grass at the unhappy children, when she re-entered the hovel. It seemed as though Cissy and Foundling Mick had understood! They shrank from her instinctively, as from hands extended to strangle them.

Still, she felt that she must act prudently. Three dead children might arouse suspicion. She would expend a little of her remaining money in feeding them; she knew how to make a little go a long way. Three or four weeks longer; that would surely be enough; but then the agent must come once more for his ninepence. She had abandoned the idea of taking the children back to the workhouse.

It was the morning of the 6th of October. Mrs Murphy, having gone out to drink, had left the children in the cabin, and the door was shut. The sick child was sinking rapidly; she could not swallow, and Cissy could only wet her lips with water. Her eyes were wide open, and she seemed to ask,—

'Why was I born? Why?'

Foundling Mick, huddled up in a corner, looked at her as he might have looked at a cage which was about to open and let out a bird.

Presently the little sufferer moaned, and he asked,—

'Is she going to die?' But he did not know what the word meant.

'Yes,' answered Cissy, 'and she will go to Heaven.'

'Can't we go to Heaven without dying?'

'No—we can't.'

A few minutes later a brief convulsion shook the frail little body, and then with one sigh the child's spirit departed.

Cissy fell on her knees terrified. Foundling Mick, to imitate her, knelt also by the side of the motionless form.

An hour later, Mrs Murphy came in, screamed 'Dead! dead!' and rushed out to proclaim her grief among her neighbours, who paid very little attention to her.

Mrs Murphy had two pieces of pressing business on hand: one was to get a doctor's certificate of the death of the child, who would be buried by the parish; the other was to get the insurance money, after as brief delay as possible. No doctor had been sent for to attend the child, but that circumstance would not hinder the dispensary practitioner from doing the needful in the case, and she must set about the matter at once. The dispensary was three miles away, and it would take her a long time to go and return, for she would be sure to stop on the way wherever drink was to be had. She set out as speedily as possible, having ordered Cissy to look after the dead child, and given herself no trouble at all about Foundling Mick; but she locked the cabin door and took the key with her.

Cissy immediately busied herself with the poor little corpse, bestowing more care upon it than the living child had ever enjoyed. She washed the face, smoothed the hair, removed the ragged chemise, and replaced it by a towel that had been hung upon a nail to dry, and would serve as a shroud for the destitute little orphan. When she had done these things in her careful, unchildlike way, so little suitable to her tender years, Cissy kissed her poor little companion on both cheeks, and Foundling Mick, who had remained in his corner, afraid to move, would have done likewise, but he was seized with terror, and dared not.

'Come! Come!' he cried out to Cissy.

'Where?'

'Outside! Come! Come!'

'No, no; we must stay here.'

And Cissy tried to quiet him. She told him also that the door was locked. But all was in vain; he continued to scream that he must get out.

'She is cold, and I am cold!' he cried. 'Come, Cissy, or she will take us with her!'

The child was wild with terror; he felt that he must die also, if he did not get away.

It was growing dusk. Cissy lighted a bit of candle which was stuck in the neck of a bottle; but then Foundling Mick was more frightened still, for shadows came, and things seemed to move about him. He loved Cissy; she was the only person who had ever caressed him in his little life; but he could not stay there—no, he could not stay.

There was a hole in the earthen floor under the broken door, and it had been roughly filled up with stones to keep out small dogs, and cats, which would otherwise have made themselves free of the cabin; to this Mick applied himself with the strange strength lent by fear to his half-starved but sturdy little frame, tearing out the stones with his hands, and scratching up the clay under them with an old shovel, in frantic haste. When the hole was empty, he called once more to Cissy, who could not have crept under the door in any case:

'Come! Come!'

'No!' said Cissy, 'I will not. She would be alone.'

Foundling Mick ran to her, put his arms round her neck and kissed her, and then, laying himself flat on the floor, wriggled through the hole, and disappeared on the outside of the door. Cissy, who concluded that he would make his way to the nearest dwelling, and thought only of the severe punishment which he would be certain to receive on Mrs Murphy's return, sat quietly by the side of the dead child.

We know what really did befall Foundling Mick, who had strayed into the country, knowing nothing of neighbours, and how he had been picked up by the itinerant showman.

CHAPTER 12

The Return

Foundling Mick was happy, and did not imagine that it was possible to be more happy. He lived entirely in the present, and thought nothing at all about the future.

His memory occasionally brought back to him pictures from the past. He remembered the little girl who had lived with him at the wicked woman's house. Cissy would be eleven years old now; what had become of her? Had not death set her free also as it had delivered the other child? If not, then he should find her again some day. He owed her much gratitude for her affection and care, and he would have regarded her as a sister, in his great need of attaching himself to any who had loved him.

Then there was Grip, to whom he was as grateful as to Cissy. Six months had elapsed since the burning of the poor school at Galway, six months during which he had undergone such strange vicissitudes!

What had become of Grip? Surely, he too could not be dead? It would be so much better that people like Hornpipe and Mrs Murphy should go. No one would be the worse, and there would be none to miss them. But such brutes are long-lived!

Thus argued Foundling Mick, and we may be sure he talked of his former friends to the good people at Kirwan's Farm, who were all interested in the subject.

Thereupon Murtagh MacCarthy had made inquiry, but, as we already know, he had been unable to discover anything relating to Cissy; the little girl had disappeared from R—.

An answer had been received from Galway respecting Grip. The poor lad, scarcely recovered from the injury he had received at the fire, and having no employment, had left the town, and was no doubt on the tramp in search of work. Foundling Mick felt as though it were wrong for him to be so well off when Grip was probably in a very different case. MacCarthy took an interest in Grip and would have been glad to give him work on the farm, but no one knew what had become of him.

The MacCarthy family led an industrious and regular life at Kirwan's Farm. They had few neighbours, the nearest were three miles away, and the farm was twelve miles from Tralee. MacCarthy and Murdoch visited the town on market days occasionally, but not more frequently than was necessary for their affairs.

The farm was in the parish of S—, and Kitty seldom left home except on Sundays and holy-days, when the family, with the exception of Granny, who was dispensed from the obligatory attendance at Mass by reason of her age and infirmity, went in their best attire to the parish church. These were great occasions for Foundling Mick, who presented a far different appearance from that of the ragged urchin who had hidden behind a pillar of the church in Galway lest he should be driven out. Now, he had nothing to fear; he occupied his own appointed place between Mary and Kitty, listened with delight to the singing, and followed the service with his own prayer book, a present from Granny. He was a boy to be proud of, in his neat tweed suit, which was always scrupulously brushed. Care of his clothes and person continued to be a marked characteristic of Foundling Mick.

The season was advancing. February was cold, and March was wet. The winter had not been severe, and did not seem likely to be prolonged. The sowing would be done under favourable conditions, and the tenants might hope to be able to meet the exactions of the landlords when the terrible 'rent day' should arrive, without having the penalty of eviction, entailed by a bad harvest, suspended over their heads.[2]

This was all well; nevertheless, there was a black spot on the horizon of Kirwan's Farm.

Two years previously, the second son, Pat, had gone to sea in the trading ship *Guardian,* belonging to a mercantile firm in Liverpool. Two letters from Pat had been received at the farm, after his voyage across the southern seas, but ten months had elapsed since the arrival of the second, and no farther news of him had reached his parents. The inquiries made by MacCarthy at Liverpool had not produced a satisfactory result; he learned only that Messrs Maxwell were uneasy respecting the fate of the *Guardian.* Naturally, the chief topic of conversation at the farm was Pat, and the post-cart was looked for with eager expectation, fully shared by Foundling Mick, who kept watch at the gate every day for its passage. The whole family was disquieted, but Granny talked more of her fears than the others. Pat was her favourite grandchild, her 'white-headed boy'. She was very old—should she live to see him again? The old woman would confide her fears to Mick, and he would try to console her.

'He will come back,' he said. 'I don't know him; and I must know him, since he is one of the family.'

'And he will be as fond of you as the rest of us are.'

'It's a grand thing to be a sailor, Granny; only it's a pity to have to go away, and stay away so long! Couldn't a whole family go on the big sea, all together?'

'No, Micky, no. When Pat went, it fretted me greatly. It's well for them that need never part! The boy might have stayed on the farm and worked with the rest. Then we wouldn't have been fretted this way. But he couldn't content himself, he had to go. God send him safe back. Don't forget to pray for him.'

'No, Granny, I won't. I always pray for him, and for you all!'

The beginning of April saw great activity at the farm, and Foundling Mick was as busy as the best, making himself useful in every department of labour that was at all within his strength, and developing especial ability as a shepherd. After a short time the sheep were left to his proud charge, and he and Ranger, the sheepdog, were firm friends and allies.

The little boy was much more given to observe the practical than the curious side of things. He did not inquire how it was that a whole ear came from a grain, but how many grains of corn or barley the ear would produce. And he formed the intention of counting them at harvest time, and writing down the result in his cherished pocketbook. This was his nature. He would have been more ready to count the stars than to admire them.

Foundling Mick was usually alone on the pastureland with his sheep for the greater part of the day. Occasionally, however, Murdoch or Peter would stop, on their way to some other portion of the farm, not to look after the 'herd', for he might be fully trusted, but for a short talk with him.

'Well, Micky,' one of them would say, 'is your flock all right and the grass thick?'

'Very thick, Mr Murdoch.'

'And are your sheep good?'

'Very good, Peter. Ask Ranger—he never has to bite them.'

Ranger was not a handsome dog, but he was very intelligent and hard-working, and he had become a faithful companion to Mick. The two talked together for hours at a time, saying the most interesting things to each other. When the boy looked the dog in the face while speaking to him, Ranger seemed to drink in his words, and his long nose quivered; his tail waved, like the 'portable semaphore', to which an expressive canine tail has been aptly likened. The friends were of about the same age, and a perfect understanding existed between them.

Foundling Mick had his little troubles, nevertheless. In the first place were his enemies, with whom he had to reckon, the marauding birds which swarm in Ireland. He did not mind the swallows, they lived on insects only during their brief sojourn, but the impudent and greedy sparrows, the mice of the air, these attacked the grain crops, and then, the rooks and the crows, how he raged against them! He would try to chase the clouds of rooks that would settle on the newly sown fields, and set Ranger to bark at them with all the power of his lungs, but of what avail were their puny efforts? The birds would merely rise in the air, make a mocking circle, and sweep down again out of his reach as before.

And then, the scarecrows were not of the smallest use! Peter had fabricated awful figures with outstretched arms and ragged garments fluttering in the wind. Children would certainly have been frightened by them, but the birds, not in the very least! Perhaps he might contrive something more startling and less silent. After long cogitation, he hit upon a promising idea. Peter's scarecrow moved its arms when the wind was strong, it is true, but it did not speak, it did not creak. It must be made to make a noise. So Foundling Mick got Peter to fasten a rattle which the wind would turn on the head of each scarecrow, and awaited the result with joyful expectation.

The rooks and the crows arrived as usual, and on the first and second day they evinced some surprise, and even a little distress and disquiet, but on the third they took no more notice of the scarecrow with the rattle than they had taken of that futile device without it, but perched comfortably on the outstretched arms of the fluttering figure, and out-cawed the harmless clash.

Then Foundling Mick, vexed and defeated, bethought himself that something is wanting to the perfection of this lower world.

These annoyances apart, things were going well at Kirwan's Farm, and Mick was as happy there as possible. During the winter his education in 'the three Rs' had made serious progress, and now he put his accounts in order every evening. His lists comprised the eggs and chickens, the little piglings, and the large families of rabbits. All these were duly entered, with correct dates. MacCarthy observed the boy's orderly ways with pleased interest, and regularly every evening gave him the stipulated little stone, which was duly deposited in the earthenware jug. These stones had all the value of shillings to Foundling Mick. The jug contained also the golden sovereign which had been the reward of his memorable sole appearance upon the boards at Limerick, and of which he had made no mention at the farm, from some unexplained instinct. Besides, as he had no use for this coin, wanting nothing, he attributed less value to it than to the little stones which bore witness to his zeal and his good conduct.

The season had been favourable, and harvest work began earlier than usual. All the hands on the farm were fully employed, and perhaps

Foundling Mick neglected his flock just a little in his ardour to assist in the delightful task of binding, stacking, and carrying. He was so proud of helping Mary and Kitty, and of being 'wanted' everywhere! Surely the happiest and most grateful of hearts was that which beat in the bosom of the once deserted, nameless boy.

That year was one of the most prosperous that Murtagh MacCarthy had passed on Kirwan's Farm. It would have been completely happy had any news of Pat reached the family. It seemed as though the presence of Foundling Mick had brought good luck to his benefactors. The rent was paid in full, all other charges were met. The following winter, which was not a cold one, was succeeded by an early spring, so that the farmers had reasonable hope of an equally good harvest to come.

Foundling Mick had resumed his long days with Ranger and his sheep. Again he saw the fields decked in their emerald green, and heard the little noises which the corn and the barley make when the ear is swelling. He liked to see 'the plumed and bearded barley' swaying to the touch of the light wind's breath. And then, there was talk of a newcomer at the farm, one eagerly looked for, who would be warmly welcomed. Granny was very happy and smiling over the expected arrival of the child of Murdoch and Kitty in three months' time.

During the heaviest press of the harvest work in August, one of the farm labourers fell sick and was unable to continue his labour. It was necessary to find a reaper out of work somewhere in the neighbourhood, if possible, but as all the farmers were equally busy, this was not by any means sure of accomplishment, and to procure a substitute for the disabled man, MacCarthy would have to sacrifice half a day in going to S— and returning. The latter was a serious inconvenience, and Foundling Mick, who understood the difficulty, promptly offered to go to S— in the farmer's stead. MacCarthy gladly consented; he knew that Mick might safely be trusted to carry a note to the right person, and that five miles of road with which he was familiar would not trouble the boy. By leaving the farm early in the morning, he could get back by noon.

Foundling Mick started in the morning, at a deliberate pace, and with a purposeful demeanour, having in his pocket the farmer's letter to an innkeeper at S—, and a tidy little packet of bacon-sandwiches for his refreshment on the way.

The weather was fine, a light wind was blowing, and the boy's heart and step for the first three miles were as light as the breeze. Presently Foundling Mick turned into a little wood, or 'plantation' as the country people called it, in order to take a short cut which would lead him out on the high road beyond, and after he had gone about a hundred yards he stood stock-still at the sight of a man stretched on the ground at the foot of a tree.

The boy looked for a few moments at this unaccustomed object, wondering whether anything ailed the man, or whether he had merely lain down to rest at so odd a place and hour.

The man remained motionless, and Mick drew near to him. He was fast asleep, his arms were crossed, his hat was pulled down to shade his eyes. He appeared to be young, and his dust-covered clothes and clay-stained boots told of a long tramp, probably from Tralee.

Mick's attention, however, was specially attracted by the fact that the sleeper was evidently a sailor. Yes, he could tell that by his costume and by the bag that lay beside him, for it was made of tarred sailcloth. There was an address upon it, too, and the boy read it at a glance.

'Pat,' he cried, 'it is Pat!'

Yes, it was Pat, and he might have been recognised by his likeness to Murdoch and Peter. Pat, who had not been heard of for so long, and was so longed for!

Foundling Mick was on the point of awakening the sleeper, when an idea arrested him. If Pat were to turn up quite suddenly at the farm, his mother, and especially his Granny, might get such a shock as would make them ill. He had better run back and prepare Mr MacCarthy, who would arrange everything nicely. Pat's father would prepare the women for the arrival of their son and grandson. As for the message to the innkeeper at S—, no matter about that; he could take it tomorrow. Why, here was Pat, one of themselves, might not he replace the sick reaper, and no stranger at all be wanted? Of course he might! And then, the young sailor was weary (as a matter of fact he had walked on from Tralee in the night, and was tired after his railway journey), he would come on to the farm quickly when he had his sleep out. The important thing was for Foundling Mick to get there first, and to bring Pat's father and brothers out to meet him.

But why should the weary sailor have to carry his bag for the last three miles? It would be much better for Mick, who was not at all tired, and quite strong enough to carry it on his back, to take charge of it for him. Besides, it would give him so much pleasure to carry a sailor's bag! A bag that had sailed the big sea! Only think!

He took up the bag by the loop of the rope which fastened it, hitched it up on his back, and set off at full speed in the direction of the farm. He had barely regained the high road, which lay in front of him perfectly straight for half a mile, before he heard shouts behind him; but he did not slacken his pace; he was more than ever anxious to get on. The person who was shouting was, however, also running.

Pat, on waking, had missed his bag, and starting up in a fury, he caught sight of the boy just as he turned into the high road.

'Stop, stop, you young thief!' he cried; but on and on ran Foundling Mick, unheeding. It was, however, vain for him to hope that he could escape from the young sailor, especially weighted as he was with the bag; so, when the shouting pursuer was only a few yards behind him, Mick suddenly dropped his load, without turning his head, and scampered off with surprising velocity.

Pat picked up the bag and continued his pursuit. The farm came in view at the same moment when he came up with Mick, and caught him by the collar of his jacket.

MacCarthy, Murdoch, and Peter were in the yard unloading bundles of forage, and each uttered a cry of astonishment.

'Pat, my son!'

'Brother!'

In a few moments the sailor had received the fond embrace of welcome from Granny, Mary and Kitty.

Foundling Mick stood by, his eyes beaming with joy, wondering when he should be noticed.

'Ah, my robber!' exclaimed Pat.

All was explained in a few words, and Mick ran to Pat and clasped him round the neck, as though the sailor had been a mast and he was clinging to it.

Great joy reigned at the farm in those days. Pat was at home again, the family circle was once more unbroken, and times were good with them.

The crops were abundant, especially fine was the promise of potatoes, the ready-made bread of the Irish people.

'Have you come back to us for a whole year, Pat?' asked his mother.

'No, mother, only for six weeks. I don't want to give up the sea, it's a good life. In six weeks I must go back to Liverpool, and ship again on the *Guardian,* but as mate this time.'

'That's grand, Pat,' said Murdoch, and he clapped his brother on the back approvingly.

'While I'm at home,' said the young sailor, 'you must let me work for you, father.'

MacCarthy accepted the offer.

Pat was especially pleased to make acquaintance with his brother's wife, whom he rightly judged to be a worthy and amiable young woman. Murdoch's marriage had taken place during Pat's absence. Foundling Mick had his share in the rejoicing. His story was told to Pat, who was touched by it, and from that moment the two became great friends.

To Mick, Pat was quite a wonderful and important personage. A sailor—that meant something altogether out of the common. No wonder that Granny kept her hand on his sleeve while he was talking, lest he should go off again to the sea. Pat's story was speedily told; his explanation of the long time that had gone by without his having sent his parents any news of him was simple enough. The *Guardian* had run aground on one of the small islands in the Indian Ocean, and for thirteen months her crew had lived upon a desert island, without any communication with the rest of the world. At length by dint of incessant labour they had succeeded in floating the ship. Vessel and cargo were all saved, and Pat had distinguished himself so much by his zeal and courage, that, on the recommendation of the captain, Messrs Maxwell, of Liverpool, the owners, had re-engaged him as mate for an approaching voyage to Liverpool.

CHAPTER 13

Change

The next day the MacCarthy household resumed its customary routine, and Kirwan's Farm had gained a sturdy workman to replace the disabled labourer.

The state of things was, then, fairly prosperous, but not all his toil and frugality could avail to enable MacCarthy to accumulate any savings, or permit him to contemplate the possibility of even one bad harvest without grave alarm. He lived on his earnings at the present, but what of the future? Ah, that future of the Irish tenant farmer, always at the mercy of the climate! On this Murdoch's thoughts were constantly fixed, and his brooding made him hate more and more deeply a social condition which could have no solution except in the abolition of landlordism, and the restoration of the soil to the cultivators by means of payments at stated intervals.

In September Kitty's baby, a girl, was born. The newcomer was welcomed warmly by every member of the family, and Foundling Mick's happiness when he was permitted to kiss the infant was supreme. The christening was fixed for an early day, and a 'party' was arranged for the occasion. Pat would be able to be present, as his ship was not to sail until late in the month. The baby was to be named Jane, Granny was to be godmother, for the good old lady's pleasure only, as it was not to be supposed the child would ever profit by her vicarious care, temporal or spiritual, and it was Granny that made the startling proposal that Foundling Mick should be godfather. What! The orphan child, the foundling? Yes, Granny considered that to constitute a 'spiritual affinity' would be the very best way to consolidate the tie between Mick and his benefactors, and Granny's wish was law. To be sure he was very young, not eight years old 'all out', and might be regarded as hardly admissible, but Granny disposed of this objection, timidly offered by Kitty, by an ingenious argument. If the godfather were too young, she said, the godmother's years would make up for that; their united ages came to 84, they would divide the number, and each claim 42, surely a discreet and proper time of life! Everything else was in the boy's favour; he was hard-working, honest, devoted, loved, esteemed, appreciated by all at the farm.

On the 26th of September the whole party repaired to the parish church, which Granny had not entered for a considerable time. The women were taken there in the farm-cart; the men went on foot. On their arrival the parish priest raised an unexpected difficulty.

'Who's the godfather?' he asked.

'Foundling Mick,' replied Murdoch.

'What's his age?'

'Seven and a half,'

'That's rather young; but it is not forbidden. He has some other name beside Foundling Mick, I suppose?'

'We don't know whether he has or not, father,' answered Granny.

Turning to the boy, the priest said,—

'You must have a Christian name of your own.'

'I have not, sir.'

'Can it be that he is unbaptised?'

On this point Foundling Mick was entirely ignorant. It would seem surprising that MacCarthy and his wife, who were such good, pious, practical Catholics, had not thought about this matter; but the fact is, it had never entered their minds that anybody could be unbaptised. No one could answer, and Mick was put to confusion. Would this doubt which no one could solve be an insurmountable objection to his becoming godfather to little Jane? Then came Murdoch to the rescue with a timely suggestion.

'Well, if he hasn't been christened, father, can't your reverence christen him now?'

'But if he has been christened?' said Granny.

'Never mind,' interrupted Peter, 'he'll only be a Christian twice over. Christen him first.'

'I can do that,' said the priest, smiling at this novel experience, 'but he will want a godfather and godmother on his own account.'

'I will stand for him,' said MacCarthy.

'And so will I,' said Mary.

'What shall his name be?' asked his reverence.

After a few minutes' consultation it was agreed that that name of the archangel which had been given by chance to the child should be retained, and he was promptly baptised 'Michael'. He then proudly officiated, by the side of Granny, as godfather to little Jane, and the family returned to the farm, where the day was kept as a holiday, and several neighbours came to partake of the homely but plentiful dinner which was provided on the occasion. This family festival afforded Mick his first glimpse of social amenities.

And now we have to pass away from these pleasant scenes and prosperous days, and, with a brief mention of the extreme severity of the ensuing winter, in which disastrous floods occurred in the province of Munster and did great damage in Co. Kerry in particular, take up the fortunes of the MacCarthy family at a later period. Those fortunes were at a low ebb at the beginning of the winter of 1881, as will be evident from a brief review of the disasters in which the occupants of Kirwan's Farm, in common with all the other tenants on the estate of the Earl of C—, were involved in the interval which we have allowed to elapse.

Weather of such severity as had not been known in Ireland within a generation. Floods which had destroyed crops, farm buildings and stock, and so damaged the dwelling-house that MacCarthy had been obliged to expend the little money which he gathered together for the working of the farm in the spring, on repairs, to keep it habitable, without receiving any assistance or even the smallest abatement of rent from Mr Eldon, the agent, who acted for the absentee Scotch landlord, had been succeeded by the last worst trouble that can come to the Irish agriculturist. The harvest had proved hopelessly deficient, and now the potato crop was utterly ruined! What was to become of the small farmers? Where were they to find means for the payment of the next gale of rent and the next instalment of the heavy taxation imposed upon their unfortunate class in Ireland? We have seen that MacCarthy, although in better times he had lived decently, and honestly discharged all his obligations, however unreasonable and tyrannical these were held to be by his son Murdoch, and by the farmer himself in his soul's conscience, had been inevitably unable to accumulate any savings. Now he was face to face with ruin, and want stared the industrious, frugal, pious family in the face. What was to be done? The misfortune that had fallen on the country ought to have been regarded and treated as a common misfortune, but well the tenants knew this would not be so; they, and they only, would have to pay the penalty of 'the dispensation of God'; those who could not satisfy the collector when he should come round, must prepare for eviction and starvation.

Where were the happy days of Foundling Mick's remembrance now? Where were the animals for him to tend, the busy population of the poultry-yard for him to reckon? There was but little work for the men to do now, and less for him, and during those long days the family watched the gradual but certain fading away of the loved and revered grandmother.

The disasters that had befallen the district had reawakened the ever-smouldering agrarian discontent. Boycotting was rife in the district—a useless proceeding which proved ruinous to both farmers and landlords. Agitation was rife in Kerry, and Murdoch MacCarthy threw himself headlong into the movement. None so violent as he in his denunciation of land-grabbers: he was perpetually travelling about the country to prevent the hiring of evicted farms. His father and Peter vainly endeavoured to restrain him. And indeed, their efforts were prompted by apprehension for his safety, for how could they fail to approve of his purpose, they who had toiled so hard and so long only to fall into the depths of poverty at last, and who had now to expect eviction from Kirwan's Farm, on which their family had lived so long?

The government, 'the Castle', as that obnoxious administration was then and is still called, knowing that the cultivators of the soil would be easily 'raised', after so ruinous a year, had taken its precautions. Already bodies of mounted constabulary patrolled the country, ready to lend armed aid to the process-servers and 'emergency men', to disperse the meetings, by force, if necessary, and to arrest the most zealous of the fanatics who were made known to the police. Evidently Murdoch would soon be of that number, if, indeed, he were not already a marked man. What could the Irish do against a system which rests upon 30,000 soldiers 'encamped'—that is the word in use—in Ireland?

The anxiety and terror in which Murdoch's parents lived may readily be imagined. A step on the road would turn Mary's face pale, Kitty's eyes would tell of fear, and Granny would lift her head, then let it droop again upon her breast. Was that the tread of the police coming to the farm to arrest Murdoch, and perhaps his father and brother as well? Arrests had been made in the towns, why not in country places also? Mary had besought her son, when the agitation became very marked, to elude the measures with which the chief agents of the Land League were threatened, but where could Murdoch have hidden himself? And supposing he could have found safety in the North, where the police were not so watchful, how could he have earned a livelihood for Kitty, himself, and their child, among strangers? He remained at the farm, trusting to be able to escape if the police should come thither in search of him. A watch was kept on all comers and goers on the road. Foundling Mick and Ranger were always on the alert; no one could have approached within half a mile of the farm unperceived.

And now MacCarthy was awaiting the inevitable visit of the rent-collector, coming to demand the 'gale' due at Christmas.

The Scotch peer who was MacCarthy's landlord had never even seen his Irish estates. Even supposing this personage to have meant well towards his tenants, he did not know them, he could not take any interest in them, nor could they have recourse to him. The estate agent, Mr Eldon, who had the management of the property, lived in Dublin, and left the task of exacting the revenues at the appointed periods to his subagent, a man named Herbert, who presented himself at Kirwan's Farm twice a year. Herbert was a hard-natured, bitter-minded person, inaccessible to the emotions of pity and sympathy. He had already given a large taste of his quality in other parts of the county, mercilessly driving families from their poor homes in the bitter weather, refusing to allow time for payment when a short delay could have saved the situation. It is true that he 'had his orders', but he took a savage pleasure in carrying them out with the utmost rigour.

Great was the suspense and apprehension with which Herbert's appearance was looked for at Kirwan's Farm.

Early in the day, on the 29th of December, Foundling Mick, who has espied him from afar, ran to the house, and gave notice of Herbert's coming. The whole family, even to the infant who was in Kitty's arms, was assembled in the large room on the ground floor.

The subagent pushed the gate open, strode up to the house with a determined step—the step of a master—opened the room door—the outer door of the house was rarely shut, even in winter—and without removing his hat, or uttering a word of greeting, seated himself on a chair in front of the table, like a man much more at home than those whose dwelling he invades, took some papers out of his leather bag, and said roughly,—

'It's a hundred pounds for the two half years. I suppose we're agreed upon that, MacCarthy?'

'Yes, Mr Herbert,' replied the farmer in a slightly uncertain voice. 'It is a hundred pounds. But I have to ask for some delay. You have given it to me—'

'Delay! Oh, delay indeed!' cried Herbert, interrupting him. 'What does that mean? I hear nothing but the one tune everywhere. Is it with delays that Mr Eldon is going to satisfy his lordship?'

'It has been a bad year for us all, Mr Herbert, and you may be sure my farm came off no better than the rest.'

'That's no business of mine, MacCarthy, and I can't give you any delay.'

Foundling Mick stood in a dark corner, his arms crossed, his big eyes wide open, listening.

'Mr Herbert,' said the farmer, mildly, 'you might take compassion on us. We only ask for a little time. Half the winter is over, and it has not been too hard. We'll recover ourselves in the season that's coming.'

'Will you pay, or won't you, MacCarthy?'

'We would if we could, Mr Herbert. Do listen to me. I assure you it is impossible for us to do it.'

'Impossible!' repeated the subagent. 'Very well, then, sell your stock and get the money.'

'We have done so, all that was left after the floods. The furniture would not bring five pounds.'

'And now that you won't be able to carry on the farm at all, you reckon on paying the rent out of the next harvest? Is it a fool you take me for, MacCarthy?'

'No, Mr Herbert, God forbid. But, for God's sake, don't take our last hope from us!'

Murdoch and his brother, motionless and silent, could hardly restrain their indignation on seeing their father standing humbly before this man.

At that moment, Granny, half-raising herself in her armchair, said in distinct, grave tones,—

'Mr Herbert, I am 77 years old, and I have been on this farm for 67 years. My father had it before my husband and my son. Until now we have always paid our rent, and for the first time we ask for one year's grace. I do not believe that Lord C— wants to hunt us off the land.'

'It has nothing to do with Lord C—,' replied Herbert, roughly. 'He does not even know you. But Mr Eldon knows you, and he has given me strict orders. If you don't pay me, out of Kirwan's Farm you shall go.'

'Leave the farm!' murmured Mary, who was as white as a sheet.

'In a week.'

'And where shall we find shelter?'

'Where you please.'

Foundling Mick had seen many sad sights in his short life; he had suffered much misery himself, and yet it seemed to him that never had he beheld such a thing as this. Here was no scene of tears or cries, but it was nonetheless terrible.

Herbert now rose from his seat, and pausing before he replaced the papers in his bag, he said,—

'For the last time, will you pay?'

'And with what?'

It was Murdoch who broke in with these words, in a loud and angry voice.

Herbert knew Murdoch of old. He was aware that the young man was an active adherent of the Land League, and no doubt regarded the present as a favourable opportunity for ridding the country of him. So, as he did not think it necessary to handle Murdoch gently, he answered with a shrug of his shoulders,—

'What with? Not with what you'll make by attending meetings, mixing yourself up with rebels, and boycotting the landlords. It's by working—'

'Working!' said Murdoch, stretching out his toil-hardened hands. 'Have those hands done no work? Have my father, my brothers, and my mother sat down idle all these years in the farm? Don't say such things, Mr Herbert, for I won't hear them.'

He finished his sentence with a gesture from which the subagent drew back, and then, giving vent to all the wrath that social injustice had kindled and kept burning in his honest and manly breast, he poured out a torrent of accusation and recrimination.

A dead silence, which MacCarthy, who had listened with head bowed down to Murdoch's violent words, did not break, succeeded to this outburst. Herbert regarded the stricken group with a gaze of arrogant contempt. Then Mary rose and addressed the subagent.

'Sir,' she said, 'it is I who implore you to grant us a delay. It will enable us to pay you—a few months only. Sir, I beg you on my knees, have pity on us.'

And the poor woman sank on her knees before the man whose mere attitude was an insult.

'No more of this,' cried Murdoch sternly, as he obliged his mother to rise. 'We have borne too much. Prayers are not the answer due to such wretches as he.'

'No,' said Herbert, 'and I don't want any more of your talk. The money, the money, down on the nail, or before a week is out you'll be hunted off the farm.'

'Very well; before a week is out, so be it,' said Murdoch, 'but before another minute I'm going to fling you out of the door of this house, which is still ours.'

Then, rushing at the man, he seized him round the body, dragged him to the outer door, and thrust him forth headlong.

'Oh, Murdoch, what have you done?' cried MacCarthy.

'I've done what every Irishman ought to do to the landlords,' answered Murdoch, 'turn them out of Ireland as I have turned their agent out of this farm!'

CHAPTER 14

Catastrophe

The situation described in the foregoing chapter was that of the MacCarthy family in the beginning of 1882. Foundling Mick was then ten years old; a short life if measured by years only, but already long if tested by its trials. Only three happy years, those which he passed at the farm, were to be counted in its sum.

And now, the poverty that he had formerly known had fallen upon the beings whom he loved, the family that had become his own. Misfortune was about roughly to sever the links that united the mother, the brother, and the children. They would be forced to separate, to disperse, perhaps even to leave Ireland. This had happened to many other families of the agricultural class, why should it not be their lot also?

Emigration was in fact the destined lot of the MacCarthy family, and it was to be of speedy fulfilment. Nothing but danger to himself could come of Murdoch's proceedings, the police were everywhere, and authority, on the side of the wealthy, and deaf to the protestations of the poor, supported the merciless exactions of the landlords, while it repressed with a strong hand the demonstrations of popular feeling. It would have been prudent for Murdoch to have remained quiet under a condition of things so hopeless for the cause which he espoused, and for his own interests, but he could not be induced to take any such reasonable course, and the violence with which he had recently spoken at a meeting, appealing to the people to rise against their oppressors, had so seriously compromised him and his, that MacCarthy feared a descent upon the place by the police at any minute. And now the terrible threat of eviction had come as the culminating blow, and it was evident that the end of the beloved grandmother was approaching. During the week of perplexity and suspense which followed Herbert's visit to the farm, she became more weak hour by hour, and did not leave her bed. Foundling Mick was constantly with her, and little Jane, now two years and a half old, would sit on his knees and gaze solemnly at the aged and sunken face. How sad were Granny's thoughts concerning the future of the unconscious child! One day she said to Mick,—

'You are very fond of little Jane, aren't you?'

'Yes, Granny.'

'You will never forsake her?'

'Never.'

'You're her godfather, remember that; and you will be quite a man while she is still only a little girl. If her father and mother were gone—'

'Oh, Granny, you must not think of such things. We'll not always be so ill off. You'll get better, and sit in your big chair again, and little Jane will play about you.'

But while Mick talked in this way, his heart was heavy, and tears stood in his eyes, for he knew that Granny was very, very ill. But he must not let the tears fall, lest she should see them. And not only did he grieve for his dear old friend, but he was in constant fear of the arrival of Herbert to carry out his threat.

The dispensary doctor from S— had visited Granny some weeks previously, and had spoken to MacCarthy about the improbability of his mother's life being prolonged to the end of the winter; he had prescribed medicine for her, which Foundling Mick had fetched from the dispensary at S—, but he had also advised that his patient should have a glass of good port wine daily. The latter counsel was beyond MacCarthy's means to follow. There was no wine in the house, and no money to buy so expensive a luxury. Granny protested strongly against the mere idea of such an extravagance; her cup of tea had sufficed for her always, and she wanted no other refreshment. But Foundling Mick, being stricken to the heart by the conviction that Granny was going from them, conceived the idea that she might be kept with them a little longer if some wine could be procured for her, and formed a bold plan for getting it.

He had seen port wine at Miss Watson's table; he remembered its rich red colour, and the care with which the hotel waiter poured it into the glasses of the lady and her guests. He had gained fair ideas of the price of most things in the last three years, but he had no knowledge of the cost of wine. No matter; there lay at the bottom of the jug that held his little store of pebbles the golden coin which Miss Watson had given him, and which he had never mentioned to anybody at the farm. He could surely get a big bottle of the rich red wine for his golden coin, a bottle that would hold a good many glasses? Yes, but where? They did not sell such grand drinks at S—, he was sure of that; for did not Mr MacCarthy or Murdoch go all the way to Tralee when they wanted to get really good things for farm use or house use? Therefore, to Tralee Foundling Mick would go, without saying anything to anybody, and the big bottle of port wine Granny should have. He would not say a word about it, but just slip away in the night. Twelve miles to Tralee and twelve miles back again would be a good long tramp for a little fellow like him, but Mick did not give a thought to that part of the matter.

He could not possibly get back until late in the following day, but he did not think he would be missed; at all events, he should be very soon able to account for himself. Any uneasiness that might be felt would be explained after a short delay, and he was generally either with Granny, or on the outskirts of the farm on the watch for Mr Herbert and his myrmidons, so that he might not be missed at all. This would mean his having remarkably good luck; but he was well aware, without being at all affected on his own account by the knowledge, that the attention of the family was now so much absorbed by the terrible condition of affairs at the farm, that it had become impossible for him to attract so much of it to himself as he had done in better days. The cold wind of neglect never blew upon Foundling Mick, but he was so truly, so essentially one of themselves that he came and went unnoticed, in the sense of being specially considered, at this crisis of their fate.

On the 7th of January, at two o'clock in the morning, Foundling Mick stole into the old woman's room noiselessly as a mouse, and kissed her sleeping face. Then he let himself out at the front door, with a loving goodbye pat to Ranger, who asked him very plainly in dog's language, 'Am I not to come too?' In a few minutes he was on the high road to Tralee. It was still black night, and half his journey would have to be made in the dark, but Foundling Mick was not afraid. He had started at two o'clock a.m., and he hoped to get back before dark. At Tralee he would take a rest, and break his fast at a public house, at the cost of a few pence. Then he would buy the big bottle of wine and start on his homeward journey.

The night was fine, the sky was clear, and Foundling Mick, who was very strong and active, did the first six miles in two hours. It was then four o'clock in the morning. The darkness, very deep towards the west, was already traversed by light streaks of pale colour, and the late stars were beginning to wane; but the sun would not be above the horizon for three hours yet. Foundling Mick sat down on the stump of a tree by the wayside, and ate a cold roasted potato, which he carried in his pocket, with appetite. The road was completely empty. Foundling Mick would not have cared to meet pedestrians, but the sight of a cart faring towards Tralee, with an obliging driver of whom he might have begged a lift, would not have been unwelcome. However, there was no such thing, and he must rely solely upon his own sturdy little legs.

At half-past seven he was within two miles of Tralee, and the pale wintry dawn was extending over the landscape. At the top of the road stretching before him Foundling Mick perceived a group of men coming from the direction of the town. His first impulse was to hide himself—and yet, what should these men have to do with a child like him? All the same, he crouched behind a hedge and watched their approach unseen.

The group was composed of police; this he recognised at a glance, and it cannot be said that he was surprised to see them. But he could hardly refrain from a cry when he recognised Herbert in the midst of them, accompanied by two or three of the assistants whose faces were only too familiar at evictions.

The boy's heart sank. Was the subagent going to the farm, and were the policemen there for the purpose of arresting Murdoch? Mick could not remain still and think of this. He started again so soon as the group had passed him; and, now running, now walking, he reached Tralee shortly after eight o'clock.

Having carefully selected the grandest-looking wine merchant's shop in the town, Mick walked boldly in, asked for a big bottle of 'the best' port, and tendered his precious sovereign, his entire fortune, in payment. The bottle, carefully wrapped in paper, was handed to him, with fifteen shillings, and he left the shop, a proud and happy boy, Herbert and the police notwithstanding, to go in search of a humble breakfast of bread and milk. This he easily obtained, and by ten o'clock he was out of the town of Tralee and on his way to Kirwan's Farm.

He walked steadily and at a good pace; for although he was tired, his spirits had risen with the acquisition of the wine, and the sense of success in the accomplishment of his purpose. At two o'clock in the afternoon the footsore boy was near enough to his destination to see the roof of the farmhouse and the outline of the farm buildings in the hollow below the road. There was no wind, and the wintry day was bright with cold sunshine. Mick was surprised to perceive that no smoke from the kitchen chimney rose into the air, and he ran on as quickly as his feet would carry him until he arrived at the gate of the farm.

It was broken! All the space between the gate and the house was trodden by numerous footsteps. The haggard, the stable, the cow-house, were unroofed; the thatch had been torn off, and tumbled on the ground, only a few bare gaunt rafters remained. The door had been beaten in; the window frames had been torn out. The house had been rendered uninhabitable, so that it should no longer afford shelter to human beings! Their 'voluntary ruin' had been effected by the hand of man!

Foundling Mick stopped short, petrified by terror. He dared not enter the yard; he dared not enter the house. And yet he must do both, for if the farmer or any of his family were still there, he must know it.

He forced himself to approach the gaping door, and called aloud to Murdoch. There was no answer. Then he sank down on the threshold and began to cry.

The scene that had taken place during Foundling Mick's absence was only one among many of those abominable spectacles which have disgraced Ireland in instances beyond counting, scenes that have ended in the abandonment of not only farms but whole villages by their inhabitants. These poor people, driven from the place of their birth and their life-toil, where they had hoped to die, might they not, perhaps, try to get back to them, to force the doors, to find a refuge there that they could not get elsewhere? Certainly they might and would, so an easy method of preventing them from doing this has been resorted to. The house is simply rendered uninhabitable. A battering-ram—the latest improvement on this instrument of savage social war, is due to the scientific ingenuity of a distinguished statesman, and known as 'Balfour's Maiden'—is reared against the house, and quickly demolishes everything. The roof is stripped off, the chimney is dragged down, the hearth-place is demolished, the doors are broken, the window-frames are forced out, nothing remains but the walls. And from the moment that all the breezes blow through this ruin, that it is flooded by the rain, and the snow lies in heaps in it, the landlord and his agent may rest easy; the destitute and shelterless family cannot crouch within it any more.

After the sight of such ferocious deeds, what wonder is it that deadly hatred of the doers of them dwells in the heart of the Irish peasant?

At Kirwan's Farm, the eviction had been carried out under still more atrocious conditions, for revenge had had its share in the work of inhumanity. Herbert, who wanted to pay Murdoch for his violent conduct, had not been satisfied with merely having recourse to the usual proceedings on behalf of the agent, he had denounced the young man to the authorities, and arrived at the farm with constables armed with a warrant for his arrest.

MacCarthy, his wife, Peter, Kitty and her child were turned out of the house, while it was ransacked from top to bottom by the police. The poor old grandmother, who had been dragged out of her bed into the yard, had raised herself up from the ground for a moment to curse her own and her country's assassins, and then fallen back—dead.

At that moment, Murdoch, who might have had time to fly, flung himself upon these wretches. Mad with rage, he brandished an axe, and his father and brother also strove, like him, to defend their home. Numbers were against them; strength was on the side of the law, if that name can be given to such an outrage on all justice and humanity.

MacCarthy and his younger son were arrested together with Murdoch; their resistance to the police was undeniable. In consequence, they were deprived of the benefit of the law of 1870.

The body of the poor old woman was placed in a cart and removed, with the prisoners, under the escort of the police, and the miserable procession was closed by Mary and Kitty, the latter carrying her frightened child in her arms.

Could a more sad and ghastly spectacle be witnessed than that funereal train, composed of a captive family and the corpse of an aged woman, which took its way towards S—, followed by the gloomy looks and muttered curses of the few spectators whom it encountered on the road!

Foundling Mick, when his first thrill of terror had subsided, rushed through the dismantled ruin, calling, calling; but there was no answer.

Then he bethought him of his treasure, of the little stones which marked the number of days since he had arrived at Kirwan's Farm, and he looked about for the earthenware jug, which he found in a corner, intact, with its contents—1,540 pebbles.

And now, he must say goodbye to the place of his abode during four years and eighty days, and endeavour to rejoin the family that had been his. But first, he searches among the heap of smashed furniture for the little chest of drawers in which his small stock of linen was kept, and he fortunately found it, broken indeed; but his own particular drawer had not been pillaged. He made up the contents, to which he added the bottle of port, into a bundle, and slung it upon his shoulders. Then he scooped a hole at the foot of a tree, and buried the earthenware jug with his pebbles in it, and forgetful of his stiffness and footsoreness in the tumultuous trouble of his mind, he fled from the ruins of his home into the high road on which the shadow of the coming evening was already falling.

PART TWO

CHAPTER 15

Trelingar Castle

The Marquis of Trelingar was a great personage in fact, but a much greater in fiction, the fiction of his own conceit. Unfortunately, the fact of his importance had a wide-spreading and sinister influence upon the fate of a large number of honest and industrious persons, his tenants and others, who were more or less at the mercy of his pride and inhumanity. The Marquis was English, the Marchioness was Scotch; they enjoyed large possessions in Ireland, and not only were they entirely un-sympathetic with the people whose toil supplied the luxury in which they lived, but they regarded them with antagonism composed partly of dislike and partly of disdain. The Marquis was 50 years old, and his family had been noble for centuries. He was a much esteemed member of the Upper House, where he was an unvarying and implacable opponent of every measure whereby any class or interests except his own might hope to be benefited. His pride was almost maniacal; he was sincerely convinced that a great wrong had been done to the aristocracy (and none but aristocrats had a right to consideration) by the abolition of the extremest privileges of the feudal times; that he ought still to hold the position of a high justiciary, dispensing life and death at his good will and pleasure, and receiving the slavish homage of the lieges. He recognised no rank beneath his own as rank at all; the inferior orders of persons possessing minor titles and the undistinguished gentry were all 'common people' to this absurd and contemptible peer, whose follies were, unhappily, sources of misery to people far superior in the hierarchy of humanity. In person, he belonged to a type which is becoming rare, fortunately for the future of British aristocracy; he was tall, thin, stiff, with a parchment-coloured complexion, a flabby, high-featured face, dull eyes, and thin hair; his manner was pompous, self-conscious and awkward, his speech was hesitating and formal; in short, his physical attributes corresponded with his poor and ignorant mental condition. His marriage had been an admirable arrangement. The Marchioness was a woman 'made for him', his match in pride, in narrowness, in lack of heart, and scantness of intelligence. Harmoniously the two led together their life of grand parade; in the amity of two selfish natures they sat aloft upon their perch, resolved never to descend from it. No doubt this lord and his lady believed that they would be received with distinguished honours in the Court of Heaven, having got in by the privileged *entrée*.

The Marquis of Trelingar was not in a fuss; so plebeian a manifestation as fidgety discomposure would have belied the first principles of his manner of existence. He was seated in front of a writing table in his elaborately furnished library, but his lordship's attitude was not reposeful, he moved the papers before and at both sides of him, looked under them, searched the pockets of his morning coat, and finally touched the electric bell at his elbow, and frowningly waited a response to the summons. Almost immediately a footman appeared and stood motionless at the door.

'See whether my letter-case has fallen under the table,' said the Marquis.

John advanced, stooped, inspected the carpet, and rose with empty hands.

His lordship frowned.

'Where is her ladyship?' he asked.

'Her ladyship is in her room, my lord.'

'Where is Lord Ashton?'

'His lordship is in the park, my lord.'

'Let her ladyship know that I wish to see her as soon as possible.'

John turned round, all of a piece, and walked away to execute his lordship's orders. After the lapse of a few minutes the library door was again opened, and the Marchioness advanced into the room with a slow and stately step. She was a heaven-sent match for her husband, 40 years old, tall, thin, scraggy, angular, aquiline-nosed, low-shouldered, flat-chested; she never could have been good looking, even in her youth, but she was aristocratic in her carriage and manners, and equalled, if she did not surpass, her husband, in her lofty notions of the privileges and traditions of their 'Order'.

John placed a chair for her ladyship, and withdrew. The Marquis then solemnly addressed her.

'You will excuse me, I hope, for disturbing you and asking you to come here—'

'I am quite at liberty,' returned Lady Trelingar. (These personages never departed from the most formal courtesy in their interviews.) 'What do you wish to say to me?'

'I wish to ask you to recall everything that occurred yesterday, as accurately as possible. You remember that we left the castle yesterday, at about three o'clock in the afternoon, for the purpose of calling on Mr Laird, at N—?'

'Yes, certainly.'

'Ashton was with us.'

'Yes.'

'And the men?'

'As usual.'

'You will remember that I had with me a letter-case containing the papers relating to the lawsuit with which we are threatened by the parish authorities—'

'A gross injustice and unheard-of insolence!' said Lady Trelingar, with a significant emphasis upon the last word.

'There was a bank-note for one hundred pounds in the letter-case, in addition to the papers; but you will remember that Laird said he preferred that I should hold over both until the proper time for acting in opposition to the parish claim should have arrived, that I did not leave the letter-case or its contents at his office, and that we got back to the Castle at about seven, when it was growing dark.'

'I remember all that,' said the Marchioness, rather wondering what her pompous lord was driving at.

'Well, then,' he resumed, 'that letter-case, which I replaced in the left pocket of my overcoat, is not to be found!'

'Have you searched among the things on the table for it?'

'Yes, I have turned over all the papers, and looked everywhere.'

'Nobody has been in the room since yesterday,' said Lady Trelingar, 'except the housemaids and John. It is not likely any servant would take it; although people of that class are rarely to be trusted.'

'It is just possible it might have slipped behind the carriage cushions,' suggested the Marquis.

'They would have found it in that case. The papers are of great importance?'

'Of the greatest. If I cannot produce them we shall inevitably lose our cause.'

'That would be an abominable shame!'

'Abominable indeed, like everything else that threatens the sanctity of property in Ireland.'

His lordship was checked at the beginning of his harangue by the entrance of a third person. This was a youth of about fifteen years old, at sight of whom the Marquis exclaimed, 'Ha, Ashton, here you are!'

Lord Ashton had regular features, but a wholly insignificant face; time could not endow it with vivacity or intelligence. The instinct of race manifested itself in his carriage and demeanour; he was of gentlemanly bearing, although he had been spoilt by his mother and indulged in every caprice by the subservient dependants in the castle. In reality, he possessed none of the qualities of his age; he had neither the good impulses, the warm heart nor the natural enthusiasm of youth. He was, in fact, a sprig of effete nobility, the product to be expected from the union of two such individuals as his parents; brought up to regard all who approached him as inferiors, without pity for the poor; learned enough in matters of sport, racing, hunting, tennis and croquet, but almost entirely ignorant of all besides, notwithstanding the succession of tutors who had vainly undertaken the task of his education.

Lord Ashton was a prime specimen of the young gentlemen of high birth who are destined to become complete imbeciles, while retaining the distinction that marks their class. The number of these peculiarly English types is diminishing, but it is still considerable.

The matter in question was explained to him, and he recalled to mind that he had seen his father place the letter-case behind his back on one of the carriage cushions on leaving N—.

'Are you sure, Ashton?' asked his mother.

'Quite sure, and I don't think it could have fallen out of the carriage.'

'Then it must have been in the carriage when we returned to the Castle,' remarked Lady Trelingar, 'and we can only conclude that one of the servants has taken it.'

Lord Ashton was entirely of his mother's opinion. He had not the slightest confidence in these fellows, who are always spies even when they are not thieves, but are generally both, and with whom people of the Trelingar quality ought to be empowered to deal summarily, and would be, were it not for the detestable modern spirit. For his part, he only wished he had a footman 'all to himself', or a little groom at least; he would soon let him know what a master meant!

After some edifying talk in this tone, the worthy trio arrived at the conclusion that the letter-case had been stolen, that the thief could be none other than one of the servants, and that an inquiry must be instituted, and those upon whom suspicion should light be handed over at once to police custody.

Thereupon Lord Ashton summoned John, and a few minutes later the steward, Mr Scarlett, stood in the august presence of his employer.

Mr Scarlett was a plausible and cunning person, who successfully assumed an air of benevolence, while he ill-treated everybody over whom his power extended. He was cordially detested by all the household of Trelingar Castle; for, under cover of a mild manner and gentle tones, he exercised a grinding tyranny, without anger, without arrogance, caressing while he scratched.

The story of the letter-case was told to Scarlett. The article had undoubtedly been placed on the carriage cushion, and ought to have been found in that place. Such was the opinion of Lord and Lady Trelingar, and therefore it became the conviction of Mr Scarlett. To suggest that the letter-case might have fallen out on the road would have been disrespectful to the Marquis, and the steward did not make any suggestion of the kind; he merely ventured to 'suppose' that the papers contained in the case were of great value. Indeed, how could they be otherwise, seeing that they belonged to his lordship?

'Yes, there has been theft—theft,' repeated the Marquis, 'and the papers, to say nothing of the money, are most important. They establish my rights in the matter of this claim made by the parish.'

The attitude of the steward was a complete model of indignation, zeal, and servility, as he stood, with downcast eyes and raised hands which trembled at the mere mention of such iniquity as that implied by a parish claim against the noble lord of the soil!

'The theft can only have been committed—' he began, softly, and with hesitation.

'By one of our people,' interrupted Lord Ashton, shaking the riding-whip he carried in a truly feudal fashion.

'You will set an inquiry on foot at once,' commanded the Marquis in his most pompous tones, 'so as to discover the guilty party or parties, and you will send for a constable on the spot.'

'If the inquiry should not be successful?' asked the steward in a timid and deprecatory manner.

'The entire household shall be dismissed, Scarlett; every one of them,' was Lord Trelingar's reply.

That the letter-case had fallen out of the carriage Mr Scarlett did not entertain the smallest doubt, but this consideration did not weigh with him. A theft had to be established in order that the judgement of the Marquis might be confirmed; it was for him to establish the theft and to find the thief. After a few more words, he left the room and was about to proceed to the nearest police station, in order to secure the services of a constable (for he by no means intended to charge the servants indiscriminately with theft, unsupported by the potent symbol of the law, after the high and mighty fashion dictated by the

Marquis), when his purpose was frustrated by an unexpected incident. He was crossing the yard to order a horse to be saddled for his use, when a bell in the wall was rung, the latch of a side door was lifted, and a boy, standing in the aperture, took off his cap deferentially to the steward.

The boy was Foundling Mick.

CHAPTER 16

In Service

Nearly four months had elapsed since the never-to-be-forgotten day on which the adopted child of the MacCarthys had quitted Kirwan's Farm. All that had happened to Foundling Mick during that period may be related in a brief space.

It was already growing dark when Mick turned his back forever on the ruins of his home. Having failed to come up with the MacCarthys and the others on the road to Tralee, he thought at first of bending his steps towards Limerick, whither the constables had, he concluded, been ordered to conduct their prisoners. To find the family, and to rejoin them and share their fate, whatever that might be, was Mick's clearly indicated object. He was too young to work for them at present, in the sense of earning money to assist them, but later on he might hope to find profitable employment, and still later, when he should have made his fortune, for he would do that, he would restore them to the welfare and comfort which he had enjoyed at the farm.

In the meantime, on that lonely road, in a region waste and desolated by poverty, forsaken by the miserable creatures whom it could not feed, with the cold, dark night coming on apace, Mick had never before felt so solitary. It is rarely that children of his age are not bound by some tie, if not to a family home, at least to a charitable establishment where they are sheltered and brought up; but what was he any more than a leaf plucked from a tree and flung down upon the roadway? There was no one to take pity on him; if he should not succeed in finding the MacCarthys, what was to become of him? And if he did, and that they were not to be imprisoned, but should make up their minds, like so many others, to immigrate to the New World, what was he to do then?

Our little lad resolved to journey on in the direction of Limerick. He was unacquainted with the road, and the evening was very cold, although calm. He trudged on for two miles without meeting a living soul, and then the previous fatigue of his walk to Tralee told suddenly upon him; his knees bent under him, his feet stumbled in the ruts, his sight grew dim. But Mick would not give in; he struggled along somehow for half a mile, and then coming to a cross-road, and not knowing which direction to take, his heart and his strength failed him simultaneously, and he sank down with a pitiful moan on a patch of grass by the wayside. Almost immediately afterwards the distant barking of a dog caught his dull ear, then the sound came nearer, and presently a dog ran round the turn of the road, his nose in the searching position, his tongue protruding, and his eyes shining like a cat's. With three or four bounds, the dog was upon the boy, but not to devour, only to caress him, and make him warm by lying down at his side.

Foundling Mick soon recovered his senses. He opened his eyes, felt that a warm tongue was licking his ice-cold hands, and murmured, 'Ranger! Ranger!'

How eagerly did Mick return the joyful greeting of his faithful companion at Kirwan's Farm, while his shivering body regained warmth from the welcome contact of his four-footed friend! He felt and said to himself that he was no longer alone in the world. He and Ranger together would seek the MacCarthys. He had no doubt that Ranger had wanted to accompany them after the eviction; but why had he returned? No doubt because the land agent and the myrmidons of the law had driven him away with stones and blows. In fact this was exactly what had occurred, and Ranger, thus roughly repulsed, had returned towards the farm. Now Mick would be able to follow the track of the police; he might safely trust to the dog's instinct for rejoining the evicted family.

He began to talk with Ranger as he had been in the habit of doing during their long hours on the pastureland at Kirwan's Farm. Ranger answered him in his own fashion, uttering short barks easy to interpret.

'Come on, my doggie, come on,' said Micky, 'let us go.'

Ranger darted off with a bound in front of his young master on one of the two roads.

But the dog, remembering the ill-treatment he had received from the escort of the prisoners and the others, had no desire to take the road to Limerick; accordingly, he selected that which lies alongside the boundary of County Kerry, and leads to one of the townlets of County Cork. Foundling Mick was unconsciously increasing the distance between himself and the MacCarthys, and when day dawned, he stopped, worn out with fatigue and half dead with hunger, to ask for food and shelter at a public house a dozen miles south-east of the farm. He had just fifteen shillings in his pocket, a sum on which one cannot do much travelling, even with great economy, when there are two to be fed, and Foundling Mick was forced by his exhausted condition to remain 24 hours in the garret which was his sleeping-place and Ranger's.

In answer to his questions the publican said he knew nothing about the MacCarthys, and, indeed, evictions had been so numerous during that winter that no attention had been paid to the proceedings at Kirwan's Farm.

When Mick resumed his journey he still followed Ranger along the road to N—, in a bewildered kind of way, and did not discover his mistake until his little store was so much diminished that he knew he should have to beg his way to Limerick, and this he was resolved he would not do. He was a smart little fellow, but he was only a child, after all; in the few days that elapsed while he wandered ignorantly farther and farther from his goal, he lost the sense of time and the power of hope. To get to a town, a real town, where he might learn something of his lost friends, where, if going farther should be impossible for want of money, he might get some trifling occupation, became his only distinct idea. As he painfully toiled along the dreary high road, his great fear was that notice might be taken of his solitary condition and his tender age, that he might be questioned, stopped, and taken to a workhouse or a poor school. Any and every hardship of a wandering life rather than either of these degrading alternatives for Foundling Mick! Besides, either would mean his being separated from Ranger, and that—never, never!

'No, no!' he said, pulling the dog's big head down upon his knees. 'We could not live without each other; could we, Ranger?'

As plainly as ever such a sentiment was expressed Ranger replied, with eyes and tail and dog-talk, that the thing was morally and absolutely impossible. It would be tedious and monotonous to dwell on the boy's wanderings, and on the sinking of his hopes. With his arrival at N— the vision of rejoining the MacCarthys faded from his fancy, to return no more. He had just sixpence in the world; he was once more 'lost'. We may pass over the long weeks of his sojourn there, and resume his history in the spring. He managed to live, by selling matches in the street, sometimes, and by the doing of odd jobs in the small farms and stable yards of the place. He was not molested, he even found a few friends, as humble and almost as poor as himself.

If any one of that small number had been in a position to observe the boy closely on the 16th of April, he might have been struck by the change in his countenance and manner since the preceding day. Foundling Mick's face was overcast with anxiety, and he looked about him furtively, as though he were beset by a fear that he was watched, as he started from his poor lodging in a loft over a little chandler's shop, early in the morning, and took the road that led to Cork.

He walked as quickly as he could, and with an impatient gait as though he would fain have run, and went straight on, eyes front, heeding nothing external to his concentrated thoughts. Of course he was accompanied by Ranger, but this time the dog did not lead his young master, at whom he occasionally glanced with wistful and glistening eyes.

It was nearly noon when Foundling Mick rang the bell at the door in the wall of the stable yard at Trelingar Castle.

Scarlett was just preparing to start on his errand to K——. In the yard were Lord Ashton's dogs, and those animals, apparently displeased by the aspect of Foundling Mick, barked at him furiously.

Mick, who was afraid lest a battle, in which Ranger would be at a disadvantage, should ensue on this hostile manifestation, made a sign to that obedient animal, and Ranger trotted back and retired behind some bushes in the vicinity of the open gate.

On catching sight of the boy, Scarlett called to him to come near.

'What do you want?' he asked, harshly. Mr Scarlett, who could be all amiability to grown-up persons who were not afraid of him, made it a point to be rough with children.

But a loud voice did not frighten our little lad. He had been used to such voices when he was with Mrs Murphy, with Hornpipe, and at the poor school. He took off his cap respectfully, but before he could answer Mr Scarlett's question he was shouted at again.

'Will you tell me what it is you want here? If it's to beg you're come, just be off with yourself.'

While Scarlett was speaking the dogs continued to bark, and Foundling Mick had some difficulty in keeping clear of the horse's heels.

'I have not come to beg, sir,' answered the boy, 'I never have begged, and—'

'I suppose you would not take anything if you got the offer,' said Scarlett, ironically.

'No! Not from anybody.'

'Then what brings you here?'

'I have come to speak to Lord Trelingar.'

'To his lordship?'

'Yes, to his lordship.'

'And you imagine that he will see you?'

'I do, because it is important.'

'Important!'

'Yes, sir.'

'What is it, then?'

'I cannot tell that to anybody except Lord Trelingar.'

'Then you may be off, his lordship is not at home.'

'I will wait.'

'You won't wait here, anyway.'

'I will come back.'

'You can't speak to his lordship,' growled the steward. 'I'm the person to be spoken to, and if you don't tell me what you've got to say—'

'I can't, sir, indeed I can't. I can only tell it to Lord Trelingar, and I beg—'

'Get out, you vagabond!' shouted the steward, threatening the boy with his whip. 'Off with you, or I'll set the dogs on you!'

At the raised voice of the steward, the dogs began to approach, to the terror of Mick, lest Ranger should abandon his shelter and come to the rescue, thus complicating the position.

At this moment Lord Ashton appeared at the far end of the yard, and, coming up to the group, asked what was to do there.

'It's a boy, begging, my lord,' answered Scarlett.

'I am not begging!' repeated Mick.

'A tramp.'

'Be off, you scoundrel,' cried Lord Ashton, 'or I will set my dogs on you!'

At that moment the Marquis appeared on the scene, and perceiving that Mr Scarlett had not yet set out for K—, he inquired into the cause of this delay, and of the noise that had assailed his aristocratic ears.

'I beg pardon, my lord,' began the steward, 'this young vagabond, a beggar, insists—'

'I tell you again, sir,' persisted Mick, 'that I am not a beggar.'

'What does the boy want?' asked the Marquis.

'To speak to your lordship.'

Lord Trelingar stepped back, struck a feudal attitude, and drawing himself up, said haughtily,—

'You want to speak to me. Speak, then.'

'My lord, you went yesterday to N—'

'Yes.'

'In the afternoon?'

'Yes.'

The steward was utterly astonished. Here was the 'tramp' questioning the Marquis, and his lordship actually answering the tramp.

'My lord,' said the boy, 'have you not lost a letter-case?'

'Yes, that is the fact. Well?'

'I found it on the N— road, and I have brought it back to you.'

With this he held out to Lord Trelingar the article which had been the cause of so much trouble by its disappearance, and the origin of so much unfounded suspicion of innocent persons. Thus, at no matter what cost to his dignity and self-esteem, the Marquis was proved to be in fault, the accusation against the servants was brought to nought, and, to Mr Scarlett's profound disgust, his expedition to K— became unnecessary.

Lord Trelingar took the letter-case, which had his name and address printed inside, from the hand of Foundling Mick, and proceeded to examine its contents. Having ascertained that the papers and the bank-note were intact, he addressed the boy.

'It was you who picked up the letter-case?'

'Yes, my lord.'

'And you opened it, no doubt?'

'I did, my lord, to see who it belonged to.'

'You saw that there was a bank-note in it, but perhaps you did not know its value?'

'It is a bank-note for a hundred pounds,' answered Foundling Mick without hesitation.

'Ah! you know that, but you did not think of keeping it for yourself?'

'I am not a thief, my lord, any more than I am a beggar,' replied Mick proudly.

Lord Trelingar had closed the letter-case, and carefully transferred the bank-note to his breast pocket. The boy bowed and made a few steps backward, before his lordship, who had shown no sense of the propriety of Mick's conduct, said,—

'What reward do you ask for having brought back this letter-case?'

'Give him a few shillings,' said Lord Ashton.

'Or a few pence; it's as much as his trouble's worth,' added the steward, quickly.

Foundling Mick, indignant at such bargaining for a reward he had not demanded, remarked,—

'Neither shillings nor pence are due to me,' and walked away.

'Stop!' Lord Trelingar called after him, and the boy paused, but did not re-approach the speaker.

'How old are you?'

'Ten and a half.'

'And your father and mother?'

'I have neither father nor mother.'

'Your relations?'

'I have no relations.'

'Where do you come from?'

'From Kirwan's Farm, where I lived for four years until four months ago.'

'Why did you leave it?'

'Because the farmer was hunted out by the police.'

'Is not that one of Lord C—'s farms?' asked the Marquis, turning to Scarlett.

'Yes, my lord,' replied the steward.

'And what are you going to do now?' inquired his lordship.

'I am going back to N— where I earn my living.'

'If you like to remain at the Castle, some kind of work can be found for you.'

This was a charitable offer; yet it was the pride and not the heart of Lord Trelingar that suggested it. Foundling Mick understood this perfectly, and instead of replying at once, he paused to reflect. He was not at all attracted by either the Marquis or his son, and the rough reception he had had from Scarlett made the latter odious to him.

Then there was Ranger. They might take him into their service, but they would not have Ranger, and he could not make up his mind to part with the comrade of his good and evil days.

And yet, was not the proposal of the Marquis a stroke of luck for the poor boy who had no certainty of being able to make a livelihood of the humblest description? His reason told him that he ought to close with it, and that if he returned to N— he might repent his decision.

True, the dog was embarrassing, but he should find an opportunity of speaking on that matter. They would surely let Ranger in, if only as a watch dog, a capacity in which the faithful animal was eminently admirable. And then, he would not be employed at the Castle without some pay, and by economising—

'Well, have you made up your mind?' growled the steward, who would gladly have seen him sent off about his business without more ado.

'How much should I be paid?' asked Mick, boldly, the practical side of him coming uppermost.

'Two pounds a month,' answered the Marquis.

Two pounds a month! This seemed an immense sum to Mick, and indeed it was large wages for a child of his age.

'I thank your lordship,' said the boy, with all his native courtesy; 'I accept your lordship's offer, and will do my best to please you.'

And thus it was that Foundling Mick took his place on that very day among the servants in the Castle, with the assent of the Marchioness, and a week later was raised to the rank and dignity of groom or little 'tiger' to Lord Ashton.

And Ranger? what had become of him during that week? Had his master ventured to present him at the Castle? No, he would have been too ill received. The fact was that Lord Ashton possessed three dogs, and loved them almost as well as he loved himself. To live with them satisfied alike his tastes and his intelligence. The dogs were highly bred Scotch terriers, and excessively ill tempered; they tolerated no intruders, and their instinct towards their own kind was aggressive and combative. Therefore Ranger hung about the place at a more than respectful distance, and Mick brought him food at night, saved from his own allowance. Both the dog and his master grew thin under this arrangement; but, no matter, they were not quite parted, and better days, in which they should grow fat together, might be in store for the faithful pair.

From this time a different life began for the young hero of this melancholy history. We need not refer to the years passed with Mrs Murphy and at the poor school, but only draw the comparison with his existence at Kirwan's Farm. There he was one of the MacCarthy family; the yoke of servitude did not gall him; but here, at the Castle, he was regarded with the most complete indifference. The Marquis looked upon him in the light of one of the 'poor's boxes' into which he dropped an alms at stated periods; the Marchioness regarded him as no more than an additional animal in the place, but not at all as a pet one; and to Lord Ashton he represented a toy which had been given to him without any caution against breaking it. Scarlett formed an exception to this negative rule; he had resolved to testify his antipathy to Foundling Mick by incessantly molesting him, and he found plenty of opportunity. As for the English servants, they looked on the foundling whom his lordship had brought into the Castle as entirely beneath them, and declined to associate, beyond the inevitable meals in common, with such 'scum'; making him feel their contempt in every small detail of his service. Foundling Mick made no complaint, returned no answer, but performed his tasks to the very best of his ability. But oh! how thankful he was when night came, and after he had executed his master's last orders, he took refuge in the little room which he had all to himself.

Nevertheless, in the midst of all this ill-will and indifference, there was one woman who took an interest in Foundling Mick. She was only a laundress in the service of the Castle, named Kate Brady. Kate was 50 years of age, and had always lived on the domain; she would probably end her days there, unless Mr Scarlett should turn her out. This he had already attempted to do, for Irish Kate was not so fortunate as to please him. To this good woman Mick would sometimes confide his trouble when he had suffered any special slight or spite from the servants.

'Patience, patience!' Kate would say to him. 'Don't mind what they say. The best among them is no great things, and I don't know one that would have brought back the letter-case.'

Very likely the laundress was right, and these persons looked upon Foundling Mick as a fool for his honesty.

Fortified by his one friend, Mick was not unhappy, although he had to comply with every caprice of his young master. This state of things would last so long as the plaything had not ceased to please; but the young gentleman was so spoilt, selfish, and whimsical that it was hard to tell for how long that condition would hold good. Children always tire of their playthings, and throw them away, even if they do not break them. Foundling Mick, however, had no notion of allowing himself to be smashed. He regarded his situation at Trelingar only as a temporary expedient; he had accepted it in lieu of something better, hoping that a farther opportunity of gaining his livelihood would soon occur. His youthful ambition rose above the functions of a 'tiger'. His pride rebelled against servitude, and was humiliated by the effacement of himself in the presence of Lord Ashton, whose superior he felt himself to be. Yes, his superior, although Lord Ashton had lessons in Latin history and other things. Professors came to instruct him, trying to fill him with knowledge as a jug might be filled with water. Foundling Mick knew nothing about these fine things, but he knew how to reflect. At ten years old he was a thinker. He appraised this young sprig of nobility at his true value, and sometimes blushed at the service he was bound to do for him. How deeply he regretted the salutary and invigorating labour of the farm, and his life with the MacCarthys, of whom he could hear nothing.

An opportunity soon arose for putting the friendship of the laundress, Kate Brady, to the test.

It is well to mention here that the dispute between the parish and Lord Trelingar had been settled in favour of the latter, owing to the production of the paper which had been restored by Foundling Mick; but the boy's action seemed to be quite forgotten now, and, indeed, why should any gratitude be felt towards him?

May, June and July had passed away, and Ranger had been fed somehow; he had also shown great prudence in keeping clear of the dangers of the park. Foundling Mick had carefully stored up, and with equal care inscribed in his pocketbook, the large sum of six pounds sterling, his wages for three months.

During those three months the Marquis and Marchioness of Trelingar had been occupied in receiving and returning the visits of the great folk of the county. A portion of the summer had gone by, and the period had arrived at which the Marquis usually visited Scotland and his wife's family. This year, however, the noble family contemplated an excursion to the celebrated Lakes of Killarney, as a preliminary to the autumnal tour, and their departure was fixed for the 3rd of August.

If Foundling Mick hoped that he was to be left at the Castle, for a short spell of leisure and peace, he deceived himself. Lord Ashton would by no means dispense with the services of his little groom. Then arose a grave consideration for poor Mick. What would become of Ranger? Who would take care of him? Who would feed him?

He decided on taking Kate Brady into his confidence, and the good woman at once settled the matter for him by promising to take charge of Ranger, unknown to anybody.

'Don't be uneasy, my child,' said Kate, 'I'm a'most as fond of your dog as you are yourself, and nothing shall happen to him while you are away.'

Thereupon Foundling Mick kissed Kate Brady with fervent gratitude, and on the evening before his departure he placed Ranger in her charge, and bade farewell to the faithful animal with a comparatively light heart.

CHAPTER 17

A Young English Nobleman

Our readers will readily excuse a hiatus in the narrative of Foundling Mick's adventures at the point which that narrative has reached. The district of Killarney and its famous lakes are too well known to require, or indeed to bear, description, and a record of the tour of the noble travellers in the picturesque region to which some of the most poetic legends and the most harrowing facts in Irish history, both ancient and modern, are attached, would be only a tedious interruption of a story which boasts of only a humble hero. The travellers did not leave their several natures behind them at Trelingar Castle; their respective characteristics were freely displayed everywhere they went, and thoroughly appreciated by the intelligent people, who were quite capable of 'taking the length of the foot' of the Marquis, the Marchioness, and the lordling. Of course they were received everywhere with well-simulated respect, which was in many instances even servile, but only the few persons of rank approaching to theirs failed to note the emptiness of their heads, the coldness of their hearts, the narrowness of their minds, and the arrogance of their pretensions as those qualities deserved. They had one recommendation only; they could, and did, spend money in the places through which they passed; for their own gratification, it is true, but still the money was actually put in circulation, and that was a good thing! As for themselves, the scenes of beauty, whether mournful or majestic, the interesting people, the suggestive spectacle of the lavish loveliness of nature in sad contrast with the poverty and suffering of humanity, said nothing to these soulless personages, who visited Killarney because it was 'the thing' to do so. If the truth concerning this expedition is to be told, as it may be told in a few words, the one individual of the party who saw, admired, understood, and enjoyed the objects which it disclosed to eyes endowed with the true faculty of seeing, was poor Foundling Mick. To the nameless deserted child, the ill-used waif, the twice-orphaned exile from Kirwan's Farm, the little victim of the capricious tyranny and bullying of the ill-conditioned cub who was heir to all the Trelingar greatness, the voice of Nature spoke, on him she smiled, and to her his seared and timid heart was opened.

We pass over the incidents of the excursion, and take up the thread of our little lad's story on the auspicious day that witnessed the return of the Marquis and Marchioness with their hopeful son and heir to Trelingar Castle.

They were very glad to be done with the traditional excursion to the Lakes of Killarney and the mountainous regions of Kerry.

'It wasn't worth the trouble and fatigue,' said her ladyship, and his lordship echoed the sentiment.

As for Foundling Mick, he returned with his head full of pictures and of remembrance. His first care was to inquire of Kate Brady for news of Ranger.

Ranger was well. He came punctually every evening to the appointed place, where the kind-hearted laundress waited for him with his food. That same evening the boy and his canine friend met again; the interview was most affectionate on both sides, and they parted with poignant regret. Prudence was necessary. Ranger had been seen more than once in the neighbourhood of the Castle, and the dogs had signified the presence of an intruder on those occasions.

The Castle resumed its usual course of existence—the vegetative existence which suited such exalted personages as its owners. Lord and Lady Trelingar were to go to Scotland in September, and to London for the winter. The monotonous routine of visits began again. Foundling Mick, who had nothing to do with that side of life at the Castle, found his own little share of another side of it anything but pleasant. He was continually exposed to the malicious devices of Scarlett, who found a ready-to-hand victim in the friendless boy. On the other hand he had no respite from the whims of Lord Ashton, and he was laughed at by all the servants, indoor and outdoor, when they saw him treated like a toy jerked by wires, perpetually called, dismissed, commanded and countermanded. All this humiliated the boy profoundly. At night, when he was at last safe in his little room, he gave himself up to reflecting upon the position into which his extreme poverty had forced him. What would his post as 'tiger' to Lord Ashton lead to? Nothing. He was made for something better. To be only a servant, a machine made to obey, was unspeakably repugnant to his independent spirit; it hampered the ambition that he felt within himself. At least, when he lived at the farm, it was on the footing of equality. He was regarded as the child of the house. Where were now Granny's caresses, the affection of Mary and Kitty, the encouraging kindness of MacCarthy and his sons? He prized far more the pebbles he had received each night, and had buried amid the ruins of the farm, than the sovereigns with which his slavery was now paid by the month. While he lived at Kirwan's Farm he was learning, he was working; he was gaining the means of making a livelihood for himself one day. Here, nothing but a distasteful task without an outlook; of submission to the whims of a vainglorious, spoilt, selfish, ignorant youth. He was constantly occupied in putting in order—not the books, there were none—but everything in the young lord's disorderly rooms.

And then, the young lord's cabriolet was Mick's despair! Oh, that cabriolet! At the risk of overturning the vehicle into a ditch, Lord Ashton seemed to take delight in driving recklessly on the worst roads in the county in order to swing the little groom, holding on by the straps at the back, from side to side more violently. The dog-cart was less of an instrument of torture to Mick; in it he could sit bolt upright and steady, in the regulation attitude with his arms crossed.

There was, however, hardly a day on which the cabriolet experience had not to be gone through. In the long drives in the Trelingar district, the dashing vehicle with its smart attendant would pass by groups of ragged children, running barefooted on the stony highway, with outstretched hands, and the too familiar beggar's whine: 'Give us a ha'penny!' At the sight Foundling Mick's heart swelled; he had known such misery himself. Lord Ashton replied to the entreaties of the poor creatures by jeering at them, and threatening them with his whip, while his 'boy' longed to throw a few of the coveted ha'pence among them. But this he was too much afraid of his heartless young master to do.

Once, however, the temptation proved too strong for him. A little girl, with fair curls and blue eyes, a pretty child despite her rags and her lean, half-starved body, looked piteously at him as the dog-cart passed her, and he threw her a penny from his seat at the back. The child picked up the coin with a cry of joy, and Lord Ashton heard that unusual sound. He had caught his groom *in flagrante delicto* of charity!

'How dared you do that, boy?' he asked, angrily.

'My lord, the little girl—she was so glad—it was only a penny.'

'Just what you had thrown to yourself, when you ran the roads, eh?'

'No, never,' protested Foundling Mick, revolting against this reiterated charge of mendicancy.

'Why did you give that beggar a penny?'

'She looked at me—I looked at her.'

'I forbid you to look at the beggar children on the roads. Mind that, now.'

And Foundling Mick had to obey, but he was exasperated by the hardness of heart of this scion of a noble house. He did not again venture to give a penny to any poor creature in passing, but early in September an incident occurred which caused him to depart from the wholesome path of caution.

On that particular day, Lord Ashton had ordered his dog-cart to go to K——. As usual, Foundling Mick accompanied him, sitting back-to-back with his lordship, with folded arms, and motionless as a statue. The dog-cart reached the little town without accident; and the driver made the horse prance and foam at the mouth, much to the admiration of the idle spectators. Lord Ashton got out and went into two or three shops, while Mick stood right in front of the horse's head, to the wonder of the gaping street boys, whose envy was excited by the young groom in his trim livery.

When Lord Ashton had sufficiently displayed his equipage and himself in the town, he took the homeward road, making the horse go at a foot-pace, with all sorts of equine airs and graces. At a short distance the dog-cart encountered a tribe of beggar children who went through the usual routine of useless supplication, but on this occasion, being encouraged by the slow movement, they followed closely behind the dog-cart. Being presently deterred by the backward sweep of Lord Ashton's ever ready and merciless whip, however, all but one dropped off and stood in the road disconsolate.

That one persisted. He was a little boy of seven, full of intelligence and high spirits, truly Irish in that particular. Slow as the pace of the horse was, the little fellow had to run over the stones, which cut his bare feet, in order to keep up with the dog-cart. Still he persisted, braving the menace of the whip, and offering a bunch of heather for the sorely needed ha'penny.

Foundling Mick, in alarm lest the child should be hurt, made urgent signs to him to desist, but in vain; the little boy still ran after the dog-cart. Lord Ashton had, of course, ordered him off several times, but he persisted, and ran along so close to the wheels that he was in danger of being crushed.

A touch of the reins would have started the horse at the trot, but that did not suit Lord Ashton's humour, he chose to go at a walking-pace, and at a walking-pace he went. At last he grew weary of the child's importunity, and struck at him with the whip. The long lash, ill-directed, caught round the neck of the little boy, who was dragged along, half-strangled for a few seconds; then with a pull the lash was loosed and he fell back upon the road.

Foundling Mick jumped off the dog-cart and ran to the child, who was screaming with pain. A red line encircled his neck. Our little lad's heart swelled with indignation; he would have felt a fierce joy in flinging himself upon Lord Ashton, who might have paid dearly for his cruelty, although he was five years older than his groom.

'Come here, boy!' he shouted. He had stopped his horse.

'The child, my lord?'

'Come here, this instant!' he shouted again, and flourished his whip. 'Come! or I'll flog you too!'

It was fortunate that he did not put his threat into execution, for there is no saying what might have happened had he done so. Foundling Mick had sufficient self-control to master his feelings, and having pushed a few pence into the pocket of the little fellow's ragged jacket, he got up behind the dog-cart.

'The first time you presume to get down without orders,' said Lord Ashton, 'I shall first give you a good horsewhipping, and then turn you away!'

Mick's eyes flashed, but he made no reply. The dog-cart rolled rapidly out of sight, leaving the little boy on the roadside, quite consoled, and jingling his pennies in his hand.

From that day forward Lord Ashton's evil instincts prompted him to make his groom's life as hard as possible. Every vexation and exaction was heaped on Mick; no humiliation was spared him. All that he had formerly had to suffer physically he now had to suffer morally, and as a matter of fact, he was no less miserable than he had formerly been in Mrs Murphy's cabin, or under Hornpipe's tyranny. He constantly thought of leaving Trelingar Castle, but whither was he to go? He had heard nothing of the MacCarthys, and even if he could rejoin them what would they be able to do for him, homeless and destitute as they were? Nevertheless, he was resolved not to remain in the service of Lord Ashton.

Mick had another pressing cause of anxiety. The family at the Castle would soon be leaving Trelingar for Scotland, and ultimately England; if he should be taken with them, he must relinquish all hope of finding the MacCarthys. Then, again, there was Ranger. What would become of him?

'I will keep him,' said Kate Brady, one day, 'and take good care of him.'

'I know you would, for you are kind,' answered Mick. 'I could trust him to you, and I would pay for his food.'

'Nonsense,' said Kate, 'I did not mean that. I'm very fond of the dog.'

'No matter, he must not cost you anything; but, if I go away, I shall not see him again for the whole winter or, perhaps, ever.'

'Why, my dear? When you come back—'

'When I come back, Kate? How do I know I'll ever come back? How do I know they won't send me away, over there, where they're going, or maybe I'll go away of my own accord—'

'Go away?'

'Yes—on chance—straight before me, as I have always done.'

'Poor boy! Poor boy!'

'I wonder, Kate, whether it wouldn't be the best thing I could do, if I set off out of this at once with Ranger, and looked for work among the farmers, in a village or near a town, not too far off, on the sea coast?'

'Why, child, you're not eleven!'

'No, Kate, not quite eleven yet. Ah, if I was only twelve or thirteen, I should be big, I'd have strong arms, I'd soon find work to do. How long of coming the years are when one is poor!'

'And long of going, too,' might have been Kate Brady's answer.

Such was the tone of Mick's reflections, and he knew not what course to take. A fortuitous circumstance speedily put an end to his uncertainty.

The 13th of September arrived, and Lord and Lady Trelingar were to leave the Castle within a fortnight. Preparations for the departure had already begun, and Foundling Mick was anxious to discover whether Scarlett was to remain in charge of the Castle during the winter. He soon learned that the steward would be left there, and immediately came to the conclusion that poor Ranger's presence in the vicinity would be revealed, and Kate Brady would be forbidden to keep him in her quarters. She would have to feed him in secret, as she had hitherto done. Ah! had Mr Scarlett only known that the stray dog he had noticed once or twice, belonged to the little groom, with what glee he would have told Lord Ashton, and with what relish that worthy young aristocrat would have put a bullet into Ranger.

On this unlucky day Ranger had strayed into the neighbourhood of the Castle, contrary to his custom, and in the afternoon, by an evil chance, one of Lord Ashton's dogs espied him at some distance. Immediately on perceiving each other, the two dogs manifested their hostile sentiments by growling. There was a racial feud between them, the lordly dog could not but entertain a deep disdain of the peasant dog; but, being of an evil nature, the former was the more aggressive of the two. No sooner had he observed Ranger standing motionless on the edge of a clump of trees than he dashed down upon him, with distended jaws and fangs ready for use.

Ranger let the terrier get within half a length of him, watching him askance so as not to be taken by surprise, tail down, and planted firmly on his legs. Suddenly, after two or three more barks, the lordly dog flung himself on Ranger and bit him in the thigh, whereupon Ranger sprang at his enemy's throat and bowled him over in an instant. This skirmish was not effected without ear-piercing howls. The two other dogs shut up in the yard joined in the concert, and Lord Ashton came running out of the yard gate, accompanied by Scarlett, to behold the terrier choking in the hold of Ranger's terrible teeth. He could only scream and stamp with rage; he dared not go to the aid of his dog lest the victor should turn on him. Ranger saw the young lord, finished the terrier with one more snap of his jaw, took his teeth out of the dog's neck, and scampered off through the trees. Then Lord Ashton and Scarlett advanced, but when they reached the scene of the crime the lordly terrier was dead.

'Scarlett, Scarlett! My dog is dead!' cried Lord Ashton. 'That brute has choked my dog! Where is he? Come! We shall find him, and I will kill him!'

The steward was not by any means disposed to pursue the slayer of the terrier; nor did he find it at all difficult to restrain the ardour of that defunct animal's master, who was, as a matter of fact, terrified at the idea that Ranger might return in an offensive mood.

'Take care, my lord, take care!' said Scarlett. 'Don't attempt to go after that fierce brute. The men will catch him some other day, never fear.'

'Whose dog is he?'

'Nobody's. There are lots of those curs going about.'

'Then he'll escape.'

'Not likely, my lord. That dog has been lurking about the Castle for weeks past.'

'For weeks, Scarlett! And I have not been told, and he has not been got rid of! And now, you see, he has killed my terrier!'

It must be admitted that there was just a streak of good in the nature of this selfish and unfeeling lad; he cared for his dogs, and especially for his favourite, Ranger's victim, as he did not and could not care for any human creature. It was in a whirl of mingled grief and fury that Lord Ashton returned to the courtyard of the Castle and gave orders for the dead terrier to be brought thither. Fortunately, his lordship's 'tiger' had not witnessed this scene; for he might have allowed the secret of his intimacy with the assassin to escape him, and Ranger, on seeing Mick, might have run to him and made a compromising demonstration. But it was not long before he learned what had happened, for Lord Ashton filled Trelingar Castle with his lamentations. The Marquis and the Marchioness offered him their best 'compliments of condolence', but he refused to be comforted, and vowed a cruel vengeance upon the vile brute to whose base-born audacity he owed his bereavement. The obsequies of the terrier were performed with an absurd exaggeration of respect, and when the last spadeful of earth had been replaced upon the dog's grave in a shady corner of the park, Lord Ashton re-entered the house with a dark scowl upon his face and shut himself up in his room for the whole evening.

It is easy to imagine the uneasiness and the forebodings of Foundling Mick. Before he went to bed, he contrived to see Kate Brady (who fully shared his anxiety for the fate of Ranger) in secret.

'You must be on your guard, my boy,' she said earnestly, 'and above all take care that they don't find out that he is your dog. It would all come down upon you, and I don't know what might happen.'

Foundling Mick thought little enough about the possibility of his being held responsible for the death of the terrier. He was thinking only that now it would be very hard, if not impossible, for him to continue to take care of Ranger. The steward would keep a look out for him in the neighbourhood of the Castle, and even though the sagacious creature was to keep out of sight successfully, how should he get to Kate at night, and how could she contrive to feed him secretly?

Our lad passed a wakeful night; he was far more anxious about Ranger than on his own account, and the course of his reflections led him to consider whether he had not better leave Lord Ashton's service on the morrow. After his thoughtful fashion he examined the matter coolly, weighing the for and against, and finally decided on putting the project that had occupied his mind for some weeks into execution.

He did not fall asleep until three o'clock in the morning. On awaking, he jumped out of bed in great surprise that he had not been aroused by the imperious summons of his master's bell, and instantly took up the thread of his thoughts. Looked at by daylight his decision remained unaltered. He would leave the Castle that very day, assigning as his reason that he felt himself unsuited to the occupation of a groom. No one had the right to prevent his departure, and he resigned himself beforehand to any insult that his demand might provoke. Then, in the prevision of a rough and immediate expulsion, Foundling Mick carefully dressed himself in the clothes he had worn at the farm, for he had preserved them, and although a good deal the worse for wear, the garments were clean and decent. He put into his pocket the accumulated wages of his three months' service; but it was his purpose, after he had respectfully informed Lord Trelingar of his intention of leaving the Castle, to ask his lordship for the fortnight's pay then due to him. He would try to see Kate Brady, and bid her farewell without getting her into trouble, and then, when he should have picked up Ranger at one or other of the poor animal's haunts, the two friends would turn their backs on Trelingar Castle with common and uncommon satisfaction.

It was nearly nine o'clock when Mick went down to the stable yard, and great was his astonishment to learn that Lord Ashton had gone out an hour earlier. Generally, the boy had to attend at his master's toilet, and he dreaded no duty of the day more, or with greater reason, for the young gentleman delighted in taunting, ridiculing, and abusing him during its fulfilment.

Mick's surprise was quickly followed by well-founded apprehension when he perceived that Bill (one of the stablemen) and the surviving terriers were not in their respective places. At this moment Kate appeared at the door of the laundry, made a sign to him to draw near, and said in a low voice, 'Lord Ashton has gone out with Bill and the two dogs. They are going to hunt Ranger.'

Mick could not answer, he was choked with grief and anger.

'Take care, my boy; here comes the steward, and you must not—'

'Ranger must not be killed,' said the boy, impetuously, 'and I shall—'

Scarlett, who had overheard this colloquy, came up to the speakers and called out to Mick roughly,—

'What's that you're saying, boy, and what are you doing there?'

Mick, not wishing to enter into a discussion with the steward, answered simply,—

'I wish to speak to Lord Ashton.'

'You can speak to him when he returns,' replied Scarlett, 'after he has caught that brute of a dog.'

'He will not catch him,' said Mick, with forced calmness.

'Indeed!'

'No, Mr Scarlett, and if he does catch him, I tell you he will not kill him.'

'And why?'

'Because I'll prevent him. I, Mr Scarlett. The dog is mine, and I shall not let him be killed.'

And Mick, leaving the steward confounded by this answer, rushed out of the yard, and sped away towards the plantation with incredible swiftness. For half an hour he vainly searched for any trace of Lord Ashton, hearing no sound to guide him. At length the barking of dogs became audible, but at a distance. He ran with all his speed in the direction of the sounds (he had recognised the 'tongue' of the terriers), and presently came to a thick grove of coniferous trees which extended all along the edge of a great pond, one of the features of the domains of Trelingar. No doubt they were hunting Ranger in that direction. Presently, Mick could distinguish the words of the unseen speakers; the dogs were silent.

'Attention, my lord! We have him now.'

'Yes, yes, Bill! here! here!'

The dogs again barked furiously, and, as Mick ran into the grove towards the voices, he was startled by a shot.

'Missed! missed!' cried Lord Ashton. 'Your turn now, Bill; mind *you* don't miss!'

A second shot was fired near enough for Mick to see the flash through the foliage.

'He's got it this time,' cried Bill, while Lord Ashton's dogs barked furiously.

Foundling Mick's legs gave way as though the bullet had struck himself, and he was falling, when the branches within about six feet of him were moved with a slight noise, and through a gap in the paling a dog appeared. The animal's coat was wet, and he foamed at the mouth. It was Ranger, who had been hit in the side by Bill's bullet, and had jumped into the pond.

Ranger recognised his master, who instantly caught him by the muzzle, and held his mouth firmly shut while he dragged him into a thicket, trembling lest the pursuers should come again upon the victim. But this did not happen. The boy and the dog lay safely hidden amid the underwood, while their enemies, tired by the cruel sport of the morning, passed so near them that Mick heard Lord Ashton say to Bill, in a tone of gloomy suggestiveness,—

'I wish I had caught him alive!'

CHAPTER 18

Eighteen Years between Them

Foundling Mick drew a deeper breath than he had ever before drawn in his life, so soon as Lord Ashton, Bill and the dogs had disappeared. And we may be sure Ranger did the same when after a time Mick ventured to let go his hold of the dog's jaws, saying to him,—

'Don't bark, Ranger; don't bark!'

Ranger did not bark.

It was fortunate that Foundling Mick, having thoroughly made up his mind that morning to leave Trelingar, had dressed himself in his old clothes, tied up his little bundle, and put his purse in his pocket. This spared him the unpleasant necessity of re-entering the Castle, where Lord Ashton would very soon learn who was the owner of the slayer of his favourite dog. What sort of reception Mick would have met with from him may easily be guessed.

It is true that by not reappearing he sacrificed the wages due to him, and which he intended to claim, but he resigned himself to that necessity. He was out of Trelingar Castle; he had escaped from Lord Ashton and Scarlett, and that was all he and his dog desired. His only thought now was to get as far off as possible in the shortest time; at the pond side he was only two miles away from the Castle gates; there must be no lingering so near his late detested prison. He had mechanically carried his little bundle under his arm when hurrying out of the stable yard after his rash speech to the steward, and it had fallen on the ground when he used his two hands to prevent Ranger from barking. With a warning gesture well understood by the dog, Mick left him, retraced his steps to the spot at which he had appeared after his plunge into the pond, and picked up the small roll of linen that constituted his wardrobe. Then, after a cursory examination of Ranger's wound, a very slight one, for Bill's bullet had merely grazed the dog's skin, he and his companion made their way out of the plantation and started off at a great pace on the high road, where neither pedestrian nor vehicle was visible. Ranger was not too much hurt to be in good spirits, and he expressed his joy in dog fashion, but Foundling Mick, although he exulted in his emancipation, was anxious about the future.

This time, however, he knew where he was going, and it was intentionally that he took a southern direction, for it was his purpose to make for Cork. From thence ships sail—merchant ships—large ones, real ones, not small coasting vessels or mere fishing-boats such as he was familiar with at Westport or Galway. Our lad found a great attraction in the idea of these ships; things commercial had an irresistible attraction for him.

The chief matter was to get to Cork; the journey on foot would take time, and must cost some money; but not much, for Mick would try to earn something by the way, as he had done before. The weather was fine, the road was good; there was neither mud nor dust; excellent conditions for a long walk.

Let us briefly record that the tired boy and dog found themselves two days later within three miles of Woodside, where Mick proposed to remain and rest for a night before entering upon the serious task of seeking employment in the fair city of Cork. They were walking along a path by the side of a little river, an affluent of the far-famed Lee, when Ranger suddenly stopped, and uttered a low growl.

Foundling Mick stopped also, and looked forwards and backwards along the road. There was nothing to be seen.

'What's the matter, Ranger?'

Ranger barked this time, and then bounded away to the brink of the river.

'He's thirsty,' said Mick to himself, 'and for that matter, so am I.' Then he too turned off the raised path towards the river; but he had taken only two steps, when the dog, with a loud bark, sprang into the water.

Mick ran forward, reached the edge, and was about to recall the dog, when he perceived the cause of Ranger's action. This was a drowning child, whom the dog had seized by his clothes, or rather by his rags, and was striving to drag to the bank. But the current was running strongly, and Ranger had a tough job to effect his feat of salvage. Mick could swim; it will be remembered that Grip had taught him; he promptly pulled off his jacket, and was kicking off his shoes, preparatory to joining Ranger in the river, when the dog deposited the child on the slope at Mick's feet. Mick seized the unconscious form, and carried it to a safe place. The rescued child was a little boy, seven years old at the most; his eyes were shut, and his head hung helplessly over Mick's arm. What was the surprise of the older lad to recognise in the pale face from which he cleared away the wet hair, that of the little boy whom Lord Ashton had slashed with his driving whip on the road to Trelingar.

The child must have been wandering ever since upon the roads! His haggard face, his thin, light body, told of all that he had suffered, of fatigue, cold and hunger. Mick put his hand on the child's stomach; it was as flat as an empty bag. He employed all his little skill to restore the poor human waif to consciousness, an operation closely observed by Ranger, and after some time he succeeded. The child breathed, opened his eyes, and said, feebly,—

'I'm hungry.'

Foundling Mick still had in his bundle some of the provisions for the day's tramp, consisting of a few slices of cold bacon, a hunch of bread, a piece of cheese, and some cold potatoes. He put a mouthful of the bread between the child's lips, and he swallowed it eagerly. After a few minutes

Mick fed him very moderately, and he regained some strength. Then he fixed his eyes on Mick, and said,—

'You! you!'

'Yes. You remember me?'

'On the road—I don't know when—'

'But I know,' said Mick, soothingly.

'Oh! don't leave me!'

'No, no! I'll take care of you. Where were you going?'

'Nowhere.'

'Where do you live?'

'I don't know. Nowhere.'

'How did you fall into the river? Were you getting a drink?'

'No; I fell in—on purpose.'

'On purpose?'

'Yes, yes. But I don't want to do it now—if you stay with me.'

'I'll stay; never fear.'

Foundling Mick's eyes filled with tears at the terrible idea of this child of seven, driven to seek death by the despair that comes of destitution, abandonment, hunger!

The little boy again closed his eyes, and Mick asked him no more questions. There would be time enough for them afterwards. And besides, did he not know the story? Was it not that of all poor forsaken creatures? Was it not the story of Foundling Mick himself, except that he, being gifted with exceptional strength of mind, would not ever have thought of taking that way out of his troubles.

What was to be done? The child could not possibly walk to Woodside, nor could Mick carry him thither. Night was approaching, and it was essential to find a shelter. Neither a farmhouse, a cabin nor a public house was within sight. On the left of the road was a large plantation of fine umbrageous trees; the wanderers might pass the night in its shelter at the foot of one of those forest-lords, on a grassy bed, by the side of a fire of sticks. At sunrise, when the child should have regained his strength, the two would be able to reach Woodside, and perhaps, even Cork. There was enough food remaining to afford them a frugal supper, and a morsel to spare for breakfast in the morning. Having arranged this plan in his mind in a few seconds, Mick took up the sleeping boy in his arms, crossed the road, and entered the plantation on the other side.

Within a few feet of the edge the plantation was almost dark, and Mick made his way with some little difficulty towards a group of majestic trees where the space was more open. There it was his good fortune to find a stump, about three feet high, the remains of a giant elm which had been blown down. The whole depth of the stump, which was five feet in diameter, and had wide-spreading roots, was filled with leaves, and as no rain had fallen for some days, these were dry; before the searcher's eyes was a bed ready prepared for his *protégé*—Foundling Mick's *protégé!*—one in which he too might lie down, if he did not mind a tight fit. Mick undressed the sleeping child, rubbed his body as nearly dry as possible, and placed him deep among the leaves, with a wisp of grass for a pillow, and then set to work to gather materials for a fire. He did not forget that the light might be seen and might attract attention to his act of 'trespass', but he was indifferent to this contingency. If anyone should think it worthwhile to investigate the origin of the light in the wayside wood, that individual could hardly be so formidable as Mr Scarlett; it was not likely his destiny had conducted Mick to a second Trelingar. He soon collected a little heap of twigs, bits of timber and dry leaves, and kindled a fire by the aid of the matches which he had prudently included in his small purchases on the day before. This done, he carefully dried the little boy's ragged clothes, and hung them on a neighbouring branch. And now it was time to think of supper. Ranger at least was decidedly of that opinion, and his master adjudged to him the larger portion of the meal. When the two had eaten, Mick wrapped up the remnants, with a view to breakfast, and confiding his bundle and the child's clothes to Ranger with unhesitating confidence, he climbed into the hollow tree-trunk, clasped its occupant in his arms, and before long was sleeping soundly, while Ranger kept unwinking watch upon the wanderers.

In the morning, the little waif awoke first, much surprised to find himself in so good a bed. Ranger saluted him with a soft-toned protecting bark. Was he not to some extent his preserver? Mick opened his eyes almost immediately, and the child put his arms round his neck and kissed him.

'What is your name?' he asked.

'Foundling Mick. What's yours?'

'Dick.'

'All right, Dick. Come and dress yourself.'

Dick did as he was desired, promptly. He was in the best of spirits; he hardly remembered that only yesterday he had wanted to drown himself. He had got a big brother now, one who had consoled him, and given him pennies, on the road to Trelingar Castle. He gave himself up at once to that youthful confidence with its characteristic natural familiarity, which is remarkable in Irish children. As for Foundling Mick, his feelings towards Dick were almost fatherly. Conscientiousness was very strong in the nameless boy, and his meeting with Dick had invested him with a whole set of new duties.

And was not Dick pleased when he had on a clean shirt of Mick's underneath his dry clothes? Did he not open his eyes, as well as his mouth, at sight of a slice of bread, a bit of cheese, and a big potato, warmed in the ashes? Was not that breakfast the best he had ever eaten in his life?

Dick had not known his father, but, more favoured by fate in that one respect than Foundling Mick, he had known his mother, who had died of want, two, or three, years? (Dick did not know exactly) previously. Then he had been taken into a refuge somewhere—he did not know the name of the place—but soon there was no more money, and the refuge was closed. Dick found himself in the street; he did not know why. Dick did not know anything! He had lived on the roads, sleeping where he could sleep, eating whatever he could get to eat. He did the best he could, poor little Dick! until the day came when, after fasting for forty-eight hours, he thought the best he could do was to die.

Such was his history, as he related it, while he ate his big potato, and in it there was nothing new or startling to the former pauper 'boarder' of Mrs Murphy, pauper handle-turner to Hornpipe's puppets, pauper pupil at the Galway poor school!

But suddenly, in the current of his talk, the child's intelligent countenance changed, he turned pale.

'What's the matter?' asked Mick.

'You're not going to leave me alone?'

'No, Dick.'

'You'll take me with you?'

'Yes, where I am going,'

Where was that? Dick did not ask, or care to know, provided Mick took him 'there' also.

'But your mammy and your daddy?'

'I have no mammy and no daddy.'

'Ah!' cried Dick, 'I'll love you.'

'And I'll love you, Dick, and we'll try to get on somehow together.'

'Ah, you'll see how I can run after cars,' said Dick, all elate again, 'and the ha'pence I pick up I'll give to you.' The little fellow had no notion of any other profession than the beggar's.

'No, Dick, you must not run after the cars any more.'

'Why?'

'Because it is not right to beg.'

'Ah!' said Dick, and relapsed into thought.

'Tell me, have you good legs?'

'Yes, but they're little.'

'Well, we are going to have a long trot today, to get to Cork this evening.'

'To Cork?'

'Yes. It is a fine town, beyond there—with boats—'

'Boats. Yes, I know.'

'And the sea. Have you ever seen it?'

'No.'

'You will see it, then. It goes ever, ever so far! And now we must be off.'

The wanderers, attended by Ranger, returned to the edge of the plantation, and took to the high road, which presently turned away from the bank of the little river and bordered the 'silver Lee'. After a time they passed, or were passed by, several vehicles, and Dick, yielding to the influence of habit, started off to pursue one of these with the old cry, 'Gi' me a ha'penny', but Foundling Mick caught hold of him.

'I told you, you weren't to do that any more,' he said sternly.

'But why?'

'Because it is not right to beg.'

'Not even when you're hungry?'

Mick did not answer, and Dick felt uneasy about the prospects of dinner, until he found himself sitting at a table in a decent little tavern, where the big brother, the little brother and the dog had a good meal.

Dick could not believe his eyes. Mick actually had a purse, and the purse had silver shillings in it, even after the score was paid.

'How did you get those shillings?' asked Dick, wondering.

'I earned them, Dick, by working.'

'By working! I'd like to work too, but I don't know how.'

'I'll teach you, Dick.'

'Now?'

'No, not now, but when we get to Cork.'

'How soon will that be?'

'This evening, if you're not too tired.'

'No, no, no. I can go on!'

And, after a good rest, they resumed their way. At six o'clock in the evening, they reached one of the suburbs of the great southern city, and found a humble lodging for the night.

CHAPTER 19

Seven Months in Cork

Foundling Mick had wanted to come to Cork, and he had come thither, under conditions, it is true, not precisely favourable to the realisation of his plans for the future. Formerly when he had roamed about the sea-beach at Galway, and when he had listened to Pat MacCarthy's tales of his voyages, the boy's young imagination employed itself extensively with commercial matters. To buy cargoes in other countries and sell them again in his own—what a dream! But he had reflected a good deal since his departure from Trelingar Castle, and he knew that a long course of training, beginning at the low estate of cabin boy, must lie between himself in his present state of wandering and poverty and the captain of a good ship, sailing from one continent to another. And now that he had Dick and Ranger to provide for, how could he think of going to sea? If he were to forsake these two, what would become of them? Since he had saved Dick's life, with Ranger's assistance, it was his duty to furnish him with a livelihood.

Next day Foundling Mick bargained with the keeper of the lodging-house for the use of a garret and a humble bed, and felt that he had taken a great step in advance. The rent of the garret was twopence per day, payable each morning. As for meals, Dick, Ranger and Mick would take those where they could find them. Early in the morning the three sallied forth.

'What about the ships?' said Dick.

'What ships?'

'The ships you promised I was to see.'

'Wait until we get to the bank of the river.'

They pursued their course in the desired direction through a long and squalid suburb, and on the way Foundling Mick bought a loaf at a small baker's shop. He cut up their frugal breakfast with the knife which had been given to him at the farm, and the boys trudged on, well content, eating the bread as they went, and in due time they reached the quays of the River Lee, where they saw several small craft, but no vessels capable of crossing St George's Channel first and after that the Atlantic Ocean. In fact, the real port is Queenstown (formerly Cobh), and swift river steamers called ferry boats carry passengers down the estuary of the Lee to the sea. Dick was not to be deceived by the very moderately marine aspect of the quays, and began to question Foundling Mick, as he had done in the matter of the ships.

'What about the sea?' said he.

'The sea! oh, it is farther off, Dick; but we shall end by getting to it, I think.'

And, in fact, Dick's big brother speedily discovered the river-steamer service, and that for a few pence they might be taken to Queenstown, where there was real sea. He could afford this expenditure, just for once on their first day in Cork, especially as Ranger would travel free of charge. The river voyage was quite entrancing pleasure to the boys; they stood in the bow of the boat, and gazed with delight upon the panorama of the banks, with the buildings of various kinds which seemed to glide away from their sight.

At length they reached the fine harbour of Queenstown, and Dick asked his companion,—

'Is *this* the sea?'

'No, only a little bit of it.'

'Is it much bigger?'

'Yes! you can't see where it leaves off.'

But the ferry boat did not go beyond Queenstown, and Dick did not see what he so much longed to behold, the 'wide open sea'. He saw any number of ships, however, more than he could ever have believed to exist, and indeed Foundling Mick was equally astonished. There the vessels were in scores, some anchored or moored, some coming in, others going out, and while Dick gazed with widely opened eyes upon all this animation in the bay, Foundling Mick was thinking of the commercial aspect of the scene, of the cargoes, the bales of wool and cotton, the barrels of wine, the cases of sugar, and saying to himself that these were bought and sold, and that all this meant trade.

They returned on a ferry boat to Cork, feeling almost bewildered by what they had seen. The excursion had been delightful, but it had cost a good deal, for they had been obliged to eat during the day. On the morrow they would need to look out for means of earning more than they would be obliged to expend; if they could not do this, the precious sovereigns must melt like ice in a warm hand. In the meantime the best place for them was the flock-bed in the garret, and thither they repaired.

It is unnecessary to enter into details of the existence of Foundling Mick and his little friend, Dick, during the six months which ensued upon their arrival at Cork. The winter, which was long and hard, would probably have been fatal to children less accustomed to cold and hunger. Necessity made a man of the little lad of eleven; he managed to live, and Dick with him, but many a night they lay down to rest hungry, even for them. Yet never did they ask alms. Dick had been made to understand that to beg was disgraceful. But they were incessantly on the look out for jobs of every kind; horses to hold, cabs to call, bags and parcels to carry—sometimes tolerably heavy ones—for railway travellers, etc., etc. Foundling Mick meant to make the remnant of the wages he had earned at Trelingar Castle last as long as possible. On his arrival at Cork, he had been obliged to expend a portion of his little store on clothes and shoes for Dick, whose pride and joy in the possession of a full suit, brand new, 'at thirteen shillings', surpassed description. How could Dick be allowed to go barefoot and in rags while his big brother was decently clad? But after this inevitable expense had been incurred, they would do their best to live on the day's earnings. They stuck to their rule, although many a time when their stomachs were empty they envied Ranger, who contrived somehow to pick up his living to his own satisfaction in the streets.

The rent of the garret was not in arrear at any time, and the lodging-house keeper, who took an interest in this strange pair of children, occasionally gave them a hot meal; which they did not hesitate to accept.

Foundling Mick was resolved to keep his two pounds intact, because he was watching his opportunity to 'go into business' with the money. This was the phrase he used, and when Dick heard him employ it he would open his eyes widely. Then Mick explained that 'going into business' meant buying things and selling them again for more than they had cost.

'Things to eat?' asked Dick.

'Things to eat, or other things, as may be.'

'I would rather have the things to eat.'

'Why, Dick?'

'Because, if any of them weren't sold, we could eat them ourselves!'

'I see you know something about business already, Dick! The important part is to choose what one buys well, and then one can always sell at a profit.'

Foundling Mick was constantly thinking on this matter, and he made some encouraging attempts. With letter-paper, pencils and matches he did not do well, there was too much competition in merchandise of that kind; but he succeeded better in selling newspapers in the neighbourhood of the railway station. There was something interesting and attractive about the boys' looks, their cleanliness, and their good manners, and after a while they got steady custom for their humble wares, daily papers, railway guides, and little books of various sorts. In a month after they had begun this kind of trade Mick and Dick each had a flat basket suspended from his shoulders by a strap; on this papers and books were ranged in order, with the titles and illustrations skilfully displayed, and change always ready for the buyers. Of course, Ranger never left his master, and he soon learned to take a newspaper in his mouth and offer it to a passer-by with an insinuating frisk of his tail, generally successful. As Ranger took very kindly to his share of the business, Foundling Mick presently equipped him with a light basket strapped to his back in which the day's newspapers were carefully arranged, with a waterproof cover in case of rain, and a little money-box hung from his collar for the reception of the purchasers' pence. This bright idea of Mick's was very successful; everybody talked of the little newsboys near the station and their four-footed assistant, and Ranger had more custom for his 'news tray' than the boys had for theirs.

Presently, Foundling Mick ventured on an extension of his business; he added smart boxes of cigar lights, cheap cigars, screws of snuff, etc., to his stock, and Ranger had his share of these also to dispose of. What a good supper, and what plentiful patting the dear dog came in for at night, when the three friends were snug in their garret and the day's work was done!

Foundling Mick had soon discovered that Dick was very sharp and intelligent. The little fellow of seven was of a less practical turn of mind than the older lad but of a more gleeful disposition, and he loved to indulge his high spirits. He could not either read, write or cipher, so Foundling Mick had at once set about teaching him his alphabet. Was it not necessary that he should be able to distinguish the titles of the newspapers that he had to sell? Dick took to learning, and his application was equal to his teacher's patience. He soon passed on from the big letters of the headings to the small ones of the columns. Then he began to learn writing and arithmetic, and found those arts more difficult. Yet, he got on very well, and, assisted by his lively imagination, he fancied himself managing Foundling Mick's shop in the handsomest street in Cork, with a superb shop-front and a grand bookseller's sign. Foundling Mick gave the little fellow a small percentage on their sales, and Dick had always a few well-earned pence in his pocket, so that he could occasionally give the often-asked-for 'ha'penny' to the little beggar children who held out their hands to him. Did he not remember well the time when he 'ran the roads' behind the cars?

It will readily be believed that Foundling Mick, acting upon a special instinct, kept his accounts with great regularity; so much for the rent of the garret, so much for meals, washing, fire and light. Each morning he wrote down in his notebook the sum required for the purchase of goods, and in the evening he balanced his expenditure with his receipts. He knew how to buy, he knew how to sell, and all was profit. At the end of that year (1882) he would have put ten pounds in his cash-box, had he possessed such an article. But, although he had no cash-box, he had a friend, a bookseller in the town, who had taken an interest in him from the first, and this kind man allowed him to deposit his weekly gains with him, and paid him a trifle of interest on the little sums, just to give the boy 'more heart'.

With the success that he was achieving by dint of economy and intelligence, ambition also came to Foundling Mick, the reasonable and legitimate ambition to augment his business. Perhaps he might have done so, in time, by settling himself finally in Cork. But his thoughts were turned towards a more important city, even Dublin, the capital. It was very far off to be sure, but it was not impossible. Take care, Foundling Mick. May not your practical mind be led astray? Remember the story of the substance and the shadow! Well, well, after all there is no harm in a boy's dream.

The winter was not hard, and Foundling Mick and Dick did not suffer too severely from being exposed to the weather from morning until night. Nevertheless, it was hard work, and they hailed Sunday as a blessed day of rest and recreation. In the morning the two boys cleaned up their garret, put on their well-brushed Sunday jackets, and after a better breakfast than they allowed themselves on weekdays, they attended Mass. On the conclusion of the service they returned to the lodging-house to release Ranger, and the three would then repair to the quay, and take the ferry-boat for Queenstown; two honest little citizens, out for a holiday after their week's work.

One day they treated themselves to a boating trip round the bay, and Dick got his first sight of the sea out of bounds.

'And farther off,' he asked, 'going on and on upon the water—always—what would we find?'

'A very big country, Dick.'

'Bigger than ours?'

'Thousands of times bigger, Dick, and it takes those big steamships that you see a fortnight to get to it.'

'And are there newspapers in that country?'

'Newspapers, Dick? Why, yes, hundreds of them; newspapers that sell as high as sixpence.'

'Are you sure of that?'

'Quite sure. It would take months and months to read the whole of them.'

Dick looked with great admiration at this wonderful Foundling Mick who was capable of being certain of such a thing. As for the big ships, those great steamers that put in at Queenstown, his fondest wish was to get on the deck of one of them and climb into the rigging, while Foundling Mick would have preferred to inspect the hold and the cargo.

Hitherto, however, neither one nor the other had ventured to embark without the authorisation of the captain—a personage whom they held in great awe. As for asking leave, their courage would not have extended to that by a long way. Just think of it; 'the master after God', as Foundling Mick had heard said, and repeated it to Dick. Thus the great desire of the lads remained as yet unrealised. Perhaps it may be gratified some day, and others which were awakening in them also.

CHAPTER 20

The First Fireman on the *Vulcan*

The year 1882, which had brought to Foundling Mick so much good and evil fortune, in the ruin and dispersion of the MacCarthy family, of whom he had not since heard, the three months at Trelingar Castle, his meeting with Dick, his taking up his abode at Cork and his prospering there, was now at an end. During the first quarter of the new year, if the boys' trade did not slacken, it seemed to have reached its maximum. Foundling Mick, feeling sure that it would not increase, was haunted by the idea of going to Dublin. If only an opportunity would offer! January, February, and March passed away. The lads lived as sparingly as possible, putting by penny after penny, and Foundling Mick was lucky enough to get a commission for the sale of a certain political pamphlet by Mr Parnell, which proved very profitable.

At the beginning of April, their friend had thirty pounds in his keeping, and eighteen shillings and sixpence to boot. The boys, who had never been so rich, held long conferences on the question of whether they should or should not venture to rent a little shop in the vicinity of the railway station. It would be so delightful to have a place of their own! Dick was for the shop. We can imagine it, with its display of newspapers and cheap bookseller's and stationer's wares; its shopkeeper of eleven, and its shopman of eight! Surely these children, so well worthy of interest and patronage, would not have lacked customers!

Patiently and gravely Mick revolved in his mind the for and against, feeling all the time that he was urged by some presentiment of his fate to dwell upon his idea of transporting himself and his commerce to Dublin. He was hesitating, resisting the entreaties of Dick, when an incident occurred which decided the matter.

It was Sunday, the 8th of April, and the two boys had agreed to pass the day at Queenstown. They started early, neatly dressed, with their shoes well polished, and Ranger, also brushed-up for the occasion, accompanied them. They enjoyed the 'run' on the steamboat even more than usual, because the weather was fine, and landed on the quay in high good-humour. The first thing to be thought of was a good meal, and this they proposed to procure at a neighbouring eating-house, from whence they would have a fine view of the big ships in the port. Mick and Dick were about to enter the tavern when their attention was attracted by a large vessel which had come into harbour on the previous evening and was being 'dressed' for Sunday. On questioning an old sailor in a yellow cap, they learned that it was the *Vulcan,* a steamer of nine hundred tons, coming from America, and bound on the morrow for Dublin. The boys were standing on the edge of the quay, eagerly observing the proceedings on board the *Vulcan,* when a tall young fellow, with black hands and a face smeared with coal dust, approached Foundling Mick, looked at him, shut his eyes, opened his big mouth, and exclaimed,—

'It's you; it's really you!'

Foundling Mick was taken aback, much more so was Dick. Here was a stranger, and a black one, addressing him. There must be a mistake! But the Negro, wagging his head gleefully, became still more demonstrative.

'It's myself,' he said. 'Don't you know me? It's me, the poor school—Grip!'

'Grip!' cried Foundling Mick, and rushed into the tall young fellow's arms with such precipitation that he came out of them nearly as black as Grip himself. What a joyful meeting that was! The former superintendent of Mr Mulvany's scholastic establishment was now a vigorous, active, well set-up young man of twenty, bearing no resemblance to the ragged lad of the Galway poor school, with the exception that he still had the same pleasant countenance.

Mick could not leave off exclaiming, 'Grip! Grip! it is you; it is really you!'

'Yes, it's me, and I've never forgotten you, my boy!'

'And you are a sailor?'

'No, I'm a fireman on board the *Vulcan.*'

Thereupon he had to explain the duties of a fireman to Dick, who had been hastily presented to Mick's former protector at the poor school.

'He's a sort of brother,' said Mick. 'I picked him up on the road. He knows you well, Grip, I've often told him about us two. Oh, Grip, what a lot of things you have to tell me! It's six years since we parted.'

'And yourself, Mick?'

'Oh, yes, I've a lot to tell you. Come and breakfast with us, we were just going in there.' He pointed to the eating-house.

'No, no,' said Grip. 'It's you that must breakfast with me; but come on board first.'

'On board the *Vulcan?*'

'Yes.'

On board—both of them? Dick and Mick could hardly believe their ears. It was as though Grip had quietly proposed to take them into paradise.

'But our dog?'

'What dog?'

'Ranger. Look, he's making friends with you.'

'So he's your dog,' and with this Grip gave a cordial pat to the delighted animal.

'And our friend, a friend of your own sort, Grip.'

'The captain?' suggested Mick, with some natural hesitation.

'The captain's ashore, and the boatswain's mate will make you as welcome as a couple of lords. Besides, I must clean myself up a bit now that I'm off duty.'

'And are you free for the whole day?'

'Yes, for the whole day.'

'It's a lucky thing we came to Queenstown, Dick.'

'It's just that, Mick.'

'And I've blackened you as well, so you'll want a wash, Foundling Mick,—is it that you're called still?'

'It is, Grip.'

'I'm glad of it. Come along.'

In two minutes the three friends were on board the *Vulcan,* and the first fireman, who had received a friendly nod from the second mate in passing, took his guests down to the scene of his labours, and to his narrow sleeping quarters, where they found a basin and fresh water, and Grip proceeded to wash and dress himself. During this process he briefly related his own history since the hurried and unconscious parting between Foundling Mick and himself.

He had been taken to the hospital after the fire at the school, and was found to be severely hurt. There he remained for six weeks, when he was dismissed in good health, but entirely destitute. The poor school was in process of rebuilding, but Grip felt that he could not return to his former life there. No, that was impossible, now that Foundling Mick was gone. Grip knew that he had been taken away by a grand lady, but whither? This he did not know, and all his efforts to discover the truth after he came out of the hospital proved unsuccessful. So then, Grip left Galway, and took to a wandering life in the adjacent country places. Sometimes he got work at the farms, but no certain employment, and this troubled him sorely. A year later he had made his way to Dublin, with the notion of going to sea. But as he was too old at eighteen to become a cabin boy, and knew nothing of the work of a sailor, he resolved to embark as a fireman, and soon found employment on board the *Vulcan.* His post was not one of ideal felicity, but Grip was resolute, patient and industrious. He soon became accustomed to the discipline of the ship, never incurred a reprimand, and by his zeal and sobriety aroused the interest of the officers, who inquired into the story of the lad who had neither home nor kin. The *Vulcan* made voyages from Dublin to New York or other ports on the eastern seaboard of America. Grip crossed the ocean several times in two years, being charged with the filling of the bunkers and the supply of fuel. Then, becoming ambitious, he applied for the post of fireman under the orders of the engineers. He was taken on trial and proved so satisfactory, that, on the termination of his apprenticeship he was promoted to the post of first fireman, and in this distinguished position did Foundling Mick find his former school companion on the quay at Queenstown.

Grip had no taste for the coarse dissipation in which too many sailors indulge when ashore, and therefore he was able to save a little fund out of his wages, and to this he added something regularly every month. He already possessed sixty pounds at the present time, and it had never occurred to him to do anything with it except save it. To put it out at interest was an idea that never could have suggested itself to Grip.

Such was the story that Grip told in his light-hearted way. Mick followed with a narrative of his own experiences, which were of so different a kind, and these inspired Grip with profound astonishment. When it came to Dick's turn there was very little to be told. Merely that he had no life story at all; for his real history began on the day of his rescue from drowning by Ranger and Mick. Ranger's history was that of his master.

Grip would have carried his friends off to the eating-house where he proposed to give them a sumptuous meal, immediately after his toilet was finished, but they were eager to go over the *Vulcan* in the first instance, and the first fireman good-humouredly yielded the point. Nothing could exceed the pleasure which this exploration afforded the two boys, but in a different measure. The commercial side of all that they saw appealed to the deep-rooted trading instincts of Foundling Mick, the nautical and unknown to the careless and happy nature of Dick.

The good meal at the eating-house, of which the three companions disposed with the appetite of their respective ages, did not interrupt their conversation, and the interchange of reminiscences between Grip and Foundling Mick was brisk and continuous. Of course, the incidents of the seagull, and the gift of the jersey were not omitted, nor were the abominable deeds of Carker.

'What has become of the wretch?' asked Grip.

'I don't know, and I don't want to know,' answered Foundling Mick. 'The worst thing that could happen to me would be to meet him.'

'Never mind, that will never happen; but as you sell newspapers, I advise you to read them sometimes.'

'So I do.'

'Well then, one of these fine days you'll read that Carker is dead of hemp-fever.'

'Hanged! Oh, Grip!'

'Yes, hanged! And serve him right!'

Then they talked of the fire at the school-house, when Grip had saved the little boy at the peril of his own life. This was the first chance Foundling Mick had had of thanking Grip for the deed, and close was the handgrip with which he emphasised his gratitude.

Grip was then questioned concerning his travels in America. He told of the great cities of the United States, their industries and their commerce, and Foundling Mick listened so eagerly that he forgot to eat.

'And then,' Grip went on to say, 'there are big towns in England also, and if you ever go to London, to Liverpool, to Glasgow—'

'Yes, Grip, I know. I have read of them in newspapers; trading towns; but so far off.'

'Not at all far.'

'Not for sailors who go there in ships, but for others—'

'Well then, there's Dublin, isn't there?' cried Grip. 'It's not so very far. The trains take you there in a day, and there's no sea to cross.'

'Ah! Dublin!' said Mick, musingly. And he remained silent and thoughtful while Grip continued,—

'It's a very fine place, and there's thousands of businesses doing there. It's just as good as Cork for ships.'

Foundling Mick heard, and his mind travelled far.

'You ought to go and set up in Dublin,' said Grip. 'I'm sure you'd get on better than here, and if you wanted a trifle of money—'

'Dick and I have some saved,' replied Mick.

'Yes, indeed,' said Dick, proudly, producing from his pocket one shilling and sixpence.

'So have I,' said Grip, 'and I don't know what place to put it in for safety.'

'Why don't you put it in a bank somewhere?'

'I don't trust banks.'

'But then you are losing the interest it would bring in.'

'That's better than losing all one has, Micky! But you see, if I haven't confidence in other people I should have confidence in you, my boy, and if you were in Dublin, where the *Vulcan* goes to constantly, we could see each other often! That would be delightful, and I tell you again, if you want a little money to take up a trade, I'll give you all I have with a heart and a half.'

The good fellow would have done this on the spot, so happy was he to get his little Micky back again. Surely the bond that united those two would never again be broken.

'Come to Dublin,' repeated Grip. 'Shall I tell you what I think?'

'Yes, do.'

'Well, it's this. I have always had the notion that you would make a fortune—'

'And I too! I have always had the same idea,' said Mick, simply, while his eyes shone with a singular light.

'Yes, Micky. Some day I shall see you rich, very rich. But you will not make much money at Cork. Reflect on what I am saying to you now, for you must not act without reflection.'

'Of course not, Grip.'

'And now let us go for a walk.'

They set out, and many were the projects formed by the three friends while they strolled about the streets and quays of Queenstown, escorted by Ranger.

At last the moment of parting came, and Grip went with the two boys to the ferry.

'We shall meet again,' he said cheerily. 'We have not come across each other for only this meeting.'

'Yes, Grip, at Cork, the first time the *Vulcan* puts in there.'

'Why not in Dublin, for she stays there for weeks sometimes. Yes, in Dublin, if you decide.'

'Goodbye, Grip.'

Hearty farewells, in which Ranger had his share, were exchanged, and Grip gazed for a long time after the river steamboat.

CHAPTER 21

On the Way
to Dublin

A few days later, Foundling Mick, Dick
and Ranger had taken leave of the fair city
of Cork, and were wending their way
towards the Irish capital. Grip's represen-
tations had had the desired effect; they had
induced Foundling Mick to yield to the
promptings of his own inclination, to
which he had begun to listen before his
meeting with the first fireman of the
Vulcan, and to abandon the secure for the
uncertain. But the young trader had
considered the matter very carefully. At
Cork, there was no progress, no expansion
for him; Dublin, on the contrary, offered
an extensive field for his activity. Dick, it is
needless to say, was all for starting at once
so soon as his young 'principal' broached
the idea to him. Foundling Mick then
withdrew his little capital from the care of
the friendly publisher, who regarded the

boy's resolution with serious misgiving, but could not induce him to forego it, and laid out his plan for the journey.

The shortest way to reach Dublin was, of course, to take the train to Limerick and thence to the capital city; but this mode of locomotion was open to the objection that it cost money, and Mick wanted to stick to his money. The season was fine for a journey on foot and time was of little consequence. What an advantage it would be, to begin with, if, instead of costing money, the journey could be made to earn some! Supposing, instead of paying travelling expenses, the juvenile itinerants were to carry on their trade on the way, selling newspapers, pamphlets, stationery, in short all their stock-in-trade in the villages and small towns which lie between Cork and Dublin. What would be needed for this novel kind of peddling? Only a light little hand-cart such as Mick could draw, while Dick pushed it from behind when necessary—(was there a vague remembrance of the Hornpipe time in this notion?)—to carry their wares and their changes of clothing, with a waterproof covering to protect the whole from rain and dust. The country was peaceful and honest; the boys had nothing to fear, and Ranger would be a guard as well as a companion. They would take the coast road, because it leads to Waterford, Wexford, Wicklow, and other seaside health resorts and bathing places much frequented at that time of year. The journey would be long, but what matter, if they could but sell and renew their humble wares on the way, and live on their slender gains.

This programme—an adventurous one, it will be admitted, involving no small amount of self-confidence, and capacity of endurance, on the part of the leader of the expedition, and great trust, docility, and good will on that of Dick—was fully and faithfully carried out. Foundling Mick had a stroke of luck at the beginning of the enterprise; he got a light hand-cart, second-hand, from a grocer in the town, for a very small price. The little vehicle held his slender stock of merchandise conveniently, and from the first the trifling articles, all very cheap but sold at a good profit, found a ready sale. In some places they passed through the two boys created a general feeling of interest; the one as serious as any old-established shopkeeper, the other so light-hearted and childish that it was not possible to refuse to buy of him. The little party of three was kindly treated at the places where it halted for the night, and Mick did not exact too much of his companions. The boys and the dog enjoyed sundry good spells of rest. We shall not follow them step by step in the journey. At Youghal they laid in an entirely new stock of commodities, so well had they prospered since their start, and at Dungarvan a happy idea occurred to Foundling Mick. This was, to purchase some woollen articles at a very low price, which he might sell in the small villages where his other goods would not be in so much demand. It is sufficient to say that his little venture out of the usual course of his business proved successful. So they went on, and the day came on which Foundling Mick, having reached the boundary of Munster, was to pass out of the province within which he had known so much vicissitude. But he had already forgotten all those old troubles; he allowed his mind to dwell only on his three happy years at Kirwan's Farm; he thought only of the MacCarthys. Where were those good friends? He regretted them, as one regrets home and kin.

'Dick,' said he, 'did I not promise you that we would take a good rest at Waterford?'

'I think you did,' said Dick, 'but I am not tired, and if you wish to get on—'

'No. We will stay here for a few days.'

'Doing nothing?'

'There is always something to do, Dick.'

And, indeed, Foundling Mick found something very interesting to do, in studying the pleasant city and the busy port. The boys chose their lodging at a decent inn, saw their cart safely disposed of, and set out for a long stroll along the quays. What endless interest and amusement was provided for them by the vessels coming and going out! How could anybody ever tire of such a spectacle?

'Ha!' said Dick, 'supposing Grip should just chance to come upon us now?'

'No, Dick, that could not happen,' answered Mick. 'The *Vulcan* does not put in at Waterford, and I have reckoned that he must be far away now—over in America.'

'Over there?' said Dick, stretching out his arm towards the horizon bounded by the sea and sky.

'Yes, in that direction. I think he will be back by the time we get to Dublin.'

'How nice it will be to see Grip again! Will he be black this time?'

'Very likely.'

'Anyhow, that does not prevent us from caring for him.'

'No, indeed, Dick, for he cared for me when I was so wretched.'

'Yes, as you did for me!' answered the little fellow, whose eyes sparkled with gratitude.

Three days later they were at Wexford; their little cart was amply supplied, and they pushed along cheerily, by way of Arklow and Wicklow, and so, by the beautiful road which borders the coastline to Bray, where they did some profitable business on the strand. Their cart was empty when they sought a night's rest in the fashionable seaside town, and after a long sleep, and a look round at the Wicklow hills, the shining sea, and Howth in the distance, they started in the morning for the unknown goal of their hopes—Dublin.

CHAPTER 22

Dublin

Again we spare our reader the details of the last stage of the journey of our two lads; nor shall we dwell upon their first sight of the Irish capital, for they reached the city footsore and weary, and having found a decent lodging in Patrick Street, and seen their hand-cart securely sheltered in an outhouse, they retired to much needed rest, promising themselves an early start on a tour of investigation in the morning.

The boys were, in fact, afoot early, much to the contrary of the generality of the dwellers in Patrick Street, and they set out, pretty much at random, accompanied by Ranger, resolved to have a good look at everything on their way, but to make for the riverside and landing-stage as directly as observation and inquiry would enable them. The poplin factories, the distilleries, the vast breweries of Guinness and Co. and D'Arcy and Sons, the public buildings, railway stations, etc., should all have their turn in due time, but the first, the chief object, the prime necessity, was to discover whether the *Vulcan* had arrived, and they might have the felicity of finding her first fireman at leisure to welcome them to this strange place whither he had, in a measure, guided them. No doubt the boys went a good deal astray, and probably doubled the distance, but they passed through a fine quarter of the city, and saw some grand sights, between the poor neighbourhood in which their lodging was situated, and Carlisle Bridge, with its noble view of the quays on either side. Many were the expressions of astonishment and admiration which they interchanged, but they made no pause, pressing steadily on until the forest of masts in the distance below Carlisle Bridge came into view, and their goal was near. Was the *Vulcan* among those ships? They would know her again most certainly. Who ever fails to recognise a ship he has gone all over from stem to stern,—especially with such a guide as Grip?

The *Vulcan* was not alongside the quays of the Liffey; possibly she had not yet arrived; or she might be in the dock, or under repair.

Foundling Mick and Dick followed the quay, going down the river on the left bank. Dick was too much taken up with the notion of the *Vulcan* to pay any attention to the Custom House, a magnificent structure, but strangely dull and inanimate as a centre of business. Foundling Mick paused for a moment to contemplate it. Should he ever have important transactions with that great place? What could be more enviable than to have to pay duties on cargoes brought from distant lands? Was such a satisfaction ever to be his?

The boys arrived at the Victoria Docks. What a number of ships, loading and unloading, the great basin, which forms the heart of the trading city, contained!

'There she is!' cried Dick, 'the *Vulcan*! There! There!' He was right. The *Vulcan* was at the quay, taking in her cargo.

A few minutes later, Grip, who was off duty, stepped ashore and joined his two friends.

'At last, here you are!' he repeated, with a cordial grasp of the hand for each.

Then the three friends strolled back along the quay towards the point at which the Royal Canal debouches on the Liffey. This was a quiet spot and they could talk at their ease. Grip wanted to hear all about their proceedings from the time of his departure from Queenstown to the moment of this happy meeting, and he listened with both wonder and interest to Foundling Mick's narrative of their long but lucrative tramp, while he had been crossing the Atlantic Ocean twice. He was eager to learn particulars; the boys had to recall everything that had happened to them, and every impression they had formed of the country and the people. He regarded Foundling Mick with unconcealed admiration. What an instinct the boy had for commercial affairs! What a genius for buying and selling! Why, he knew at least as much about figures as Mr Mulvany! And when Foundling Mick told him that his capital now amounted to one hundred and fifty pounds—safely bestowed about his person—Grip exclaimed,—

'Then you are as rich as myself, my boy, only what it took me six years to earn you have made in six months! I say again what I said before, you'll do well in your business; you'll make a fortune.'

'Where?' asked Mick.

'Everywhere. Anywhere you may go. In Dublin, if you stay here; somewhere else if you don't.'

'And what about me?' said Dick.

'You'll do right well also,' said Grip, encouragingly, 'so as you never do anything without consulting the boss.'

'Who? The boss?'

'Why, Mick, of course. Don't you think he looks like a boss?'

'We will talk about that,' said Mick.

'Yes, after breakfast,' replied Grip. 'I am free all day. I know the town as well as I know the *Vulcan*'s furnaces. I must pilot you, and we'll see Dublin together. Then you will know what it will be best for you to do.'

The three friends procured a good meal at a tavern much frequented by sailors, and while they sat at table Grip related his last two ocean trips, to the great contentment of Dick. Foundling Mick listened in thoughtful silence. He was much older than his years by the development of his intelligence, the gravity of his ideas, and the permanent tension of his mind. He might have been twenty years old at his birth and thirty now!

Grip took the boys to the centre of the city, the rich quarter which contrasts so strongly with the poor, for there is but little transition in the capital of Ireland. He showed them the fine bridges and Sackville Street[3], with its statues, Nelson's pillar, the vast post office, its handsome houses and fine shops. Alas! also its poor and shabby pedestrians, and many signs, impossible of concealment, of the poverty that abounds in Dublin, and which no authority or watchfulness can hinder from obtruding itself upon the sight of the well-to-do inhabitants. Foundling Mick took particular notice of the great number of young boys who are employed in selling papers, the leading journals, both Catholic and Protestant, Conservative and Nationalist, having their respective offices in the streets on either side of Nelson's pillar.

'Ha!' said Grip, looking about him, 'what a number of newspaper boys there are hereabouts, and it's just the same down on the quays and at the railway stations.'

'No business to be done in that way,' said Foundling Mick, nodding his head decisively. 'It succeeded in Cork, but it won't do here.'

They continued their walk, and Grip pointed out the principal buildings, the post office, which would be the depository of a vast correspondence in the future, he persisted in saying, between Mr Foundling Mick, Merchant, and all the big commercial towns at home and abroad. Then came the Four Courts, and Grip told Mick he might admire the building, but avoid it when he should have money to lose, for it was a greater consumer of hard-earned wealth than the *Vulcan* was of coals. Before a superb edifice, of aspect at once classic and palatial, Grip paused, and gravely saluted it.

'The Bank of Ireland, once the Parliament House, and will be again, please God! Dick, there's cellars full of gold as big as houses inside there, my boy. And it's there Mick will be putting his money for safety some day.'

And so he went on with his merry exaggerations, all coming from his heart. Mick only half heard him, so fixed was his attention upon this spacious edifice wherein so many accumulated fortunes formed 'heaps of thousands on top of each other', according to the fireman of the *Vulcan*. After they had explored the principal streets, and made the circuit of St Stephen's Green, the three friends got into a tramcar and were conveyed to the entrance of the Phoenix Park. We need not expatiate upon their delight with the great expanse, the noble trees, and the various uses of this unequalled public resort. After they had gazed at the Viceregal

Lodge, and speculated on their chances of getting a glimpse of the Lord Lieutenant—a stroke of luck which was withheld—it was time for them to part, so they returned by the tram to Carlisle Bridge, Grip turned off along the quay, and the two boys, once more thoroughly tired out, made their way to Patrick Street. It had been arranged that they should see Grip every day until the sailing of the *Vulcan*. But before they parted the following colloquy had taken place between Grip and Foundling Mick.

'Well, Mick,' asked Grip, 'has any good idea come into your head today?'

'About what I'll do, is it?'

'Yes, have you made your mind up to anything?'

'No, I haven't, Grip, but I've made it up against something, I'll not try newspaper-selling here. There's too many in the trade.'

'That's what I think too, Mick.'

'And as for hawking things in the street in the cart, I don't know. What is there to sell in that way? Besides there are a great many at that trade, too, I am sure. No—perhaps,' he went on, in an anxious, hesitating tone, 'it would be the best plan to set up for myself, to rent a little shop—'

'Just the very thing, my boy!'

'A shop in a part of the town where there's a good deal of traffic, not rich people, you know, but people that want cheap things, and are constantly coming and going. Some place in the Liberties, now.'

'You could not do better.'

'But what should we sell?' asked Dick.

'Useful things,' replied Foundling Mick, 'things that are most generally wanted.'

'Things to eat, then, cakes?'

'You greedy little chap!' exclaimed Grip, 'cakes aren't useful.'

'Yes, they are—for they're good—'

'That is not enough,' said Mick, 'our wares must be necessary above all. However, we shall see. I will go about in that quarter and see into things. There are second-hand places where there's a look of good business. I think a sort of bazaar—'

'A bazaar! That's it!' cried Grip, whose mind's eye already beheld Foundling Mick's shop with a gaily painted front, and a sign with his name in gold letters.

'I'll think of it, Grip. We must not be too impatient. We must think well before we decide.'

'And don't forget, Mick, that all my money is at your service. I don't know what to do with it, and it is a great bother to have it always about me.'

'Always about you?'

'In my belt, Mick.'

'Why don't you put it out?'

'Well, I will, with you. Will you have it?'

'We'll see, later on, if our trade does well. It is not the money we're short of, it's the way to use it, with profit and without too much risk.'

'Don't be afraid, my boy. I tell you again, you will make a fortune. That's sure and certain. I can see you with hundreds and thousands of pounds.'

'When does the *Vulcan* start, Grip?'

'In a week.'

'And when does she come back?'

'Not for two months, for we have to go to Boston, to Baltimore, and I don't know where else; anywhere that we get a cargo to take.'

'And another to bring back!' said Foundling Mick, with a sigh.

CHAPTER 23

The Boys' Bazaar

Our hero was at this time eleven and a half years old; Dick was eight,—their combined ages falling short of one legal majority. The idea of Foundling Mick starting in business, founding a commercial house! Could there be anyone but Grip, that is to say a person who loved him with a blind, unreasoning affection, to believe that he would succeed from the beginning, that his trade would become extended, and that he would make a fortune?

Nevertheless, it is a fact that two months after the arrival of the boys in Dublin, Bedford Street boasted a bazaar, which had the privilege of attracting attention, and also customers, in that humble but busy quarter of the town. The commercial experience of the young shopkeeper, gained at Cork, and during his long tramp with his hand-cart, had convinced him that purchasers can always be found for articles of necessity, provided they are of good quality and reasonable price.

The Boys' Bazaar was a real shop with a real signboard, and the inscription, 'Mick, Dick and Co'. Ranger was, no doubt, the Co. Foundling Mick was lucky in the first instance in encountering a good-natured and sympathetic person in Mr O'Brien, the owner of the ground-floor shop, and the small two-storeyed house above it. Great was his surprise when application was made to him by a boy of Mick's age to be allowed to rent the place, which had been vacant for several months. The answers which Foundling Mick made to his questions were, however, so serious and sensible that he took a liking to the lad at once, perceiving that he had no common intelligence to deal with. Mick concluded his straightforward statement of his circumstances, wishes and intentions by offering a year's rent in advance for the shop, and Mr O'Brien, who had listened with patient attention to all the boy had to say, took the offer into serious consideration, instead of turning him out at once as a fool or an impostor. The story of this poor forlorn creature, his struggles against poverty and abandonment, the trials he had undergone, his little trade in Cork, his peddling tramp from thence to the capital, the whole narrative of his life, interested the kindly man, himself a retired shopkeeper, deeply. In the past of Foundling Mick's life—the past of a child of his age!—he perceived so sure a guarantee for the future that he was quite convinced by it, and not only agreed to let the shop to Mick, but resolved to help the boy with his advice, and to watch his first attempts with vigilance.

A year's rent was paid in advance, and Foundling Mick became a responsible shopkeeper in Bedford Street. His premises were not extensive, they consisted of the shop, with a 'return' for the accommodation of goods, and a glass door which gave admission to a fair-sized back room communicating with and lighted from the back yard; the latter was common to the proprietor of the shop and the lodgers who occupied the two floors above. A side door opened from the shop into the passage, which extended from the front or 'private' door to the back door opening on the yard, and gave access to the staircase. The house was compact and in good repair, and the lodgers, Foundling Mick's neighbours, were quiet, respectable people, who were not a little surprised when they discovered that the new tenants beneath them were a pair of children.

Foundling Mick and Dick had not much need of a kitchen, but the accommodation of their back room in that respect was not to be despised, and to them seemed sumptuous, for it included a convenient cooking-stove, a sink, a small dresser and a roomy cupboard. The boys would not trouble the stove or crowd the cupboard, for the present, to any inconvenient extent, they would just eat how and where they could, as frugally as possible, at times when there were no customers to be served. The customers were to be above and before everything!

And why should not customers come to this little shop, which was so carefully conducted, and arranged with so much intelligence and propriety? It offered a great choice of articles. Our young trader had expended some of the money that remained after he had paid his year's rent in buying, of wholesale dealers and manufacturers, the various merchandise which occupied the shelves and was displayed upon the counter of the Boys' Bazaar.

He had also bought the humble furniture of the back room at a second-hand dealer's close by, a bed, a table, a press to hold clothes and linen; mere necessaries, indeed, but wonderful treasures to the two boys, and these things with the shop furniture of desk, account-books, pens, ink, etc., added to the rent, made a great hole in the hundred and fifty pounds which they had brought to Dublin. Therefore it was necessary to be exceedingly prudent, for a reserve fund was indispensable. The stock would be replaced as it was sold out, and the bazaar always sufficiently supplied.

Needless to say that the accounts were kept with the utmost regularity in daybook and ledger—Foundling Mick's ledger!—and the condition of the cash-box—Foundling Mick's cash-box!—was verified each evening. Mr Mulvany's own books were not in more perfect order. And now, what was sold at the Boys' Bazaar? A little of everything that was wanted in that quarter of the town. Foundling Mick established a kind of fusion of all the trades, and announced that 'everything' might be had from him at low prices, stationers' wares, ironmongers' wares, booksellers' wares, gardening tools, rakes, spades, balls, tops, toys of every kind and to suit every taste. How dearly Dick loved the toy department! How carefully he dusted the toys he longed to handle—especially the boats, the boats at sixpence apiece!

We have not space to follow day by day the progress of the Boys' Bazaar in the esteem and also in the confidence of the public. Suffice it to say that the unique establishment was a success from the first. Mr O'Brien was astonished at Foundling Mick's capacity for business. To buy and to sell is well, but to know how to buy and sell is better, it is all. Mr O'Brien had done these good things in his own time, but he had begun at 25 years of age, not at twelve; hence he shared the ideas of Grip, and confidently expected that Foundling Mick would make a fortune. But he would sometimes say: 'Don't go too fast, my boy!'

'No, sir,' Mick would answer, 'I will go slowly and carefully, for there's a long road to travel, and I must spare my legs.'

It must be observed, in order to explain its phenomenal prosperity, that the fame of the Boys' Bazaar had spread rapidly in Dublin. A shop set up and kept by two boys, the older of the two at the age when boys are at school, the younger in the toy period of life, was the sort of thing to attract attention, bring customers, and make the concern fashionable. Foundling Mick had gone to the expense of a few advertisements in the daily papers at so much a line, but the *Freeman's Journal* and the *Irish Times* gave him gratuitous paragraphs, which did the Boys' Bazaar solid service. Real ladies actually took the trouble of coming from the genteel quarters of the town, and were waited upon by Foundling Mick with the most scrupulous politeness, while Dick pleased them by his lively ways, his quick intelligence, his bright eyes and his curly head. Then the toy-shelves were emptied in no time, the carts, the boats, and the sand-buckets and spades were carried off by the dozen, and children were brought to buy their own toys from a little shopkeeper of their own age.

Whether this happy state of things would last was a question, but in any case, Foundling Mick devoted himself to his business with indomitable industry and keen intelligence.

As a matter of course, Grip's first thought on the arrival of the *Vulcan* at Dublin, was to visit his friends. To describe him as 'astonished' is insufficient, he was transfixed with wonder and admiration. Never had he seen anything like the shop in Bedford Street, and, according to him, since it boasted the Boys' Bazaar, Bedford Street itself might have challenged comparison with Sackville Street in Dublin, the Strand in

London, Broadway in New York, and the *Boulevard des Italiens* in Paris. At each visit he regarded it as an obligation that he should buy one thing or another 'to keep trade going'. Today it would be a pocketbook to replace one which he had never had; tomorrow it would be a pretty painted boat, that he wanted to give to the children of one of his comrades on the *Vulcan* who was not a father. His grandest purchase was a mock meerschaum pipe with an amber mouthpiece of yellow glass. And he would repeat to Foundling Mick, to whom he insisted on handing the price of his purchases,—

'Ha! my boy, you're getting on! Look at yourself, now, there you are, skipper of the Boys' Bazaar, and you have only to keep your steam up! It's a long day to the time when we were ragged boys in the Galway school and shivered with cold and hunger in the garret! By-the-bye, that ruffian, Carker, has he been hanged?'

'Not yet, that I know of, Grip.'

'It will come! It will come, I tell you, and you must be sure to send me a paper with a report of the performance.'

Then Grip returned on board, the *Vulcan* steamed out of port again, and after a few weeks the fireman reappeared at the Boy's Bazaar and began to ruin himself in superfluous purchases as before.

One day Foundling Mick said to him,—

'You still believe, Grip, that I shall make a fortune?'

'Believe it, my boy! Just as sure as I believe that Carker will swing at the end of a rope.'

This was Grip's notion of the most forcible asseveration of certitude here below.

'Well, my dear Grip, don't you think at all of the future for yourself?'

'I? Why should I think about it? Haven't I an employment I would not change for anything?'

'A hard one, and ill paid.'

'What? Four pounds a month, and fed, and lodged, and warmed— indeed roasted sometimes?'

'And in a ship!' put in Dick, who remained constant to his earliest ideal of bliss.

'No matter, Grip,' resumed Mick, 'a fireman has never yet made a fortune, and we are intended by God to make our fortunes in this world.'

'Are you so sure of that?' asked Grip, with a dubious shake of the head. 'Is it in His commandments?'

'Yes,' answered Mick, promptly. 'He desires that we should grow rich, not only to be happy ourselves, but to make those happy who deserve to be so, yet are not.' And then the boy's mind wandered afar; to Cissy, his companion in Mrs Murphy's cabin, and to the MacCarthys, of whom he could get no tidings, to little Jenny —all poor and suffering, no doubt, while he ...

'Stay, Grip,' he said, 'think well what you will answer to this. Why should you not remain on land?'

'Leave the *Vulcan*?'

'Yes—leave the *Vulcan* and be our partner. You know—Mick, Dick and Co.? Well, Co. is not sufficiently represented, and if you would join us—'

'Do, Grip, do, dear Grip!' entreated Dick. 'It would make us both so happy if you would.'

'Me, too,' said Grip, who was touched by this proposal, 'but there's something I must say—'

'Say it, Grip.'

'Well, then, I'm too tall!'

'Too tall?'

'Yes. If a long lath of a fellow like me made his appearance in the shop it wouldn't be the same thing at all. It wouldn't be the Boys' Bazaar. Mick, Dick and Co. must be little fellows if they're to draw customers. I should injure the firm, I should do you a wrong. It's because you're children that you're doing so well.'

'Perhaps you're right, Grip,' said Foundling Mick, regretfully, 'but we shall grow.'

'We are growing!' added Dick, raising himself on tiptoe.

'Of course you are, and take care you don't grow too quick.'

'We can't help that, Grip.'

'No, you can't. That's why you must try to make sure of all you can while you are boys. Now, I am five feet six and a little over, and in your line nothing over five feet is any use! However, if I cannot be your partner, Mick, you know my money is yours all the same.'

'I don't want it.'

'Well, well, just as you like; but if you take it into your head to extend your trade ...'

'We could not do it with only us two.'

'Well, then, why don't you hire a woman to do your housework?'

'I had thought of that, Grip, and Mr O'Brien advised me to do it.'

'He is right—bravo, Mr O'Brien. You don't know any good servant whom you could trust?'

'No, Grip.'

'Look about you; you'll find one, never fear.'

'Wait a minute, I've thought of some one—an old friend—Kate Brady!'

At the sound of this name Ranger intervened with a joyous bark, and wagged his tail hilariously.

'Ah, you remember her, Ranger!' said his young master, fondly caressing the dog. 'Kate! Our good Kate!'

Ranger bounded towards the door as though he awaited only an order from his master to rush away at the top of his speed to Trelingar Castle and bring Kate to the Boys' Bazaar.

Grip was then told all about Kate, and was immediately convinced that nothing could be better than to send for her and to install her at once in the kitchen. Fortunately, the upper floor of the house was to let; a room might be rented for the occupation of the partners, and a corner of the kitchen screened off for Kate. She need not show at all; her grown-up-ness would not be detrimental to the firm of Mick, Dick and Co.

But was she still at Trelingar Castle? Was she still living?

Foundling Mick wrote by the same day's post, and the next day but one he received a letter, written in a large legible hand. Forty-eight hours later, Kate arrived at the Kingsbridge Station.

She was warmly welcomed by her former *protégé*, who hugged her fervently, and by Ranger, who jumped at her and laid his paws on her shoulders. She could respond to this welcome only by tears, and when she was installed in her kitchen, and had been introduced to Dick, she wept afresh for joy.

On that day Grip had the honour and happiness of partaking with his young friends of the first dinner cooked by their own housekeeper in their own house. On the morrow the *Vulcan* set out to sea, and the happiest fireman afloat was in her engine room.

It may be asked whether Kate was to have wages? She would have been content with board and lodging only, these being given her by her 'dear child'; but such was not Foundling Mick's notion of the right method of doing things. She was not to be worse off, instead of better, for serving him whose existence at Trelingar Castle she only had made endurable. Wages she should have, and all the care and comfort that the boys in their small way could give her.

Very soon Foundling Mick discovered the economical value of the bold step he had taken. Kate kept the shop and the rooms in perfect order; cleanliness reigned in that little domain; their clothes and the scanty household linen were washed and mended; their food was purchased with judgement and admirably cooked, at less cost than the comfortless meals at a small eating-house in the neighbourhood on which they had hitherto subsisted. Kate was in short a model servant, her capacity was equal to her honesty—that great quality which had exposed her to the ridicule of the servants at Trelingar Castle. But why should we waste time by recalling to mind the Trelingar people in gilded saloon or servants' hall? Let the marquis and his happily adapted consort vegetate in their pompous uselessness, and let us trouble ourselves no more with those samples of the great.

It is really important, on the other hand, to mention that the year 1883 ended in a very respectable balance to the credit of Mick, Dick and Co. The resources of the Boys' Bazaar hardly sufficed for the demands of Christmas and the New Year. The toys-shelves were cleared twenty times over. To say nothing of other toys, Dick sold every kind of craft, even to clockwork steamboats, by scores, and all the boy-partners' wares were disposed of in proportion. Foundling Mick had no cause to repent of having left Cork and renounced the sale of newspapers. Mr O'Brien continued to take a lively interest in the young head partner in this unique firm, and to give Foundling Mick wise counsel, which was respectfully accepted; not so the aid in money, which he had also offered when he had tested the feasibility of the enterprise and the worth and ability of his young friend. Foundling Mick would not borrow, would not incur responsibility; would not share either loss or gain. In the case of Mr O'Brien, as in that of Grip, he respectfully declined a loan.

In short, at the end of six months, Foundling Mick had a very good right to be satisfied; he had trebled his capital since his arrival in Dublin.

CHAPTER 24

Found

'Any persons who may be possessed of information of any kind respecting the family of Murtagh MacCarthy, formerly the tenant of Kirwan's Farm, in the parish of S—, County of Kerry, are earnestly requested to transmit the same to Mick, Dick and Co., the Boys' Bazaar, Bedford Street, Dublin.'

The above advertisement was inserted in several of the Irish papers at the beginning of the New Year, and Mick had neither compunction nor regret in expending the money which this proceeding cost. Could the adopted child forget his best friends, especially when fortune was smiling on his modest efforts? It was his bounden duty to endeavour by every means in his power to find them, and come to their assistance. What would be his joy and thankfulness if he could ever repay to them any part of all their care and affection!

Whither had these good people gone in search of shelter after the destruction of the farm? Had they remained in Ireland, earning hard their daily bread? Had they exiled themselves, for the sake of Murdoch's safety, in some far-distant land, in Australia or America? Was Pat still traversing the sea? The thought that his benefactor and his family were in want was a constant and sore grief to Foundling Mick.

No result was attained by the advertisement. Had Murdoch been in a prison in Ireland news of him would have been received. The conclusion to be drawn was that the whole family had emigrated. Whither? How was Mick to solve that question? Would they succeed in making a new country for themselves in the far colony? Had they forsaken the old land for good and all?

Mr O'Brien applied himself to the solution of the matter that was troubling the spirit of his young friend, and discovered, through one of his correspondents in Belfast, that six members of the MacCarthy family had sailed for Melbourne two years previously. He had no means of tracing them farther. Then Foundling Mick applied to Messrs Maxwell for information respecting Pat, but there also failure awaited him. He received for answer that Pat had quitted the service of the firm fifteen months before, and no one knew on what ship he had embarked. One chance remained. Pat might return to one of the Irish ports and learn there that inquiry was being made respecting his family. This was a slender chance, it must be admitted, but Mick clung to it nevertheless, and his good friend O'Brien also tried to cheer him up.

'I should not be surprised,' he said to the boy one day, 'if you were to see all the MacCarthys again.'

'See them—in Australia—thousands of miles away! Oh, no, Mr O'Brien.'

'Why should you talk in that way, my boy? Is not Australia next door to us? There is no distance nowadays. Steam has suppressed it. They will come back to this country, I am sure. Irish people do not abandon Ireland, and, if they have succeeded over there—'

'Is it reasonable to hope, Mr O'Brien?'

'Certainly it is; if they are hard-working and intelligent as you say.'

'Industry and intelligence are not always enough, sir. Luck is wanted too, and the MacCarthys never had any luck.'

'What they had not formerly they may yet have, Mick. Do you suppose that I have always been lucky? No, I had many ups and downs, affairs that I could not manage, reverses of fortune, until the day that saw me master of the situation. And look at yourself, Mick, are you not an example? Did not you begin by being the sport of poverty and wretchedness, and how is it with you now?'

'What you say is true, Mr O'Brien, and sometimes I wonder whether it is not all a dream.'

'No, Mick, it is sound, solid reality. It is very extraordinary, for you have gone far beyond what could have been expected from a mere child, as you actually are. A little lad of twelve! But reason is not always to be measured by age, and by reason you have been continually guided.'

'By reason? Yes, perhaps—and yet, when I think of my present situation, it seems to me that chance has something to do with it.'

'There is less of chance in life than you think, and things are more closely linked together than is generally supposed. You will observe that a piece of ill, rarely fails to be accompanied by a piece of good, fortune.'

'Do you think so, Mr O'Brien?'

'Yes, and I believe it all the more that there is no doubt of it in your own case, my boy. This reflection occurs to me whenever I think of what your existence has been. You were sent to Mrs Murphy; that was evil fortune—'

'And good fortune that I knew Cissy there, and the first kindness I ever received was from her. What has become of her, my little companion, and shall I ever see her again? Yes, that was good fortune.'

'And it was well also that Mrs Murphy was an abominable old hag, for otherwise you would have been left with her until the time came for your being taken back to the workhouse. Then you ran away, and this threw you into the hands of the puppet-showman—'

'Oh! the monster!'

'It was well he was such a wretch, for otherwise you would still have been in his service, tramping the country with him and his puppets. Then you were put into the poor school at Galway—'

'Where I met Grip, who has been so good to me; who saved my life at the risk of his own.'

'And this led to your being taken up by that foolish actress. Quite another existence, I acknowledge, but it would not have resulted in any honourable and worthy career, and I regard it as fortunate that after having amused herself with you, one fine day she forsook you.'

'I don't resent it to her, Mr O'Brien. After all, she did take pity on me, she was good to me—and, since then, I have come to understand many things. So then, following out your reasoning, it is due to her forsaking me that I was received into the MacCarthy family at Kirwan's Farm—'

'Just so, and there again—'

'Oh, Mr O'Brien, you can never persuade me that the ruin of those good people could possibly be a fortunate circumstance.'

'Yes, and no,' said Mr O'Brien gravely.

'No, Mr O'Brien, no! And though I may be a successful man some day, I shall always regret that the starting-point of my good fortune should have been MacCarthy's ruin. I would willingly have passed my whole life at the farm as a son of the house—'

'I understand your feelings perfectly; but for all that it is no less true that this series of circumstances will enable you, I hope, one day to recompense those good people for what they did for you.'

'But it would be so much better if they had not required assistance from anyone.'

'Well, well, I will not insist, and I respect your feelings. But let us go on arguing and come to Trelingar Castle.'

'Ah! those horrid people, the lord, and the lady, and their odious son! What humiliation I had to endure there. That was the worst part of my existence.'

'And, according to my line of reasoning, it is well that it was so. If you had been well treated at Trelingar Castle, you would probably be there still.'

'In the position of a groom! No, no, Mr O'Brien, never. I was only waiting while there—so soon as I had saved something, I—'

'Ah! by-the-bye,' interposed Mr O'Brien, 'Kate must be enchanted that an accident brought you into the Castle.'

'Yes, the dear woman.'

'And Dick must be enchanted that an accident took you out of it, for otherwise you would not have met him on the high road, you would not have saved his life, you would not have brought him to Cork, where you both worked so bravely, and where you found Grip. And at this moment, you would not be in Dublin—'

'Talking with the best of men, who has become our friend,' answered Foundling Mick eagerly, and he clasped the good man's hand with fervent gratitude.

'And who will not spare you his advice when he sees you need it.'

'Thank you, Mr O'Brien. Yes, you are right, and your experience cannot err. The things of life are linked together! God grant that I may yet be useful to all those whom I love and who have loved me!'

The business of the Boys' Bazaar continued to prosper. Public favour was not capricious in its regard, and before long Mr O'Brien had a second shop to let which adjoined the Boys' Bazaar, and Foundling Mick took it for his new enterprise. What was that? A grocery business, no less, and soon a flourishing one. All the neighbours bought their groceries at the, extended Boys' Bazaar, and Kate had a hand in the sale now, she was not out of place among the serious articles of household consumption, while the partners attended most to the fancy goods, and Dick in particular presided with even increased zeal over the toys. The whole of the floor above the first shop now belonged to the firm, the boys had a comfortable sitting-room as well as their neat bedroom, and Kate no longer had to be 'screened off' in a corner of the kitchen. A more orderly and respectable little household could not have been found. And how hard they worked, those two! The day was hardly long enough for their commerce, and when the evening came there were the books—Foundling Mick's unfailing joy—to be made up, and the receipts to be verified. Dick's education was progressing also, and the visits of Grip were punctual and regular. Let us pass over an interval of monotonous occupation and steadily augmenting prosperity, but which was not marked by any incident more special than Foundling Mick's success in persuading Grip to transfer his savings from his belt to the Post Office Savings' Bank; and take up the fortunes of the Boys' Bazaar at a more advanced point.

In January 1885 Foundling Mick had entered his fourteenth year, and Dick was nine and a half. The two boys were in perfect health, well grown for their respective ages, and strong. The ills of their early years had left no traces upon them. The bazaar was in the full tide of prosperity, and the firm actually found it necessary to procure assistance in keeping their books. Mr Simpson, a trustworthy young man, recommended by Mr O'Brien, had been engaged in the capacity of book-keeper. Foundling Mick had money in the Bank of Ireland by this time, and was unmistakably on the road to fortune. He had not relinquished his efforts to discover the fate of the MacCarthys, but he was still unsuccessful, and this failure was the black spot on his horizon. The agent in Melbourne whom he had employed failed to trace the emigrants beyond that city. Nothing had been heard of Pat after he left Messrs Maxwell's service, and it was not impossible that he was with his parents in Australia.

Foundling Mick did not allow his thoughts to dwell on any of those whom he had known, except the MacCarthys and Cissy. As for Mrs Murphy, Hornpipe, Mr Mulvany, and the august house of Trelingar, he put them as far from his mind as though they never had existed.

'And Carker? Has he been hanged?'

This was Grip's invariable question each time that he turned up at the Boys' Bazaar on landing from the *Vulcan*. The invariable reply was that nothing had been heard of Carker. Then Grip would look over the police reports in the newspapers accumulated since his last departure, and having failed to discover any reference to his former schoolfellow, he would say,—

'Let us wait! We must have patience!'

'But why may not this Carker have become an estimable person?' asked Mr O'Brien one day, in a remonstrating mood.

'He!' cried Grip, 'he, that rascal! Why, it would turn one against good behaviour!'

Kate, who knew the story of the Galway school and its pupils, was entirely of Grip's opinion.

It was November and winter had set in severely. The weather was such as might fairly predispose anybody to remain indoors, nevertheless, Foundling Mick started by an early train for Belfast. The occasion for his forsaking the Boys' Bazaar for even a short time was a misunderstanding with a wholesale firm in Belfast, with whom the lad had recently had certain dealings, and Mr O'Brien, who deprecated very strongly anything that might possibly involve a lawsuit, had advised his young friend to settle the matter in person. Mick acted on this prudent counsel, and duly arrived at Belfast, without the slightest prevision that the day would be one to be marked henceforth in his life for remembrance. He looked about him on his arrival at the important commercial city of the north of Ireland, with the intelligent interest which such a seat of industry could not fail to inspire in a mind of the cast of Foundling Mick's, and promised himself an inspection of the main points of interest after he should have finished his business with Messrs MacMullen, to whose warehouse he repaired forthwith. Mick was conducted after a short delay to the private room of the head of the firm, and received politely, but with unconcealed surprise, by Mr Alexander MacMullen. The interview was a satisfactory one, the misunderstanding was easily removed, the relations between the Belfast merchant and his young customer (whose intelligence and smartness in the discussion of the matter in question astonished that astute person equally with his youth and self-possession) were placed upon a sure footing, and Foundling Mick found himself free to see a good deal of the city before dark. He had heard, and read in the newspapers, much about the division between classes and creeds in Belfast; he knew that capital and labour were upon terms anything but friendly there, and that in the northern capital the hardships which the Irish poor have to endure everywhere, have the aggravation of detestation of their religion, and a bitter persecuting spirit on the part of the wealthy and powerful classes; but he also knew that the Irish faith has never been shaken, and that no efforts to impose an alien creed upon the Irish race has succeeded; so that the strife rages always without result. But these things concerned Foundling Mick not at all; he was interested in the trade of Belfast, not in its factions, and he walked briskly through the town, not failing to observe all its features, and to admire the evidences of its industry and prosperity, but not loitering, for the day was very cold, and he wanted to see as much as possible before he should have to return to the station, where he intended to dine before starting for Dublin. He was turning his steps in the direction of the station, and having taken what his accurate eye told him was a short cut through a narrow street—for Foundling Mick possessed the bump of locality—had emerged upon a broad thoroughfare, when he found himself in front of a great factory. An angry crowd was assembled before the doors of the building, and the concourse blocked the street. Foundling Mick had to get through the mass somehow, and in doing this he learned the cause of the tumult. It was pay-day, and a number of male and female 'hands', already discontent, had come to protest against a decrease of their wages which had been announced for the next week. These poor people had been refused a hearing, and their anger was thoroughly roused. Muttered threats had been followed by shouts, and the doors and windows of the factory were assailed by showers of stones. At the moment when Mick had all but wormed his way to the edge of the crowd on the factory side of the street, a body of police rushed upon the malcontents with intent to disperse the assemblage, and arrest the ringleaders.

Foundling Mick, fearing lest he should have no time for his dinner at the station, tried to get away, but could not succeed, and only escaped from being trodden down in the charge, by forcing himself into a doorway, just as five or six workmen, brutally struck by the truncheons of the police, fell down alongside the factory wall.

Close to him, just beyond the doorstep, lay a young girl —a factory hand, pale, thin and sickly looking—who was eighteen years old, but might have been twelve from her appearance. She had been dashed down and lay there moaning, and feebly imploring help. Foundling Mick started at the sound of her voice. It reached him like a far-off remembrance. His heart beat quickly; he could not speak, and he was unable to move near to the prostrate figure. In a few minutes the crush was lessened, the crowd was giving way before authority (supported by truncheons), and the way was cleared in front of the doorway in which he stood. He bent over the girl; she was insensible. He raised her head, turned her face so that a gleam from a gas lamp was thrown upon it, and murmured, 'Cissy! Cissy!' It was Cissy, but she did not hear him.

Without a moment's hesitation he procured assistance, had the fainting girl placed in a cab, and conveyed her to the railway station. She recovered sufficiently before they arrived there to be able to walk along the platform without attracting attention from either busy officials or self-engrossed travellers, and when the train started she was comfortably ensconced in a corner seat of a first class carriage, without any other passengers, and Foundling Mick was kneeling by her side, holding her hands in his, and speaking to her in words of consolation and endearment which she was still unable to comprehend.

In such fashion was accomplished the abduction of Cissy by Foundling Mick; and who had so good a right to carry her away from her misery as he whom she had so often defended against ill-treatment in Mrs Murphy's wretched cabin?

CHAPTER 25

A Change of Colour and Condition

A happier little party than that which was assembled in the Boys' Bazaar on the following day could not have been discovered in all Ireland, or for that matter in all Europe, or perhaps anywhere short of Paradise. Cissy had been installed in the best room, and Foundling Mick was by her bedside at every spare moment. She had come to herself completely, recollected what had happened, and recognised in the vigorous and well-grown youth who had rescued her, the little child who had escaped from Mrs Murphy's den through a mousehole, so to speak.

And she, who was but seven years old then, and was now eighteen, worn out by toil and want, could she ever become the handsome young woman she might have been had she not lived in the vitiated atmosphere of factories?

It was ten years since they had met, and yet Foundling Mick had recognised Cissy by her voice, more surely than he would have known her by her face. Cissy, for her part, had not forgotten any of the incidents of their woeful childhood. It was of these that they talked, holding each other's hands, looking together into that miserable past as into a mirror.

As for Kate Brady, she could not hide her emotion. Dick's joy found utterance in the strangest exclamations addressed to Ranger, who responded with short barks of sympathy. Mr O'Brien, who had called early at the Bazaar to learn how Foundling Mick had fared in his mission, was much touched by the simple story. They had all heard of Cissy; it was not like the arrival of a stranger, however interesting; it was the coming home of Foundling Mick's elder sister.

Grip's presence only was wanted to complete the content of the little party, and no doubt he would have recognised his 'boy's' Cissy at the first glance. But the *Vulcan* was expected to arrive very shortly, and then all would be right.

Cissy's history may be told in a few lines; it is that of too many of the Irish children. Six months after the disappearance of Foundling Mick, Mrs Murphy died in a drunken fit, and Cissy was taken back to the workhouse at R—, where she remained for two years. She was then sent to a linen factory in Belfast, where she earned a few pence a day in the midst of the unwholesome flax dust, pushed about and beaten, having none to defend her, but always gentle, nevertheless, amiable, docile and seemingly inured to the hardships of existence.

Cissy did not contemplate any possible amelioration of this state of things. And, at the moment when she felt most sure that it was destined to remain always the same, it was suddenly changed by the touch of a hand—the hand of a child who had received from her the first caress he had ever known, and who was now at the head of a prosperous house of business. Yes! he had taken her away from her hateful life at Belfast, and here she was, in his house, and about to be the mistress of it! Yes! the mistress, he told her over and over again; not the servant.

Cissy a servant! Would Kate Brady hear of such a thing? Or Dick? Or Foundling Mick permit it?

'So you wish to keep me with you?' she said.

'Wish it, Cissy!'

'But at least I may work, so as not to be a burthen to you?'

'Yes, Cissy.'

'Then what shall I do?'

'Nothing, Cissy.'

And to this he adhered. Nevertheless, a week later, in the full exercise of her own sweet will, Cissy was installed behind the counter, having been instructed in the duties of a saleswoman. And the Boys' Bazaar was all the more frequented on account of her presence there; for the new and happy life to which she was introduced soon told on her, and she became as pretty as she was amiable and intelligent.

Cissy's greatest wish was for the arrival of the first fireman of the *Vulcan*. She knew all about Grip's conduct during the wretched years of the poor school; that he had succeeded her as Foundling Mick's protector, and that but for him Mick must have perished in the fire. The first fireman might reckon on a warm welcome on his return, but that happy event was unexpectedly deferred. Owing to certain commercial necessities, the year 1886 came to a close before the *Vulcan* appeared once more in the Irish Sea.

On the last day of that year Mr O'Brien had the pleasure of congratulating his young friend on the fact that the capital of the Boys' Bazaar had reached a sum of over £4,000 free of all debts. He expressed his gratification in the kindest manner, and at the same time recommended Mick to act with great prudence.

'It is often more difficult to keep one's gains,' he said, 'than to acquire them.'

'I know you are right, sir,' replied Foundling Mick, 'and I shall not let myself be led away. But I do wish the money in the Bank was doing something more profitable. It is money that's asleep, and sleepers are not workers. Now, Mr O'Brien, if some good opportunity were to arise?'

'It would not be enough for it to be good, Mick, it would have to be excellent.'

'In that case, then, I am sure you would be the first to advise me—'

'To profit by it? Certainly, provided you did so in your own line of business.'

'That is just what I mean, Mr O'Brien. I should never think of running risks in operations that I know nothing about. But one may endeavour to extend one's trade while acting with prudence.'

'On those conditions it would be hard if I didn't approve, my boy, and if I hear of anything that would be perfectly safe,—well—we shall see!'

Mr O'Brien was as cautious as he was sagacious, and did not think proper to pledge himself any farther.

The 23rd of February was a date to be marked with a red cross in the calendar of the Boys' Bazaar, for, on that day, Dick having mounted a step-ladder in the shop in order to get at the topmost toy-shelf, very nearly tumbled off on being hailed from below.

'Ahoy, there, parrot-perch! ahoy!'

'Grip!' cried Dick, and slid down the ladder, as a boy slips down a stair-rail.

'It's myself, Dick! How's Mick, my lad? And Kate? And Mr O'Brien? I don't think I've left out anyone, eh?'

'Not anyone? Not me, Grip?'

Who said these words? A young girl who came from the back of the shop, and held out her two hands to the first fireman of the *Vulcan*.

'Beg pardon, miss,' said Grip, in some confusion. 'I— I don't—'

'Why, it's Cissy, Grip! Cissy! Cissy!' repeated Dick, with shouts of laughter.

Those were pleasant days that followed the completion of the little company at the Boys' Bazaar. It might truly have been called a 'family' party, although not one of its members was related to any of the others, and all belonged to the class of the 'disinherited'. Whenever he was free from his fireman's duties, Grip was to be found at the Boys' Bazaar, and it was not long before Foundling Mick became aware (but prior to Grip's making the discovery) that there was an attraction at the shop counter, which had exerted its charm from the first, was growing stronger every day, and from which the first fireman of the *Vulcan* had neither the power nor the desire to escape. What would you have? It is the common lot!

'Is not my big sister a pretty girl?' was the ingenuous question put to Grip by Foundling Mick one day.

'Your big sister, my boy! But if she wasn't, she would be, all the same! If she was ugly, she wouldn't be, all the same!'

'Grip! What do you mean?'

'Oh, I'm talking stupidness, I know; but I can't express myself, that's the reason. If I could express myself—'

On the contrary, he expressed himself very well, in Kate Brady's opinion at least, and in less than in three weeks after Grip's appearance on the scene she said to Foundling Mick,—

'Our Grip is changing his skin. He used to be black, and now he's getting back to his own white colour. I don't think he will be on the *Vulcan* much longer!'

This was the opinion of Mr O'Brien also. Nevertheless, on the 15th of March, when the *Vulcan* steamed out of port, bound for New York, her first fireman was on board, having been accompanied to the water's edge by the whole family.

He returned on the 15th of May, and it seemed that the change in his colour was more distinct. He was received with the usual warmth, but he was not so demonstrative on his own part, and his demeanour towards Cissy bordered on the ceremonious. She was more serious and reserved than before, especially when by any chance she found herself alone with Grip. Somehow, the evenings did not pass so pleasantly as before, and when the hour came for Grip's withdrawal, Foundling Mick would say,—

'Tomorrow, old fellow?'

'No, not tomorrow, Mick. There's too much to be done. I can't possibly come.'

The next day Grip would arrive exactly as he had done the day before, or perhaps an hour earlier, and most certainly his skin became whiter each time.

It will be evident to the reader that Grip was in a psychological condition favourable to his acceptance of Foundling Mick's proposal that he should relinquish his employment on board the *Vulcan*, and become a partner in the house of Mick, Dick & Co. Foundling Mick was aware of this, but he took good care not to sound Grip on the subject. He judged it better to let the advance be made by Grip himself.

About the beginning of June the advance was made in the following fashion.

'Business is brisk, Mick, isn't it?' asked Grip.

'You can judge for yourself. The shops are pretty full.'

'Yes; there are a lot of customers.'

'Yes, indeed, Grip; especially since Cissy's been at the counter.'

'That's not surprising. I can't think why in all Dublin, or even in all Ireland, any one should want to buy anything unless she sells it!'

'Well, it certainly would be hard to find a nicer girl.'

'Or more—more—' replied Grip, who was quite unequal to finding a comparative worthy of Cissy.

'And so intelligent,' added Mick.

'So, then, things are all right?'

'I've told you so.'

'And Mr Simpson?'

'He's very well.'

'I was not asking for him,' said Grip, with some irritation. 'What do I care about Mr Simpson's health?'

'But I do, Grip. He is very useful to us. He's an excellent book-keeper.'

'And understands his business?'

'Perfectly.'

'I think he is rather old.'

'No—he does not look so.'

'Hm!'

The conversation stopped there, and when Foundling Mick repeated it to Mr O'Brien and Kate Brady, each of them listened with a smile.

Even that rogue of a Dick let himself into the joke, and a few days afterwards said to Grip,—

'Is not the *Vulcan* starting soon?'

'So they say,' answered Grip, and his countenance fell perceptibly.

'And then,' resumed Dick, 'you will light the furnace by only looking at it.'

As a fact the remarkably fine eyes of the first fireman were sparkling at the moment, but no doubt that was because Cissy was going about the shop, in her pleasant, smiling way, and presently she paused to say,—

'Grip, would you reach up to that box of chocolate? I am not tall enough.'

Grip reached up to the box.

'Would you just hand down that sugar-loaf? I am not strong enough.'

Grip handed down the sugar-loaf.

'Will your trip be a long one?' inquired Dick, whose roguish tone and laughing eyes seemed to mock poor Grip.

'Very long, I think,' said the fireman, shaking his head. 'At least five weeks.'

'Five weeks! Why, that's nothing! I thought you were going to say five months!'

'Five months? Why not five years?' exclaimed Grip, in the tone of a poor wretch who has been sentenced to imprisonment.

'Then you are very happy, Grip?'

'And why not? Of course I am.'

'You're a big fool!' said Dick, and he ran away with a grin on his roguish face.

The fact was, that Grip's life was not exactly lively since he chose to pass it mostly with his head in an angle of the wall. It was therefore just as well that he should go, since he could not make up his mind to stay, and accordingly he did go, on the 22nd of June.

During Grip's absence on this occasion, Mick, Dick & Co. did a very successful stroke of business, with the approval of Mr O'Brien. This was the purchase of the patent of a rather expensive mechanical toy from the inventor, a person known to Mr O'Brien. The novel article of commerce took the fancy of the customers at once, and the receipts of the Boys' Bazaar were raised both directly and indirectly by its vogue. Numbers of children of the 'gentry' wanted the toy, numbers of mothers bought it for them, and rarely failed to discover that other purchases might be made on Foundling Mick's premises with an advantage over the shops in a more fashionable quarter. So well were things looking that Mick indulged in the calculation of how much he might be able to give Cissy for her 'fortune', when Grip should be induced to have his mind made up for him on the important point of matrimony. That Cissy would have Grip if he could summon up courage to ask her, Mick was quite certain, in fact everybody in the house knew that. And why not? Grip was a fine, handsome young man, and Cissy was well aware of all his good qualities. Of course, she believed that her feelings were unsuspected by anybody.

It ensued from this condition of things, that on the return of the *Vulcan*, on the 29th of July, the first fireman was more awkward, embarrassed and moody—in short, more unhappy—than before. His ship was to start again on the 15th of September. Would he go with her this time?

Foundling Mick had made up his mind on one point. His sister Cissy should not marry a fireman. He intended to impose, as a first condition, that Grip should relinquish his post on the *Vulcan*, and enter the firm in the character of a partner. If he would not do this, then no Cissy for Grip.

One day when the disconsolate one was hanging about the kitchen where Kate Brady was at work—he was more at ease with that good woman—Kate said to him with apparent carelessness,—

'Haven't you remarked, Grip, that our Cissy grows prettier and prettier?'

'No, I haven't,' replied Grip, 'I haven't remarked it. Why should I remark it? I don't look—'

'Ah! you don't look? Well, then, open your eyes, and you will see what a pretty girl our girl is. Do you know that she is close on nineteen?'

'What, already?'—Grip knew Cissy's age accurately — 'You must be mistaken, Kate.'

'I'm not in the least mistaken; she's just nineteen, and she ought to be getting married. Mick must look out for a good, honest boy for her, about 26 or 27, just like yourself, you know. Someone we could all trust with her; not a sailor, though, not a sailor! People that go to sea, no, no! Sea-faring folks needn't be coming this way. And Mr Mick will give her a snug little fortune, I'm thinking—'

'She doesn't want it.'

'That's true, Grip, but a little money's a good thing in setting-up house. Our young master has someone in his eye, I think.'

'Is it someone that comes to the Bazaar often?'

'Yes, pretty often.'

'Do I know him?'

'No, it seems you don't know him,' answered Kate, looking at Grip, who looked away from her.

'And—does Cissy like him?' asked Grip, as though the words stuck in his throat.

'Well,—we're not altogether sure. When people can't make up their minds to speak—'

'What stupid fools some people are!' said Grip.

'That's just what I think,' rejoined Kate, readily.

In spite of this very broad hint, the first fireman embarked on the *Vulcan* a week later; but when he returned on the 29th of October, it was evident that he had formed a great resolution. He did not, however, speak at once. The ship was to be laid up for repairs, and Grip had two months before him.

He had walked into the Bazaar immediately after his arrival, and finding Kate Brady dusting the shop, had asked her point blank,—

'Is Cissy married?'

'No,' replied Kate, 'but she soon will be. It's coming.'

As the *Vulcan* was in the repairing dock, Grip had nothing to do on board, and so he was much with his friends. Indeed, short of living there altogether, he could hardly have been more constant to the Boys' Bazaar. And yet, things did not progress. In fact the *Vulcan* had been repaired, was in process of lading, and within a week of putting to sea, and that unbearable Grip had not yet opened his handsome mouth, when an unexpected occurrence that had a reflex action upon the lagging swain took place.

A letter arrived from Australia, addressed to Mr O'Brien, and containing the following news:—

Mr and Mrs MacCarthy, Murdoch, his wife and their little girl, with Peter and Pat, who had rejoined them, had just sailed from the port of Melbourne for Ireland. Fortune had not smiled upon them, and they were returning to their own country well nigh as poor as when they left its shores. They were on board the *Queensland*, a sailing ship; the voyage would no doubt be slow and difficult, and their arrival could not be anticipated for nearly three months from the date of their departure.

Foundling Mick was greatly relieved by the arrival of this letter. To have any news at all of his friends was a boon of price, but the nature of the news grieved him sorely. However, he would be able to help them. How ardently did he long to be tenfold more prosperous, so that they might have tenfold the aid he could now offer them.

Foundling Mick requested Mr O'Brien to let him have this letter, and Mr O'Brien consented to do so. Mick locked it up in his safe, and, strange to say, did not allude to it after that day. Indeed, after the receipt of the letter, he seemed to avoid any mention of the former occupants of Kirwan's Farm.

Grip took the news very seriously. It had an aspect personal to himself of which he entirely disapproved. These MacCarthys, these two brothers,

Peter and Pat, were coming back; no doubt they were very fine fellows, and Foundling Mick was greatly attached to them. What if Cissy should think one of them a specially fine fellow, and Foundling Mick discover that he would be the best of husbands for the girl whom Mick regarded as an elder sister? In short, Grip became frightfully jealous, and on a certain day in December he made up his mind that there must be an end to this state of things. He had only just reached that conclusion when Foundling Mick took him aside, and asked him to come into his private room, as he had something to say to him.

The stricken Grip followed Mick, with a pale face and a sinking heart.

When they were seated face to face, Foundling Mick said, in a business-like tone,—

'I am probably going to undertake a rather important affair, and I shall want your money.'

'At last!' said Grip, 'you haven't been too quick about it. How much do you want?'

'All you have in the Savings' Bank.'

'Take what you want, then.'

'Here's your book. Sign, please, so that I may draw out the money today.'

Grip opened the book and signed.

'As for the interest,' said Mick, 'I shan't say anything—'

'That does not matter.'

'Because—from this day forth you are in the "house" of Mick, Dick & Co.'

'As what?'

'As a partner.'

'But—my ship?'

'You will give up your berth.'

'And—my business?'

'You will leave it.'

'Why should I leave it?'

'Because you're going to marry Cissy.'

'I'm going—to marry—Cissy!' repeated Grip in bewilderment.

'Yes; she wishes it.'

'Ah! It is she—'

'Yes! And as you wish it also—'

'I? I wish it—'

Grip did not know what he was saying, or understand a word of the farther discourse of Foundling Mick. He took up his hat, put it on his head, took it off, placed it on a chair, and sat down upon it without perceiving that it was there.

'No matter,' said Foundling Mick. 'Any way, you'll have to buy a new one for the wedding.'

No doubt he did buy a new hat for the occasion, but he never had any clear idea of how his marriage was brought about. Even Cissy herself could not extricate him from the confusion and bewilderment in which he passed the intervening days. It came to pass, however, that on the 24th of December, Christmas Eve, Grip put on a black coat, as though he were going to a funeral, and Cissy arrayed herself in a white gown, as though she were going to a party, Mr O'Brien, Foundling Mick, and Dick assumed their best clothes, and Kate Brady made a noble appearance in a black silk gown and a shawl of many colours, the gift of her young master. Thus festively attired, the whole party proceeded in two cabs to the nearest Catholic Church, and when Grip and Cissy came out, leading the way, half-an-hour later, they were safely and certainly man and wife.

CHAPTER 26

The Voyage
of the *Doris*

On the 15th of March, nearly three
months after the marriage of Grip and
Cissy, the schooner *Doris* cleared out of the
port of Londonderry, and put to sea with a
north-easterly wind. The vessel calls for our
attention simply because she carries Caesar
and his fortunes, in other words,
Foundling Mick and a mixed cargo which
is the property of Mick, Dick & Co.

How has all this happened? Briefly,
thus:—After the marriage of Grip and Cissy,
the business of the Boys' Bazaar became very
brisk, and there was a great to-do in
enlarging the shop, putting up new shelves
and various fittings: in these operations
Grip, who had hardly yet realised the fact
that he was actually Cissy's husband and his
'boys' partner, displayed the utmost activity
and handiness. Everything was in perfect
order for the New Year, and with that season

of beginning again the custom of the Bazaar notably increased. At the opening of 1887, Foundling Mick would have had nothing to desire but for the anxiety concerning the MacCarthys which continually oppressed him. His mind was full of his projects for their future security and welfare. But what of the *Queensland*? Tedious as the voyage must needs be, it was full time, and more, for news of the ship. At length Foundling Mick, who read the announcements in the *Shipping Gazette* assiduously, learned, on the 14th of March, that the steamer *Burnside* had passed the sailingship *Queensland* on the 3rd. The *Queensland* was then in the Atlantic, and might be expected to reach Queenstown in three weeks. Until then there was nothing for it but patience.

A few days later Foundling Mick's attention was attracted by an announcement in a daily paper among the items of commercial news to the effect that on the fifteenth of the current month, the cargo of the schooner *Doris* from Hamburg would be sold under a decree of the Court of Bankruptcy for the creditors by public auction at Londonderry; the said cargo consisting of one hundred and fifty tons of various merchandise.

Foundling Mick thought deeply over this announcement. The idea had occurred to him that he might conduct a profitable operation in the matter. Under the circumstances the cargo of the *Doris* would certainly be sold at a low price. He immediately consulted Mr O'Brien concerning this bold project, and his steady-going old friend, having read the notice and reflected upon it with the gravity of a man who does nothing lightly, replied as follows:—

'Yes, there's good business to be done in this. All these goods, if they go cheap, can be sold at a large profit, but on two conditions; that they are of excellent quality, and that they can be bought fifty per cent, under the market price.'

'That's what I was thinking, Mr O'Brien,' answered Foundling Mick, 'and the only way to know about the cargo of the *Doris* is to see it. I shall start for Londonderry this evening.'

'You are right, my boy, and I will go with you,' said Mr O'Brien.

Foundling Mick endeavoured to express his gratitude for such a proof of Mr O'Brien's regard, but the worthy gentleman stopped him by saying simply,—

'Let us try to turn this opportunity to good account—that is all I ask.'

Foundling Mick then informed Grip and Cissy that he was going to Londonderry by the evening train, on business which had the full approbation of Mr O'Brien. Almost the whole of his capital would be involved in the contemplated operation, but with a secure result, and his adviser and friend would be with him. He confided the Boys' Bazaar to the care of the newly married couple during his absence of 48 hours.

Mr O'Brien and Foundling Mick left Dublin that evening. Short as the separation was to be, Dick regarded it ruefully. He had not been parted from Foundling Mick for a day, since the auspicious occasion on which the latter had aided Ranger in his gallant act of salvage, and he would dearly have liked to accompany the senior partner.

The cargo of the *Doris* was closely examined by Mr O'Brien, who pronounced it to be suited in kind and quality to the requirements of Mick, Dick & Co. If he should be able to buy it at a low price he would realise a large profit, even to the quadrupling of his capital. Mr O'Brien would not have hesitated to make the purchase on his own account. He advised Foundling Mick to anticipate the sale by auction, by making a private offer to the creditors, Messrs Harrington.

This was good advice, and Foundling Mick acted on it, with success. He came to an advantageous agreement with Messrs Harrington, and obtained the cargo at a rate all the more advantageous that he offered to pay ready money. If Messrs Harrington were astonished at the youth of the purchaser, they were still more surprised by the intelligence with which he discussed this important transaction. Mr O'Brien offered his security, and the affair was settled on the spot by a draft on the Bank of Ireland.

Three thousand five hundred pounds, almost all Foundling Mick's capital, was the price at which he became the owner of the cargo of the *Doris*. It was not surprising that after the completion of the transaction he experienced an emotion which he did not try to restrain.

The simplest method of conveying the cargo to Dublin was to employ the *Doris* for that purpose. The skipper asked nothing better, and with a fair wind the passage would occupy only two days.

Having settled this point, Mr O'Brien and his young companion had only to take the evening train. Then an idea occurred to Foundling Mick:

he proposed to Mr O'Brien that they should return to Dublin on the *Doris*. Mr O'Brien, who had the best reasons for disliking a sea passage, however brief, declined, but was quite content that Mick should make the little trip.

'It tempts me, Mr O'Brien,' said Mick. 'It is a short run, and I would rather not lose sight of my cargo.'

Mr O'Brien returned alone to Dublin, where he arrived at early dawn, and precisely at the same moment the *Doris* put to sea.

The wind, coming from the north-west, was favourable. If it did not change, the passage would be excellent. But it was the month of March, and nearing the equinox the weather is apt to be treacherous in the Irish Sea. The *Doris* was commanded by a coasting captain named Cleary, and its crew consisted of eight sailors. They were all old hands, and familiar with the coast of Ireland.

The first day's voyage promised favourably, and Foundling Mick greatly enjoyed the entirely novel sensation of being at sea. He was no more seasick than a cabin boy. Nevertheless, the thought of that precious cargo in the hold of the vessel, and of the abyss which had but to open to swallow up all his fortune, would occur to him.

He wished Dick were on board. He would have been so pleased to make a voyage 'in earnest' this time, not only on a *Vulcan* moored to the quay in Cork or in Dublin. If Foundling Mick had foreseen that he was to return to Dublin by sea, he would certainly have taken Dick to Belfast with him and treated him to the trip, and then Dick would have had no wish ungratified.

The north-east wind continued to favour the schooner's course until the afternoon. Foundling Mick remained on the deck all day, had his meals there, and resolved to stay until the cold of night should oblige him to resort to the captain's cabin. Decidedly, his first maritime excursion would leave none but the pleasantest impressions, and he congratulated himself upon having thought of escorting his cargo in person. He should feel proud on entering the port of Dublin with the *Doris,* and he was sure that Grip and Cissy and Dick would be at the quay to meet him.

Between four and five the weather changed; great masses of vapour piled themselves up in the east, and the sky became murky and threatening. Foundling Mick turned away from the bulwarks and observed the captain's face. It had changed with the weather, and was overcast and anxious.

'Well, captain?' said Mick, in surprise.

'I don't like it,' was the answer, and Captain Cleary returned to his lookout to the west.

The wind had fallen off, the sails began to flap against the masts, and the *Doris* rolled heavily under the influence of a long swell which stretched over the sea. The captain suggested that Foundling Mick should go below; but the swell did not affect him, and he remained on deck. From that moment the signs of tempest increased, and night fell upon the *Doris* battling with a storm which only those who have witnessed such scenes of atmospheric strife could have believed to be possible in so short a time. All space seemed filled with piercing, whistling sounds, before which the sea-birds flew in terror towards the land. Then in an instant the schooner was struck, and shivered from her keel to her topmast-head. The wildest confusion reigned, everything that could roll rolled and tumbled about, and it became very difficult to remain on deck.

'Go below, sir,' said Captain Cleary to Mick.

'Captain, let me—'

'No—go below, I tell you, or you will be swept overboard by a sea.'

Foundling Mick obeyed. He carried a heavy heart with him to the cabin; but his trouble was not so great on his own account as on that of the cargo in peril. His whole fortune was on board, and might be lost—all the good he hoped to do might be rendered impossible.

An hour later the mainmast fell with a terrific crash, the ship heeled over to starboard, and as the cargo was displaced in the hold, being unable to right herself, she was in danger of filling over the bulwarks.

Foundling Mick, who had been thrown against the bulkhead of the cabin, scrambled up on his hands and knees, and strove to ascertain the meaning of the tumult on deck. Was the ship actually going down?

No; but the captain, finding it impossible to right her, and fearing that she must founder, was making preparations to abandon the schooner. Notwithstanding the inclination of the vessel, which rendered the operation very dangerous, the long boat had been launched, and all hands were about to get into it.

Foundling Mick understood the position when he heard the captain shouting to him to come on deck.

What! leave the ship and all she contained in her hold? No, that could not be! Were there but one solitary chance of saving her, Foundling Mick would run that chance, even at the peril of his life. He knew the maritime law; if the sea did not swallow it up, an abandoned ship belongs to the first person who boards her.

The cries were repeated; the captain shouted to Mick again and again, but there was no reply.

'Where can he be?' asked the captain.

'We are sinking!' shouted the sailors.

'The boy! the boy!'

'We cannot wait.'

'I must find him.'

The captain hurried down into the cabin, but Foundling Mick was not there. Again he shouted, but in vain.

'Where is he? Where is he?' demanded the unfortunate and bewildered captain.

'He may have come on deck,' said a sailor.

'He has gone overboard,' said another.

'We are sinking—we are sinking!' cried the whole crew in chorus.

All this passed amid a scene of the wildest tumult, with the *Doris* rolling fearfully, so that every moment she seemed to be about to turn keel upwards.

The captain returned to the deck. Foundling Mick must have ventured on deck in the terrible darkness, and been swept into the sea! At the moment of the captain's reappearance the schooner plunged more deeply into the hollow between two mountain-like waves, and then rose for a brief space, which enabled him with the crew to get into the long boat, at the imminent risk of being swamped, and pull away from the side before, as they believed, she must go down.

The *Doris* was without captain and crew, but she was not an abandoned ship, she was not derelict, for Foundling Mick had not forsaken her.

He was alone, every moment he was menaced with death; the next might see him swallowed up by the seething sea; but he did not despair. He was sustained by an extraordinary presentiment which inspired him with confidence. He managed to regain the deck, and crawled to the bulwarks under the wind at a place where the sea was not coming in. What a multitude of thoughts came crowding upon him. This was, perhaps, the last time he should think of those whom he loved, of the MacCarthys, of Grip, Cissy, Dick, Kate and Mr O'Brien, and he implored the aid of God, beseeching Him to spare his life for their sake also.

The night came to an end. The tempest abated with the first rays of the sun. Still the sea continued to heave under the influence of a persistent swell. Foundling Mick turned his eyes in the direction of the land, but there was no coastline to be discerned, and seaward not a sail, not even a fishing boat. Indeed, if there had been, it could hardly have perceived the dismasted wreck, half-hidden between the crests of the waves as it rolled in their trough.

And yet, the only chance of safety was being seen by a craft of some kind, for if the *Doris* continued to drive towards the west, she must inevitably be lost with all she carried, on the reefs which lay along the seaboard.

Foundling Mick was entirely helpless; by no effort of his could he direct the motion of the unwieldy, disabled vessel towards the fishing-grounds, and he had tried in vain to fix a piece of canvas to a still standing spar, to serve as a signal. He was in the hands of God only.

The day wore on without any aggravation of danger to the ship. She still drifted at the same inclination, but the sea was falling, and the wind was abating hour by hour. Foundling Mick ate food in order to preserve his strength, and not for an instant—we insist on this point—not for an instant, having retained the clearness of his intelligence, did he allow despair to lay hold on him. He kept one thing steadily before him, he was defending his right.

At four o'clock he saw smoke to eastward, and half an hour later a large steamer came distinctly into sight, going north, and at a distance of five or six miles from the *Doris*. Foundling Mick made signals with a flag attached to a boat hook, but they were not seen, and the big ship vanished from his sight.

Even then, such was the extraordinary courage of the boy, he did not despond. Darkness was coming on and he could not count on meeting any other craft that day. There was nothing to indicate that he was approaching the shore. There would be no moonlight, and the darkening sky was cloud-laden. The wind, however, was moderate, and the sea much less tumultuous.

As the temperature was low, it was better for the solitary navigator to go below when the night fell, for it would be impossible to distinguish any object at even half a cable's length. Foundling Mick was greatly fatigued and unable to keep awake. He wrapped himself in a blanket, lay down on the planks alongside the bulkhead of the cabin and fell into a sound sleep.

At dawn of day he was awakened by loud sounds from without, and sat up, listening. Was the *Doris* drifting on to the shore, or had a vessel met her at sunrise?

'We are first,' shouted some men's voices.

'No, no, we are!' answered others.

Foundling Mick at once understood what had happened. No doubt the *Doris* had been sighted from early dawn; two boats' crews had hurried to get alongside her, and were now disputing which of the two she should belong to. The rival parties had boarded the wreck, and were now attacking each other.

Foundling Mick would only have to show himself to put an end to the conflict, but he took good care not to do so. These men might turn against him, and might not hesitate to toss him overboard, so as to avoid any ulterior claim. Without losing a moment, he must hide himself. He promptly crept into the hold and crouched down between the bales of goods. After a while, the tumult ceased, peace had been made. The belligerents had agreed to sell the cargo and divide the proceeds, after they should have taken the abandoned ship into port.

The crews were those of two fishing-smacks which had set out from Dublin Bay at sunrise, and sighted the wreck of the schooner four or five miles out. They then raced for the prize, but both arrived at the same time, hence a quarrel, blows and finally a bargain over the booty. Ah! these fishers would have made a good haul that morning.

Foundling Mick was barely stowed away safely in the hold, when the respective owners of the two smacks came tumbling down into the cabin, and we may judge how much pleased he was to be out of their sight when he heard one say to the other,—

'It's a good job there's not a single soul on the schooner.'

The other made answer,—'If there was, itself, he wouldn't be long there.' Half an hour later the hull of the *Doris* was in tow to the two smacks, which were urged by sail and oar as rapidly as possible towards

Dublin Bay. As it was low tide, the smacks made for Kingstown, and on their arrival at the landing-place, the salvage men found a crowd assembled. The arrival of the *Doris* had been signalled, and Mr O'Brien, Grip, Cissy and Dick were in the front rank of the assemblage. They had been informed of the salvage.

What was their grief on learning that the fishing boats had brought back only an abandoned hull. Foundling Mick was not on board—Foundling Mick had perished! The little group was overwhelmed by the dreadful news.

At this moment a harbour official, whose duty it was to conduct the inquiry respecting the salvage, and who was empowered to deliver up the ship to its lawful claimants, arrived on the scene. What a stroke of luck for the salvage men!

But, on a sudden, a head appeared above the cabin stairs followed by the figure of a stalwart youth. What a cry of joy was uttered by Foundling Mick's 'own', and by what a shout of rage did the fishermen answer it!

In an instant Foundling Mick was on the quay, and clasped in Cissy's arms. He greeted the others with a grasp of their hands, and then advanced towards the official.

'The *Doris* has never been abandoned,' he said, in a clear, firm voice, 'and all that it contains is mine.'

All discussion was useless. Foundling Mick's presence on board had saved that rich cargo, which remained his property, as the *Doris* remained the property of Captain Cleary and his men, who had been picked up at sea on the previous day. The fishermen had to rest satisfied with the reward to which they were legitimately entitled.

An hour later the Boys' Bazaar was the scene of a most happy reunion, in which Kate Brady and Ranger had their full share of recognition and pleasure. Foundling Mick's first experience of the sea had been singularly perilous; nevertheless, Dick presently sidled up to him and said,—

'Ah! if I could have been with you on board!'

'All the same, Dick?'

'All the same!'

CHAPTER 27

The Wages of Foundling Mick

The young senior partner in the firm of Mick, Dick & Co. was clearly on the high road to fortune, thanks to his intelligence, and, let it be said, to his courage also. His conduct in the matter of the *Doris* bore ample testimony to both.

One thing was still wanting to his happiness; the MacCarthys had not yet arrived. He had arranged with Mr Bennett, an agent at Queenstown, that he was to be informed by telegraph of the signalling of the *Queensland*, but the notice of that event tarried, and although Foundling Mick was not alarmed, he found it difficult to be patient.

Meanwhile, the Boys' Bazaar had become doubly fashionable, for the fame of Foundling Mick's exploit had spread in the city and in the suburbs, and his customers of all classes were very numerous. Mr

O'Brien's expectation that the capital engaged in the purchase of the cargo of the *Doris* would be quadrupled, was in a fair way to be not only realised but surpassed. The Bazaar was extended on both sides, and a shopman was added to Foundling Mick's staff. The toy department had ceased to be of the foremost importance, and Dick was now able to help Mick in the heavier part of their business. The hand of a woman of intelligence and taste was recognised in all the arrangements over which Cissy presided, and she herself was highly ornamental at the counter, where she was ably seconded by Grip, who had by this time thoroughly mastered the truth that his marriage was a fact, not a dream. The first fireman of the *Vulcan* was turned into the best and most loving of husbands, and there was every reason to believe that he would one day have an opportunity of developing and displaying the parental virtues also.

At length, on the 5th of April, a telegram was delivered at the Boys' Bazaar in the morning. Dick received it, and immediately shouted, from the shop,—

'News! News!'

Foundling Mick came running in at the sound, and snatched the welcome mustard-coloured envelope from Dick's outstretched hand. Cissy and Grip, followed by Mr O'Brien, joined him while he was devouring with his eyes the following message:—

> Queenstown, 5th April, 9.25 a.m.
> To Foundling Mick, Boys' Bazaar, Bedford St, Dublin.
> *Queensland* just come into dock. MacCarthy family on board. We await your orders.
>
> BENNETT

Foundling Mick was almost choked with emotion. His heart stopped beating, and a burst of tears relieved him after a moment. He then merely said,—

'That is well,' and went away to his own room. When he returned, he said nothing about the telegram, or the MacCarthys, much to the surprise of Mr and Mrs Grip, Dick and Kate. He went about his business as usual, and only 'troubled' Mr Simpson for a cheque for one hundred pounds, concerning which, or its destination, he said nothing whatever.

Four days elapsed, and Holy Saturday came. Easter Day fell, that year, on the 10th of April.

In the morning, Foundling Mick collected all his staff and said to them,—

'The Bazaar will be closed until Wednesday morning.'

On this intimation, Mr Simpson and the shopman withdrew, and then Mick asked Grip, Cissy and Dick whether they would not like to make a little excursion during the three days of vacation.

'I would for one,' cried Dick. 'Where are we going to?'

'Into the County Kerry,' answered Mick. 'I wish to see it again.'

Cissy looked at him.

'You really wish us to go with you?' she asked.

'Indeed I do.'

'Then I'm to be of the party?' said Grip.

'Certainly.'

'And Ranger?' asked Dick.

'Ranger also.'

It was arranged that Kate Brady should be left in charge of the Bazaar, and that the excursionists should leave Dublin by the four o'clock train for Tralee, where they were to sleep. On the following day Foundling Mick promised that he would explain the rest of the programme. They then dispersed, each to make preparations respectively for an absence of three days.

At four o'clock the travellers were at the railway station. Grip and Dick were in the highest spirits; but Cissy, who was of a less expansive disposition, was quietly observant of Foundling Mick, who remained impenetrable.

'Tralee,' said Mrs Grip to herself, 'Kirwan's Farm is not very far from Tralee. Is he going back there?'

Ranger was placed in the guard's van with a special recommendation, backed by a bright shilling, to the care of that official, and then Foundling Mick and his companions took their seats—in a first-class carriage, if you please!

Foundling Mick, who knew Tralee, took his friends to the best hotel on their arrival at that town; they had an excellent though unusually late supper, and slept soundly in their strange quarters.

The following morning, Easter Sunday, while Dick was opening his eyes and stretching himself, and Cissy was at her toilet, assiduously waited upon by Grip, Foundling Mick was out walking about the town. He recognised the inn to which Mr MacCarthy used to go and he with him, the marketplace which had first inspired him with a taste for trade, the wine merchant's shop where he had bought the bottle of port for Granny. He returned early to the hotel for breakfast, and at eight o'clock a smart jaunting-car with a capital horse was brought to the door, and the party started for S——, where Foundling Mick proposed that they should hear the Easter Day mass. The bell was ringing when they arrived at the church at ten o'clock. Foundling Mick entered the sacred edifice with a pale face and a beating heart. Here the double baptism of himself and his godchild had been celebrated. Ranger was left in the porch, and Cissy walked by Mick's side; there was no one in the church to recognise Murtagh MacCarthy's adopted child in the well-grown, well-looking, well-dressed youth who bore himself during the service with unaffected reverence and devotion.

After Mass came a good luncheon at the one good inn which S—— boasted, and again the jaunting-car was put in requisition to convey the excursionists to Kirwan's Farm. So much Foundling Mick had told them, but they all felt that there was something kept back, something that moved their young benefactor profoundly.

Foundling Mick's eyes were wet with tears as the swift wheels bore him along the road he had so often trodden with MacCarthy and Mary, with Kitty, and even Granny when she was able to go out. How mournful the place looked. It was easy to see that the country was abandoned. Ruins everywhere! and such ruins!—made to force the evicted people to quit their last shelter. In many places notices were affixed to the walls, indicating that such and such a farm, or field, was to be let or sold. And who would have ventured to buy or rent these, since their only harvest was poverty!

At length, at a turn of the road, Kirwan's Farm came in sight, and a sob escaped from Foundling Mick's breast.

'It was there—' he murmured.

The farm was in a wretched state. The hedges were destroyed, the central door had been smashed to pieces, the outbuildings were half pulled down, the farmyard was overgrown with thistles and weeds, the house was roofless, the windows were smashed, the walls were full of holes. For five years, the rain, the snow, the wind and even the sun had done their worst with it. Nothing could be more lamentable than those empty rooms, open to all the blasts. A sad sight was the place where Foundling Mick had slept beside Granny's bed.

'Yes, it is the farm!' he repeated, and it seemed as though he dared not enter.

Dick, Grip, and Cissy kept back a little behind him, in silence. Ranger came and went uneasily, sniffing the ground; no doubt he too was picking up his old recollection. Of a sudden the dog stopped, his eyes sparkled, his tail quivered.

A group of persons had appeared before the yard gate,— four men, two women, and a little girl. These people were poorly dressed, and seemed to have suffered. The oldest of them stepped out from the group and came towards Grip, whose age indicated him as the chief personage among those strangers.

'Sir,' said he, 'an appointment has been made with us at this place—by you, no doubt?'

'By me?' replied Grip, looking at him in surprise.

'Yes; when we landed at Queenstown a sum of one hundred pounds was given to us by the shipowners, who had been directed to send us on to Tralee—'

At this moment Ranger barked wildly with joy, and fawned upon the older of the two women with the most significant demonstrations of affection.

'Ah!' she exclaimed, 'it is Ranger! our dog Ranger! I know him!'

'And do you not know me too, mother? Do you not know me?' cried Mick.

'Is it he? It is our child!'

How shall the inexpressible be expressed? How shall the scene that ensued be depicted? Not at all; it may be imagined by all humane, tender, grateful hearts, and best by those to whom sorrow and suffering are familiar; but it cannot be described.

When something like calmness had been restored, and Foundling Mick had almost devoured his god-daughter with kisses, the reunited friends seated themselves on a pile of stones in the yard and began to talk. The lamentable story of the MacCarthys may be related here in a few lines although it was made long in the telling by Foundling Mick's eager and impatient questioning. After the eviction, and Granny's death, they had been taken to Limerick, where Murdoch was imprisoned for some months. When he was set free, the family went to Belfast and embarked on an emigrant ship for Melbourne in Australia. Soon after their arrival in the colony, they were joined by Pat. And then began a weary succession of efforts and failures: sometimes they got work together, at others they were separated. At last, after five years, they had left the country in which they had not been able at any time to do more than earn the humblest subsistence, to try whether their native land, for which they pined as only Irish hearts can pine, would be always so pitiless to them. Times, they had heard, were not quite so bad for the poor 'at home' as they had been. The laws had been ameliorated in certain respects, and the landlords' claws cut to some extent. English public opinion was growing enlightened, and being brought to bear upon the condition of the Irish race. At all events the MacCarthys *must* go 'home'; let their fate be what it might, they would meet it in their own country. And so they had come 'home'.

Foundling Mick listened, and looked at these poor people, with profound emotion. MacCarthy was much aged, Murdoch was grave and sombre as he had been in the old time, Pat and Peter were weather-beaten and dejected, Mrs MacCarthy had lost the briskness and spirit of the busy farmer's wife of other days. What had become of Kitty's grand and gentle beauty? she looked fever-stricken, and Jenny was not so strong and rosy as she ought to be at her happy age. The boy's heart was rent at the spectacle.

Cissy, who was seated between Mrs MacCarthy and her daughter-in-law, said, in a soft, low tone to the former,—

'Take comfort, ma'am. Your troubles are over—over like ours—thanks to your adopted child.'

'To him! What can he do for us?'

'You—my boy?' repeated MacCarthy.

Foundling Mick was incapable of answering him.

'Why have you brought us back to this place, which recalls our miserable past?' asked Murdoch. 'Foundling Mick, what made you wish to put us face to face with these recollections?'

The same question was on the lips of all the others. Not one of them but wondered what could have been Mick's intention in bringing the MacCarthys to meet him at Kirwan's Farm.

'Come!' he answered, when he had mastered himself with difficulty. 'Come, my father, my mother, my brothers, come with me!'

They followed him to the middle of the farmyard, where, in the midst of weeds and coarse grass, there still stood a small green fir-tree.

'Jenny,' said he, addressing the little girl. 'You see that tree? I planted it the day you were born. It is eight years old, like you!'

Kitty, to whom his words recalled the time when she was happy, and hoped that her happiness might be lasting, burst into tears.

'Jenny, my darling—' resumed Mick, 'you see this knife; it was Granny's first gift to me, your great-grandmother, I mean, but you hardly knew her.'

At that name, evoked in the midst of these ruins, MacCarthy and his wife quivered with the pain of remembrance.

'Jenny,' continued Mick, 'take this knife, and dig up the clay at the foot of the tree.'

Jenny knelt down, without understanding him, put aside the grass, and made a hole in the spot to which he pointed. Presently the knife struck upon something hard. It was an earthenware jug, which had remained unharmed in the clay.

'Take out the jug, Jenny, and empty it.'

The little girl obeyed, and all the others looked on in profound silence. The jug was found to contain a number of little pebbles, like those to be found in the bed of the adjacent river.

'Mr MacCarthy,' said Foundling Mick, 'do you remember that every evening, when you were pleased with me, you gave me a little stone?'

'Yes, my boy, I do remember, and there was not one single day but you deserved to have one.'

'They represent the time that I passed at Kirwan's Farm. Very well, count them, Jenny. You know how to reckon, don't you?'

'Oh, yes!' replied the little girl. And she began to count the stones, making little piles of them by the hundred.

'Fifteen hundred and forty,' she said.

'That is right,' answered Foundling Mick. 'That makes more than four years I lived in your family, my Jenny; your family which had become mine.'

'And those stones,' said Mr MacCarthy, hanging down his head, 'are the only wages you ever received from me; these stones that I hoped to change into shillings.'

'And which are going to change into sovereigns for you, my father,' said Foundling Mick, solemnly.

Neither Mr MacCarthy nor any of his family could believe, could comprehend that they heard. Such a fortune as that? Was Foundling Mick mad?

Cissy guessed their thoughts, and said,—

'No, no, dear friends; his heart is as sane as his mind, and it is his heart that speaks!'

'Yes, father, mother, you my brothers, Murdoch, Pat, and Peter, and you, Kitty, and you, my godchild, yes, I have the happiness of giving you back a part of what you gave me. This farm is for sale. You shall buy it. You shall rebuild the old house. Money shall not be wanting, and you will have no more Herberts to fear. You shall be your own masters, in your own home!'

And then Foundling Mick told the story of his life since the day he had left Kirwan's Farm, and explained his present position. Fifteen hundred and forty pounds, which he placed at the disposal of MacCarthy, was a large fortune for an Irish farmer. And on that soil which had been watered by so many tears of sorrow, those of joy and gratitude fell fast.

The MacCarthy family remained for the three Easter days with Foundling Mick and his friends at S—; then the latter returned to Dublin, and on the Wednesday the Bazaar re-opened its doors.

A year elapsed—the year 1887, which must be reckoned one of the happiest in the lives of the humble folk of our veracious history. The young senior partner was full sixteen years old. His fortune was made. It is true that a part of that fortune belonged to Mr and Mrs Grip, and to Dick; but the fact was of no importance, seeing that those three persons formed with himself one and the same harmonious family, to whom a division of interests was simply inconceivable.

The MacCarthys, having purchased two hundred acres of land on favourable terms, have rebuilt the farmhouse, renewed the farming materials, and bought new stock. Health and strength have been restored to them at the same time with happiness and ease. Just think of it; mere Irish tenants who had long suffered under the lash of landlordism, now in their own home, no longer slaving to pay an impossible rent to pitiless masters!

Foundling Mick does not forget, he never will forget, that he is their adopted child, and one day he may be united to them by a closer tie. Jenny is nearly ten years old, and promises to be a handsome girl. To be sure she is Foundling Mick's god-daughter, but in due time a dispensation may settle that difficulty of spiritual affinity, and then, why not? Why not indeed? Ranger, an old dog now, would probably think the earlier it is settled the better.

THE END.

NOTES

[1] M. Jules Verne draws very largely upon his imagination here, as elsewhere, in this narrative. The practice to which he refers did not at any time prevail in Ireland, and has been considerably suppressed in England.

[2] It is since 1870 that the tenant farmers were secured by law from being expelled from their holdings without compensation for improvements made at their cost.

[3] Now O'Connell Street. The reconstructed bridge, once Carlisle, is now O'Connell Bridge.

A Chronology of Jules Verne

William Butcher

1828 8 February: birth in Nantes of Jules Verne, to Pierre, a lawyer, and Sophie, of distant Scottish descent. The parents have links with reactionary milieux and the slave trade. They move to 2 Quai Jean-Bart, with a magnificent view over the Loire.

1829 Birth of brother, Paul, followed by sisters Anna (1837), Mathilde (1839) and Marie (1842).

1834–7 Boarding school. The Vernes spend the summers in bucolic countryside with a buccaneer uncle, where Jules writes his travel dreams. His cousins drown in the Loire.

1837–9 École Saint-Stanislas. Performs well in geography, translation and singing. For half the year, the Vernes stay in Chantenay, overlooking the Loire. Jules's boat sinks near an island, and he re-enacts Crusoe. Runs away to sea, but is caught by his father.

1840–2 Petit séminaire de Saint-Donitien. The family move to 6 Rue Jean-Jacques Rousseau. Jules writes in various genres, his father predicting a future as a 'savant'.

1843–6 Collège royal de Nantes. In love with his cousin Caroline. Writes plays and short prose pieces. Misses a year's studies, but easily passes *baccalauréat*.

1847 Studies law in the Latin Quarter. Fruitless passion for Herminie Arnault-Grossetière, dedicating scores of poems to her.

1848–9 In the literary salons meets Dumas *père* and *fils*, and perhaps Victor Hugo. Law degree.

1850 Comedy 'Broken Straws' runs for twelve nights.

1851 Publishes short stories 'Drama in Mexico' and 'Drama in the Air'. Works as private tutor, bank clerk and law clerk.

1852–5 Secretary of the Théâtre lyrique. Publishes three more stories and one of his operettas is performed. Visits brothels.

1856	Meets a young widow with two daughters.
1857	Marries Honorine, becomes a stockbroker and moves frequently. Publishes first book, *The Salon of 1857*.
1859–60	Visits Scotland and England and writes *Backwards to Britain*.
1861	Travels to Norway and Denmark. Birth of only child, Michel.
1863	*Five Weeks in a Balloon*.
1864	*Adventures of Captain Hatteras* and *Journey to the Centre of the Earth*. *Paris in the Twentieth Century* is brutally rejected by publisher Jules Hetzel.
1865	*From the Earth to the Moon* and *Captain Grant's Children*. A contract specifies 200,000 words a year.
1866	'Geography of France and her Colonies'. Summer residence in fishing village of Le Crotoy.
1867	With Paul to America on the *Great Eastern*.
1868	Buys a boat, the *Saint-Michel*, and visits London.
1869	*Twenty Thousand Leagues under the Seas* and *Round the Moon*.
1870	Hetzel rejects an early draft of *The Mysterious Island*. Verne has a mistress in Paris. During the Franco–Prussian War, he serves in the National Guard.
1871	Moves to Amiens. Father dies.
1872	*Around the World in Eighty Days* and *The Fur Country*.
1873–4	*The Mysterious Island* and *The Chancellor*. Begins collaboration with Adolphe d'Ennery on successful stage adaptations.
1876–7	*Michel Strogoff*, *Hector Servadac* and *The Child of the Cavern*. Buys second, then third boat, the *Saint-Michel II* and *III*. Wife critically ill, but recovers. Michel rebels and is sent to a reformatory.
1878	*The Boy Captain*. Sails to Lisbon and Algiers.
1879–80	*The Begum's Fortune*, *The Tribulations of a Chinese in China* and *The Steam House*. Verne sails to Edinburgh and visits the Hebrides.
1881	*The Giant Raft*. Sails to Rotterdam and Copenhagen.

1882	*The Green Ray* and *The School for Robinsons*. Moves to a larger house.
1883–4	*Keraban the Inflexible*. Takes Honorine on a tour of the Mediterranean and is received in private audience by Pope Leo XIII.
1885	*Mathias Sandorf*. Sells *Saint-Michel III*.
1886	*The Clipper of the Clouds*. Paul's son, Gaston, fires twice at Verne, laming him for life. Hetzel dies.
1887	*North against South*. Mother dies.
1888	*Two Years Vacation*. Local councillor on a Republican list.
1889	*The Purchase of the North Pole* and 'In the Year 2889' (signed Jules Verne but written by Michel).
1890	Stomach problems.
1892	*Carpathian Castle*.
1893	*Foundling Mick*.
1895	*Propeller Island*.
1896–7	*For the Flag* and *An Antarctic Mystery*. Health deteriorates. Brother dies.
1901	*The Village in the Treetops*.
1904	*The Master of the World*.
1905	Falls ill from diabetes and dies.
1905–14	Michel takes responsibility for the manuscripts, publishing nine volumes under his father's name, although writing major parts himself.

Translating *Foundling Mick*

Kieran O'Driscoll
Centre for Translation and Textual
Studies, Dublin City University

This republication of the only translation into English of *P'tit Bonhomme*,[1] under the title *Foundling Mick* (1895),[2] one of Jules Verne's lesser known works—though a novel which is of particular interest to an Irish readership—provides an opportunity to reflect briefly upon the nature and quality of this particular translation, and, more generally, upon the history and quality of renderings into English of Verne's overall corpus of fiction.

The best-known novels forming the cornerstone of Verne's epic series of *Extraordinary Journeys*—including such titles as *Twenty Thousand Leagues under the Seas, Journey to the Centre of the Earth* and *Around the World in Eighty Days*[3]—have been retranslated into English quite frequently over the last 135 years or so.[4] The accuracy and general stylistic quality of successive renderings of Verne's novels into English have significantly improved with the passing of time, most particularly in recent decades. This trend towards increasing accuracy has accompanied the literary rehabilitation of Jules Verne from the 1950s onwards, throughout the world. The fact that many of Verne's most famous novels are now available in reliable English retranslations begs the question of how the present—indeed only—translation of the less widely known *Foundling Mick* might be evaluated in terms of its accuracy and style. Before considering this question, let us briefly examine the background to this Verne novel.

The present novel was originally published in French in 1893 under the title *P'tit Bonhomme*, which literally translates as 'little fellow'; hence, the creativity of the anonymous translator is already evident in the choice of a non-imitative rendering of the novel's title (*Foundling Mick*), which alludes to the fact that the central character is initially introduced to the reader as an abandoned waif or 'foundling'. This title simultaneously confers a name of the translator's invention on the main protagonist, to whom Verne refers throughout only by the appellation '*P'tit Bonhomme*'.

This English translation was first published in London in 1895 by Sampson Low, Marston and Company, which had already issued many of Verne's previous works in translation from the 1870s onwards. In most cases, the identity of the translators remained uncredited, such translatorial invisibility being the norm at that time.

But the present 2008 republication is not, in fact, the first time this translation has found an Irish publisher. Sometime between 1936 and 1940, according to *The Jules Verne Encyclopedia*,[5] an abridged version of the Sampson Low target text was published by The Educational Company of Ireland as part of a series called *The Talbot Library of Standard Authors*. The title was changed, on that occasion, to *A Lad of Grit*.[6] The emblem of the above educational publishers, on the title page of this 1930s edition, bears the legend 'Let Knowledge Grow From More To More'. This is a salient reminder that Verne's works were intended to combine fictional adventures with much factual detail in the realms of the physical sciences, history and geography, so that they have often been associated primarily with younger, school-going readers. Because they have always been seen as having educational benefit, many of the translations of Verne's works, over the years, have been categorised as having a pedagogical purpose, and as being fiction for younger readers, and indeed this original Irish publication of *A Lad of Grit* seems to belong to these educational and 'adventure fiction' categories.

VERNE'S EVOLVING LITERARY REPUTATION

Verne was traditionally viewed as being a writer of popular literature, of adventure and science-fiction stories aimed at younger readers. However, the last 60 years have seen an ongoing re-evaluation, by scholars and literary critics, of Verne's work, including a recognition on the part of the academic community that these novels' apparently simple, workmanlike style conceals an impressive narrative technique and a depth of themes and characterisation. They have been seen as deserving of more careful retranslation into English, as shall be discussed in more detail later in this article.

More recent translations of some of the *Extraordinary Journeys* are, therefore, not only superior to their predecessors in terms of accuracy, completeness and style, but are also accompanied, in many cases, by detailed paratextual material written by Verne scholars—who, often, are also the translators.

THE NATURE OF THE TRANSLATION OF *FOUNDLING MICK*: DESCRIPTIVE TRANSLATION STUDIES (DTS)

This translation, though somewhat abridged, and despite having been produced in the late nineteenth century—the era when Verne's works were least accurately rendered into English—is a generally faithful, accurate rendering, couched in natural though formal target language, and is eminently readable and enjoyable. The translator, though remaining faithful to source text meaning, does not adopt a slavishly literal approach: instead, this target text combines semantic fidelity with an idiomatic use of (Hiberno)–English, including the translator's own creative though accurate choices of lexis. This rendering offers a faithful representation of Verne's narrative, and of his literary style.

Descriptive Translation Studies (DTS)[7] offers a methodological apparatus for a detailed analysis of this translation of *Foundling Mick* and for an attempted explanation of the strategies and forms of translation shifts. In Toury's methodology, individual sentences and short passages of the target text (which Toury terms 'replacing segments') are compared with corresponding segments of the source text ('replaced segments').

The following is a small sample of source text segments, together with their corresponding translated segments, in order to illustrate and discuss some of the characteristics of the present translation.

Example 1—Abridgement at macro-textual level and imitative rendering of certain chapter titles

The fact that this translation is abridged is initially evident on a macro-textual, structural level, from its number of chapters in comparison with the original text. Verne's *P'tit Bonhomme* consists of two parts: the first, entitled '*Les Premiers Pas*' (translated in the 1895 version as 'Beginnings') contains sixteen chapters, whereas the target text's corresponding first part comprises only fourteen; the source text's second part, '*Dernières Étapes*' (rendered as 'Second Part') has fifteen chapters; the target text, thirteen.

On the other hand, there is a direct, largely imitative correspondence between many of the original chapter titles and their renderings, as the following instances serve to illustrate:

> First Part (Beginnings):
> ST Chapter I: '*Au fond du Connaught*' / TT Chapter I: 'In Far Connaught'
> III: '*Ragged-school*' / III: 'The Poor School'
> IV: '*L'enterrement d'une mouette*' / IV: 'Concerning a Seagull'
> V: '*Encore la ragged-school*' / V: 'More of the Poor School'

> Second Part:
> VII: '*Sept mois à Cork*' / V: 'Seven months in Cork'[8]
> VIII: '*Premier chauffeur*' / VI: 'The First Fireman on the *Vulcan*'
> XIII: '*Changement de couleur et d'état*' / XI: A Change of Colour and
>   Condition

Example 2—Non-imitative rendering of other chapter titles

In contrast, some chapter titles are rendered non-imitatively. In the following examples of differentially rendered titles, therefore, it may be said that the translator's agency and personal creativity are evident:

> First Part (Beginnings):
> II: '*Marionnettes royales*' / II: 'Little Mick'
> VII: '*Situation compromise*' / VII: 'Rocks Ahead'

<u>Example 3—Abridgement and other alterations at micro-textual level</u>

This descriptive analysis, applied to *Foundling Mick,* also reveals a certain amount of abridgement at the micro-textual level, in which sentences are shortened and sometimes omitted, and passages condensed. In the following example (Example 3) there is some omission, condensation and alteration of the novel's opening paragraph. Some of this opening passage's geographical details, together with facts provided by Verne about Ireland's political and administrative system in the nineteenth century, are omitted by the translator. For instance, some names and locations of Irish provinces are not translated. Verne's explanation of the function of the lord-lieutenant within Britain's colonial administration of late nineteenth-century Ireland is also omitted. On the other hand, other factual information such as the surface area of Ireland is made much more precise in the translation. These translatorial decisions are an example of how *Foundling Mick* is, in some respects, a target-oriented translation: culture-specific facts which are assumed to be known to a British and Irish readership are not reproduced.

The abridged nature of this translation appears to be representative of much literary translation into English in late nineteenth-century Britain, in which norms of translation seemed to include a widespread tolerance for some degree of contraction. On the other hand, present-day norms of translation would not allow a somewhat reduced version of the source text to be presented as a complete rendering.

The following example (3) also illustrates the use of non-imitative target language, which complies with norms of idiomatic usage and also shows the creative imprint of the individual translator, as in the phrase 'formerly formed a part of the insular tract of land now called the United Kingdom'. Translatorial agency is also seen to include some degree of interpretative addition, as in the choice of the phrase 'This we learn from the geologists':

*L'Irlande, dont la surface comprend vingt millions d'acres, soit
environ dix millions d'hectares, est gouvernée par un vice-roi
ou lord-lieutenant, assisté d'un Conseil privé, en vertu d'une
délégation du souverain de la Grande-Bretagne. Elle est divisée
en quatre provinces : le Leinster à l'est, le Munster au sud, le
Connaught à l'ouest, l'Ulster au nord. Le Royaume-Uni ne
formait autrefois qu'une seule île, disent les historiens. Elles
sont deux maintenant, et plus séparées par les désaccords
moraux que par les barrières physiques. Les Irlandais, amis
des Français, sont ennemis des Anglais, comme au premier
jour.* (ST, p.17)

Ireland, which has an area of 31,759 square miles, or
20,326,209 acres, formerly formed a part of the insular tract
of land now called the United Kingdom. This we learn from
the geologists; but it is history and fact that the islands are
now two, and more widely divided by moral discord than
by physical barriers. The Irish, who are friends of France,
are, as they always have been, enemies of England. (TT, p.1)

Example 4—Micro-textual abridgement (further example)

There is a further example of abridgement in the following translation
shift. In addition, the source text metaphor is modulated from '*lait*'
('milk') to 'flowing breast'. This shows the personal imprint of the
translator's creative choice:

*Ce n'est point cependant une terre bréhaigne, puisque ses enfants
se comptent par millions, et si cette mère n'a pas de lait pour ses
petits, du moins l'aiment-ils passionément.* (17)

But although the motherland has no flowing breast to give
to her children, she is passionately loved by them. (1)

<u>Example 5: Micro-textual abridgement (final example of same)</u>

The following coupled pair provides a final illustration of abridgement: in this instance, a list of poetic descriptors of Ireland is slightly altered in translation, with some omitted, and others, which do not appear in the original, added by the translator. Furthermore, the translator omits the phrase *'sa chanson ne s'échappe que de bouches maladives'* ('its song escapes only from sickly mouths' [my translation]). Specific facts—relating to population—which are not in the original, are provided in the translation. In general, the limited amount of reduction effected by the translator throughout this target text does not detract from a globally accurate rendering of the narrative essence of Verne's novel: the sequence of events and the portrayal of characters is faithfully transmitted. Certain factual and descriptive details, considered superfluous to the narrative, or already known to the target readership, are occasionally reduced or omitted:

> *Aussi lui ont-ils prodigué les plus doux noms, les plus «sweet» (sic)—mot qui revient familièrement sur leurs lèvres. C'est la «Verte Erin», et elle est verdoyante en effet. C'est la «Belle Emeraude», une émeraude sertie de granit et non d'or. C'est «l'Île des Bois», mais plus encore l'île des roches. C'est la «Terre de la Chanson», mais sa chanson ne s'échappe que de bouches maladives. C'est la «première fleur de la terre», la «première fleur des mers», mais ces fleurs se fanent vite au souffle des rafales. Pauvre Irlande ! Son nom serait plutôt l'«Île de la Misère», nom qu'elle devrait porter depuis nombre de siècles ; trois millions d'indigents sur une population de huit millions d'habitants.* (18-9)

They call her by the sweetest of names; she is 'Green Erin'—and indeed her verdure is unequalled—she is 'The Land of Song'; she is 'The Island of Saints'; she is 'The Emerald Gem of the Western World'; she is 'First flower of the earth, and first gem of the sea'. Poor Ireland! She ought to be called 'The Isle of Poverty', for that name has befitted her for many centuries. In 1845 the population of 'the most distressful country that ever yet was seen', reached its highest point, 8,295,061; in 1891 when the last Census was taken, it had fallen to 4,706,192, and the terrible preponderance of indigence is maintained at the old figures, 3 to 8. (1)

Example 6—Imitativeness and Natural Expression

Some individual replacing segments are imitative of ST form as well as of meaning, insofar as such imitativeness is consistent with TL natural usage. The following two translation shifts illustrate the simultaneous achievement of semantic fidelity and formal imitativeness:

> *Un beau pays pour les touristes, cette Irlande, mais un triste pays pour ses habitants.* (17)

> A fair country for tourists is Ireland, but a sad one for the dwellers in it. (1)

> *Ils ne peuvent la féconder, elle ne peut les nourrir—surtout dans la partie du nord.* (17)

> They cannot fertilise it, and it cannot feed them, especially in some of the northern districts. (1)

Example 7—Target Culture Orientation: use of culture-specific terms

The use of the specific term 'Mass' in the following example offers an illustration of how this translation has been specifically adapted to the target readership, and to an Irish target culture, by using a technically more accurate term than the source text's more general 'offices du matin':

> *Ce jour-là, un dimanche précisément, 17 juin 1875, la plupart des habitants s'étaient rendus à l'église pour les offices du matin.* (18)

On Sunday, the 17th of June, 1875, most of the inhabitants were at Mass ... (3)

Example 8—Semantic alteration

The following example illustrates one of the changes made by the translator to the detail of the original, in that the dog who pulls the cart in the opening chapter of the source text, becomes a pony in translation:

> *En ce moment, il n'y avait personne dans les rues de Westport, si ce n'est un individu qui poussait une charrette traînée par un grand chien maigre, un épagneul noir et feu, aux pattes déchirées par les cailloux, au poil usé par le licol. «Marionnettes royales ... marionnettes!» criait à pleins poumon cet homme.* (19)

> For the moment, there was only one person in the main street of Westport, a man who was pushing from the back a queerly shaped vehicle drawn by a small and manifestly ill-used pony, and shouting, with wasted energy in the vacant space: 'Puppets! Puppets!' (3)

Example 9—Taboo language

In the following coupled pair, the insulting language used by the travelling showman to the animal and to Mick, is only hinted at in the translation. This dilution of potentially offensive language may indicate Victorian literary norms by which the delicate sensibilities of the late nineteenth-century reader may have considered a more imitative rendering to be unacceptable. The offensive language, i.e. two phrases which literally translate as 'son of a bitch' and 'son of a dog' respectively, is diluted through the use of the word 'sworn', the phrase 'a hideous prefix' and the use of a line to suggest the taboo nature of the omitted words.

This translation shift also illustrates the ongoing omission of some lower-level, minor textual details such as *'caché dans la caisse de son véhicule* ('hidden in the box of his vehicle'). Some meaning is altered : the *'robuste animal'* becomes a 'miserable beast'. Interpretation and explicitation on the part of the translator are thus evident.

> *Et après que l'homme a dit au robuste animal :*
> *«Marcheras-tu, fils de chienne ? ...» il semble qu'il s'adresse à*
> *un autre, caché dans la caisse de son véhicule, quand il crie :*
> *«Te tairas-tu, fils de chien ?»* (19)

> And then, after the man had sworn at the miserable beast,
> he would seem to address some other lower animal, saying,
> with a hideous prefix, 'You —, will you hold your tongue?'
> (3)

Example 10—Syntactic Modification and Alteration of Proper Names

The following translation shift offers, firstly, an example of the use of syntactic alteration. A number of shorter source text sentences are combined into a longer utterance in the target text. It also illustrates the use of non-imitative, individually chosen target language forms, which preserve global accuracy in their semantic faithfulness to the replaced segment. Secondly, this shift is notable for its alteration of the name of the travelling showman from 'Thornpipe' to 'Hornpipe'. This is a humorous amendment on the translator's part, as the chosen translation resonates with a British and Irish target readership, referring as it does to a popular type of dance (or instrument, or air) in the target cultures. This is, in fact, one of several changes of name chosen by the translator: apart from the renaming of the eponymous principal protagonist, *'P'tit Bonhomme'* to 'Foundling Mick', the name of his dog is changed from 'Birk' to 'Ranger', and his co-worker in the Dublin business enterprise—'Bob' in the original—appears as 'Dick' in the translation. The shop which is set up in Dublin by Foundling Mick, which, in the source text, is designated as *'le bazar de Little Boy'* and also as *'les Petites-Poches'* becomes the 'Boys' Bazar' in the target text.

*Cet homme s'appelle Thornpipe. De quel pays est-il ? Peu
importe. Il suffit de savoir que c'est un de ces Anglo-Saxons,
comme les îles Brittaniques n'en produisent que trop parmi les
basses classes. Ce Thornpipe n'a pas plus de sensibilité qu'une
bête fauve, ni de cœur qu'un roc. (19-20)*

The man's name was Hornpipe. It matters little what was
his birthplace; enough that he was one of those Anglo–
Saxons, too frequently to be met with among the lowest
classes in the British Isles, who have no more feeling than a
wild beast, no more heart than a granite rock. (4)

MULTIPLE CAUSES OF TRANSLATION FORM

We have considered a number of examples of various types of translation
shifts which occur in *Foundling Mick*, and their probable causes. It is
useful at this point to summarise the theoretical background to the
interacting causes which are thought to work together to bring about the
particular form of individual translations.

The 'material cause' is that of the source text itself, together with the
particular source language-target language pair involved in the
translation—the differences between the language of the original text and
the language of the translation will clearly have a significant bearing on
the form of the translated text.

A further cause is the 'formal cause', that is, norms of translation,
which are cultural values influencing what is accepted as a translation at
a given point in space and time. These norms include values of natural,
idiomatic and thus non-imitative usage in the target language, values
which, as has been noted earlier, certainly apply to the present rendering
of *Foundling Mick*. Other norms are those of accurate, faithful translation;
reproduction of unusual expression in the source text; correction of
factual errors in the original and creative use of the target language.
Though such norms are often regarded as dominant norms applying to
a wide spectrum of translations in many text-genres, this is not to say

that such norms are accepted unquestioningly by all translators. Norms differ across space and time. They differ in the extent to which they are perceived as binding upon the activity of translators (thus norms may be strong or weak), and individual translators may select or reject different norms in their own unique manner.

There is then the 'final cause', which refers to the purpose or *skopos* of the translation, the use to which it is to be put and the target readership for whom it is intended. For instance, a translation of a Verne novel aimed principally at a younger readership may be abridged and simplified, and may contain illustrations (such as the 1982 Ladybird Books 'retelling' of *Around the World in Eighty Days* by Faraday).[9] On the other hand, a translation of one of Verne's works aimed at a general or scholarly target readership will tend to be complete and unabridged, and to also contain much paratextual material, including explanatory notes (such as Butcher's 1995 retranslation of *Around the World*).[10] Translation theorists also include, within this cause, such cultural and social influences on the translation as the status of the source text author at a particular time and place: thus, as has been noted earlier, the increasing canonicity of Verne's novels in recent decades has led to more accurate, thoughtful and careful retranslations of his work.

Lastly, there is the 'efficient cause', which refers to the individual aesthetic input of the translator: this input may include such features as creative choice of target language wording, modification of ST style, personal interpretation of meaning on the part of the translator or decisions to comply with certain translation norms and not with others. A comparison of different translations into English of the same literary text, whether it be by Jules Verne or any other retranslated author, tends to reveal noticeable differences in style and in general translation approach between differing individual translators. These variations are often due, to some extent, to the style and interpretation of the translator. One translator may favour the use of a colloquial or informal register of English, and may depart, to some extent, from the style of the original author, while another may prefer a more formal usage which attains closer stylistic equivalence (if the original author's style is formal, as is often the case with Verne's writings).

Certain translators may thus have a significant individual input into the translations they produce, so that agency is a salient translation cause.

The social and intellectual status of the translator may give him or her greater freedom to choose his or her own translation approaches, independently of the influence of other, competing actors in the translation network, such as publishers or dominant sets of norms. The preceding examples of translation shifts have gone some way towards illustrating the nature of the translator's creative imprint in sections of *Foundling Mick*.

VERNE'S MARGINALISATION IN NINETEENTH-CENTURY LITERARY SYSTEMS

In the light of the four above causes of translation (which are based on Aristotle's four posited causes of social phenomena, and applied to translation causality by the translation theoretician and historian, Anthony Pym,[11] it is clear that the 'final cause' of Verne's gradually increasing literary standing has had a significant bearing on the growing accuracy of translations of his work into English, from the poor translations of the 1860s onwards, to the superior renderings of the present day. The Verne scholar, Arthur Evans,[12] notes that, from 1863 to 1905, Verne's prolific output enjoyed significant popular success, but his work was not generally regarded as having any real literary merit. He suggests a number of factors which contributed to Verne's position on the margins of the French literary polysystem.

The fact that some of his novels were adapted for the theatre, and later the cinema, in his native France and elsewhere, meant that his works were seen essentially as light reading for the masses. They were therefore shunned by the academic community and by literary experts, as well as by authors such as Emile Zola, who described Verne as being, like Perrault a few centuries earlier, a children's writer and 'unliterary'. Traditionally, the French literary system was a hierarchical one which canonised 'great works', whereas Verne's novels of adventure and scientific anticipation were deemed to constitute what Evans[13] refers to as a 'radically new literary form' and as 'paraliterature' and even 'secondary literature'.

The perceived pedagogical objectives of Verne's fiction meant that it was regarded as excessively didactic, this feature being considered incompatible with literary greatness. At the same time, the Catholic Church in France was suspicious of the apparent lack of theism in the *Extraordinary Journeys*, and this hostility was connected to a general climate of anti-scientism existing at that time, which led to Verne's novels being negatively evaluated by the establishment in his native France.[14] It is evident, for instance, that Verne's detailed scientific descriptions of marine life in *Twenty Thousand Leagues*, or of earlier forms of humanity in *Journey to the Centre of the Earth*, reeked too strongly of Darwinism to be welcomed by a religious and anti-scientific Establishment.

In the United Kingdom at that time, works by Verne were similarly seen as being popular fiction aimed at the working classes. Haywood[15] points out that, in nineteenth-century Britain, there was a widely held view that the working-class reader of popular fiction was intrinsically different in his or her reading tastes to more refined readers belonging to the upper social classes. It was not considered advisable to encourage the development of literacy on the part of the 'common reader', as this might constitute a threat to the social order:

> ... the common reader 'must have coarse food: ghosts and murders' ... [There was an] intractable social division between polite and popular culture. Social and political stability derives from a restriction of literacy, not its universalization. The lower orders, addicted to their 'coarse food' of sensationalism, are incapable of refinement.[16]

Since literacy was not encouraged in the lower socio-economic groups, and as popular fiction was deemed to be an inferior genre, Verne was marginalised within the British literary system. The result was that many translations into English of his works, in the late nineteenth and early twentieth centuries, were grossly inaccurate, and characterised by severe bowdlerisation and haste. Thus, the depth of research which lies behind the extensive scientific detail of marine biology in *Twenty Thousand Leagues under the Seas*—to cite just one example—is continuously misrepresented, because it is truncated and mistranslated, by early translators. On the other hand, retranslations of this novel from the decade of the 1990s (by such translators as Butcher) have helped to enhance Verne's scientific and literary standing, by being accurate, complete and annotated. Indeed, as one of Verne's less well-known novels, *Foundling Mick* has not received the literary recognition it deserves. The present republication should help make this novel more widely appreciated.

VERNE'S REPUTATION IN THE US OF THE NINETEENTH CENTURY

In contrast to the low literary status of Verne's fiction in his native France and in Britain after 1860, his novels were more highly regarded in the United States of the late nineteenth century. Early US translators of Verne such as George Makepeace Towle (1841–93) produced largely accurate renderings of such novels as *Around the World in Eighty Days* (1873).[17]

A number of reasons may be advanced for this contrasting perception of the *Extraordinary Journeys* in the United States in this period. Verne was favourably compared to other travel and adventure novelists of prestige such as Defoe and Swift; travel literature was already popular thanks to the works of Mark Twain; and the era of technology (transcontinental railroads, telegraphic communications) and the importance of extending frontiers to the West (see Turner's *Frontier hypothesis*) meant that Verne's themes resonated strongly with an American readership. For instance, the railroad, the telegraph and the Wild West play an important part in *Around the World*. In addition, *Realism* as a literary movement was important in America and elsewhere in the 1860s. Several features belonging to this school were evident in Verne's writings: their educational value, their moral stance and their themes of individual control of destiny and of society's observation of the individual. One need only look at the eccentricity and determination of a Captain Nemo or a Phileas Fogg, and the reading public's fascination with these individuals, for evidence of the two latter features of *Realism* in Verne's fiction.

It was also considered important that the large number of immigrants living in the United States be educated in English language proficiency and in developing literacy skills, so that the reading and teaching of popular writers such as Verne, in translation, were encouraged as a matter of public policy.

THE VERNE 'RENAISSANCE'

From the 1950s onwards in France, and subsequently in English-speaking countries, Verne's works enjoyed a literary renaissance of sorts. Evans[18] attributes this reassessment of Verne's literary worth to the influence of such philosophers and literary commentators as Sartre, Moré, Barthes and Cocteau, who began to explore new and hitherto largely unsuspected depths in Verne's writing. Thus, the *Extraordinary Journeys* began to be reinterpreted in accordance with new currents of literary analysis such as structuralism and psychoanalytic criticism. This reassessment of Verne in a more favourable light led to more accurate retranslations and fresh interpretations of his works. For example, in his 1995 annotated translation of *Around the World in Eighty Days*, William Butcher interprets parts of Verne's text through Freudian theories of the subconscious, which he explains in his Introduction and endnotes, and reflects in particular translation choices. Butcher also sees certain sections of *Around the world* as containing sexual language and homosexual innuendo. These interpretations have conditioned some of his micro-textual translation choices. [19]

Evans, in his analysis of the evolving literary status of Verne's *œuvre* throughout the late-nineteenth and twentieth centuries,[20] refers to

> the sudden renaissance of public interest in Jules Verne and the scholarly (re)discovery of the *Voyages extraordinaires* in France during the 1960s and 1970s ... Defying many decades of canonical repression ... (certain French scholars) proclaimed admiration for Verne ... (Verne's writings began) gradually to emerge from hallowed oblivion.[21]

The decade of the 1990s has seen the accurate retranslation into English, with annotations, of some of Verne's most celebrated novels, by leading Verne scholars such as Walter James Miller, Frederick Paul Walter and William Butcher.[22] Verne scholars are continuing to translate some of Verne's other, heretofore less well-known novels into English, so that the deservedly high literary status of the *Extraordinary Journeys*, should continue to grow.

CONCLUSION

To conclude, the following example illustrates the change for the better in Verne's literary reputation and the care with which his works have been retranslated. An anonymous translation of *Around the World in Eighty Days*, published in Britain in 1879, was significantly truncated and grossly inaccurate. One of the many mistranslations which occur regularly throughout this target text is as follows:

> *On ne connaissait à Phileas Fogg ni femme ni enfants—ce qui peut arriver aux gens les plus honnêtes* ... (11)

> No one knew whether Fogg had a wife or children, which might be possessed by the most scrupulously honest of men (10)

This truncated and inaccurate target text seems to have been due not so much to incompetence on the part of the translator, as to likely commercial pressures from publishers to translate quickly. Almost ninety years later, in 1968, a British retranslation of this same Verne novel—by Oxford scholar of French literature Robert Baldick and his wife Jacqueline—was meticulously accurate, couched in a formal, literary style which mirrored that of Verne, and written in modern, clear, accessible and idiomatic English.[23] The Baldicks' translation of *Around the World* continues to be republished and enjoyed today. An instance of the accuracy of the Baldicks' rendering, in comparison to the poor quality of its 1879 predecessor, is provided by their precise, correct translation of the foregoing source segment:

So far as was known, Phileas Fogg had neither wife nor children—which may be the case with the best of men ... (3)

The present republication of the English translation (1895) of Verne's *P'tit Bonhomme* is a welcome initiative in continuing international endeavours to make the lesser-known works comprising the *Extraordinary Journeys* available to a twenty-first century readership. *Foundling Mick* now invites the twenty-first century reader to accompany Verne's 'little fellow' on an extraordinary journey all round the Irish coastline and a fascinating trip back in time to a crucial moment in Irish history, from the distinctive perspective of a nineteenth-century French storytelling craftsman.

NOTES

[1] Jules Verne, *P'tit bonhomme* (Paris, 1978).

[2] Jules Verne, *Foundling Mick,* trans. not known (London, 1895).

[3] In French: Jules Verne, *Voyage au centre de la terre* (Paris, 1864); Jules Verne, *Le tour de monde en quatre-vingts jours* (Paris, 1981). English translations: Jules Verne, *A journey into the interior of the earth,* trans. Frederick Amadeus Malleson (1ˢᵗ edn, London, 1879); Jules Verne, *Round the world in eighty days,* trans. not known (London, 1879); Jules Verne, *The tour of the world in eighty days,* trans. Stephen W. White (Chicago, 1885).

[4] Examples of later English translations include Jules Verne, *Around the world in eighty days,* abridged and translated by John Webber (London, 1966); Jules Verne, *Around the world in eighty days,* trans. Michael Glencross (London, 2004).

[5] Brian Taves and Stephen Michaluk, Jr, *The Jules Verne encyclopedia* (Lanham, MD, 1996).

[6] Jules Verne, *A lad of grit,* trans. not known (Dublin, *c.* 1940).

[7] Gideon Toury, *Descriptive translation studies and beyond* (Amsterdam, 1995); see also Theo Hermans, *Translation in systems: descriptive and system-oriented approaches explained* (Manchester, 1999).

[8] In this republication of the translated text, the chapters in Parts One and Two have been numbered consecutively. Therefore, in Part Two Chapter V is herein numbered Chapter 19, Chapter VI is Chapter 20 and Chapter XI is Chapter 25.

[9] Jules Verne, *Around the world in eighty days,* Retold in simplified language by Joyce Faraday (Loughborough, 1982).

[10] Jules Verne, *Around the world in eighty days,* trans. William Butcher (Oxford, 1995).

[11] Anthony Pym, *Method in translation history* (Manchester, 1998).

[12] Arthur Evans, 'Jules Verne's English translations', *Science Fiction Studies* XXXII(1) (2005), 80–104.

[13] Evans, 'Jules Verne's English translations', 80–104.

[14] William Butcher, *Jules Verne: the definitive biography* (New York, 2006).

[15] Ian Haywood, *The revolution in popular literature: print, politics and the people, 1790–1860* (Cambridge, 2004).

[16] Haywood, *The revolution in popular literature,* 2.

[17] Jules Verne, *Around the world in eighty days,* trans. George Makepeace Towle and N. D'Anvers (London, 1876).

[18] Evans, 'Jules Verne's English translations', 80–104.

[19] William Butcher, *Verne's journey to the centre of the self: space and time in the Voyages Extraordinaires* (London, 1990).

[20] Arthur B. Evans, 'Jules Verne and the French literary canon', in E.J. Smyth (ed.), *Jules Verne: narratives of modernity* (Liverpool, 2000), 11–39.

[21] Evans, 'Jules Verne and the French literary canon', 24.

[22] Jules Verne, *Twenty thousand leagues under the sea: the definitive unabridged edition,* trans. Walter J. Miller and Frederick P. Walter (Annapolis, MD, 1993).

[23] Jules Verne, *Around the world in eighty days,* trans. Robert and Jacqueline Baldick (London, 1968).

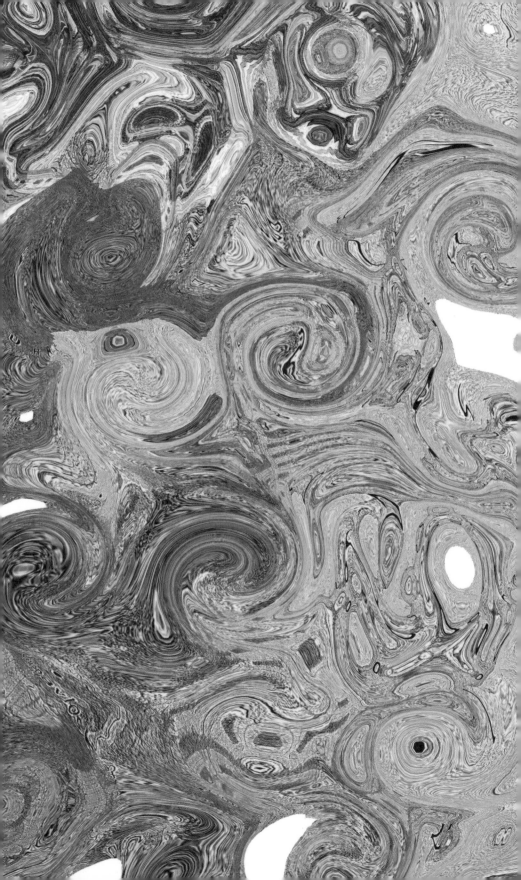

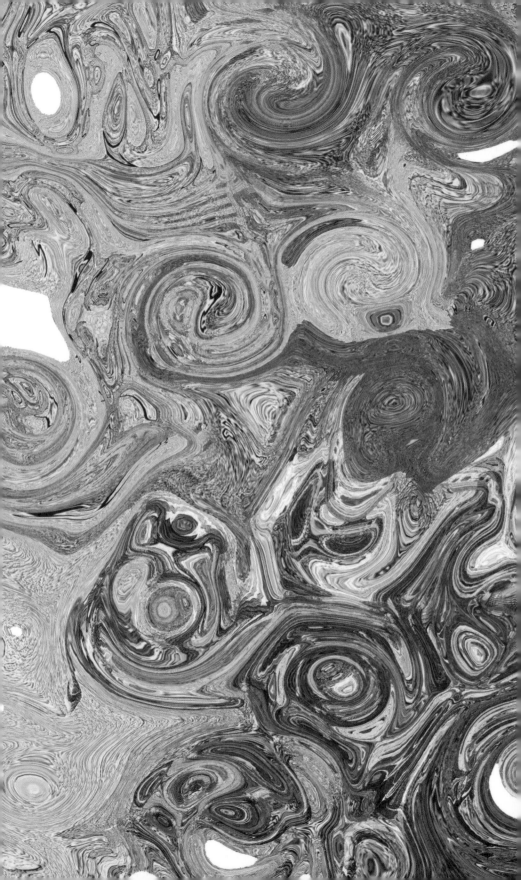